LOVE, ITALIAN STYLE

Young Lady Laura Lockridge had been taken on the Grand Tour of Europe by her father as the finishing touch in an education that had included scandalously unladylike academic studies and shockingly unfeminine athletic pursuits.

But by the time they reached Italy, Laura's horizons had broadened beyond either her or her father's most daring desires.

Laura had to learn to deal with the danger of bandits, the vengeance of a vicious nobleman, and the loss of parental protection.

And most fearfully challenging of all, she had to find out how to face the world as the wife of the elegant and masterful Marquess of Vare in public—and how to fight what she had begun to feel for him in private. . . .

# *MAD*
# *MASQUERADE*

# *MAD MASQUERADE*

by
Barbara Hazard

A SIGNET BOOK

**NEW AMERICAN LIBRARY**

A DIVISION OF PENGUIN BOOKS USA INC.

Copyright © 1985 by B. W. Hazard Ltd.

SIGNET TRADEMARK REG. U.S. PAT. OFF. AND FOREIGN COUNTRIES
REGISTERED TRADEMARK—MARCA REGISTRADA
HECHO EN DRESDEN, TN, U.S.A.

SIGNET, SIGNET CLASSIC, MENTOR, ONYX, PLUME, MERIDIAN
and NAL BOOKS are published by New American Library, a division of
Penguin Books USA Inc., 1633 Broadway, New York, New York 10019

First Printing, April, 1985

3   4   5   6   7   8   9   10   11

PRINTED IN THE UNITED STATES OF AMERICA

For Pauline
more than my sister; my friend

The author acknowledges with gratitude the information found in Christopher Hibbert's book *The Grand Tour*, published by G.P. Putnam's Sons, first American edition 1969, which was used in the preparation of this novel.

And, after all, what is a lie? 'Tis but the Truth in masquerade.

—Lord Byron, 1788–1824

# Prologue

When John de Mornay Philip Haverfield, the seventh Marquess of Vare, received an urgent message from his aunt, Lady Price, that note having the added impetus of being delivered while he was still at the breakfast table in Vare House, St. James's Place, an observer might have seen his slight frown as he read it, but any one of his acquaintances could have told you there was no doubt that he would obey her summons to call at his earliest convenience. The marquess had come into his title twelve years ago, and even then, at the age of twenty, had taken his position as head of the family seriously. He never shirked his duty, no matter how irksome or unpleasant that duty might be.

Lady Price was his father's youngest sister. She resided for most of the year in London, claiming that the quiet somnolence of the countryside gave her the megrims. The marquess had often thought that an extended stay at her late husband's estates in Sussex would have been most beneficial to her only son, for Archibald Price, although he was only twenty-four, had been on the town forever. His sojourn at Oxford had been brief; indeed, he had been sent down in a matter of weeks, as much to his relief as to those in authority at the university. At the time, he had confided to his cousin that Oxford was all a hum, and he would never have agreed to go there at all if he had known how devilishly boring it was. Did John realize that the masters had actually expected him to spend the majority of his time in study and almost constant reading? His indignant expression as he imparted this information had

11

sorely tried John's ability to keep a straight face.

Since then, the young man had amused himself with all the various activities available to a young sprig of fashion, and his cousin was sure he had never opened a book again, with the exception of the betting books at his various clubs.

The marquess reread the lady's note. Since it was not the first urgent missive that Lady Price had sent round in the past several years, it was certain that this one also involved the errant and irrepressible Lord Price. The marquess wondered what he had been up to in the month that he himself had been away in the country, and frowned again before he consulted with his secretary and prepared to walk the short distance to his aunt's town house on Jermyn Street.

Lady Price's butler, Sibley, took his hat, cane, and gloves, and managed to convey by no more than a slight tightening of his already prim lips that the marquess's surmises had been quite correct.

Lady Price was still at table in a sunny, well-appointed room at the back of the house, reading her morning post while she drank her coffee and ate the one slice of unbuttered toast that was all she allowed herself for breakfast. As Sibley announced her caller, she sprang to her feet, coming to kiss and exclaim over her nephew, even as she ordered a fresh pot of coffee and managed to strew her bills and invitations on the floor at her feet.

M'lord helped her to her seat again and took the chair facing her as he chatted lightly of the weather and of his return to London, until Sibley had restored the papers to a neat pile on the table, brought the coffee, and bowed himself out. Lady Price, who would never see fifty again, was wearing a very youthful gown of lavender muslin, her still-blond hair dressed in the latest fashion. Clarissa Price had been called the Toast of the Season the year she had been presented, and traces of that beauty were still apparent. Now the marquess noticed her strained expression, and the way her hands fluttered first to her coffee cup and then were clasped tightly together, and he steeled himself for the unpleasantness he was sure was in store for him.

At last the butler left the room at his usual stately pace, and Lady Price barely waited for him to shut the double doors behind him before she began to speak. "Dear John, the most frightful thing . . . but I knew you would not fail me!"

"Perhaps that was because I detected an even more than usual degree of urgency in your note, aunt," he replied, quirking one dark eyebrow in her direction. "I suppose I need not even hazard a guess. It is Archie, of course."

"Archie, indeed!" the lady agreed with a snap. "I am sure I am the fondest of mamas, and you know, John, I have never interfered with his pleasures, nor wearied him with lectures and scenes, but right now I could cheerfully consign my dear son to perdition, and help him there by strangling him myself!"

For her, this was a vehement statement, and the marquess was surprised. Clarissa Price had always been an easygoing parent; indeed, there were those who said she would be the ruin of her son, left as he was without a father's guidance. Lord Price had been a bruising rider to hounds, and he had come to grief in his thirtieth year mistiming a fence when his only child was three years old. Somehow the careless young widow had raised Archie without resorting to a heavy hand on the leading reins, and if her son was not noted for conventional behavior or superior sense, at least he managed to keep to a line that only the highest sticklers could fault. As for Lady Price, she had gone her own merry way, and even the worst of her son's peccadilloes up to now had moved her only to laughter and the prompt summoning of her nephew to make all right. On reflection, the marquess had to admit that her methods had served very well. Today, however, she was not amused, but worried and distraught.

"Out with it, then, ma'am! What has the young scamp done this time?" he asked in a light tone. "Painted Grosvenor Place blue? Lost his fortune on 'Change? Set up another opera dancer or two, or driven blindfold to Bath with only his groom to guide him?"

"So you heard about that mad scheme, I see. No, it is much, much worse. Oh, John, he is in love!"

Her nephew's expression did not change as he stirred his coffee. "But he always is, dear Aunt Clarissa. Either falling into it, deep in its throes, or recovering from it. I fail to see why such an ordinary occurrence has the power to overset you this way."

"But this time he informs me he is serious. John, I have never seen him quite so determined," Lady Price informed her nephew. Before he could reply, she hurried on. "John, I tell you I cannot bear it! No one, least of all I, expected Archie to fall in love with anyone suitable. I am sure I would swoon with shock if he announced his betrothal to any nice, well-brought-up young miss from a good family, but this . . . this *woman* he says he intends to marry must be all of thirty-five if she's a day, and married twice before, I must point out. You know the family, of course, why, they are so notorious, everyone in London knows the family. And I don't care if her father is a marquess and her mother the daughter of a duke, she has the morals of a barnyard cat! My poor deluded boy! And her first husband died so mysteriously, too. It is my belief that she has run through his fortune and is casting about her for a replacement. What better culprit could she find than dear, biddable, *naive* Archie with his twenty thousand pounds a year? Why, the very thought of calling such a creature 'daughter' is so repugnant I am sure I could fall into strong hysterics! I beg you to do anything you have to to detach him from her coils. Think of it, John! We would be forced to acknowledge Pamela Jones-Witherall!"

The marquess's mouth tightened, and he rose to his feet to pace the breakfast room. His aunt watched him, her eyes wide with tears and her hands clasped to her heart. The Marquess of Vare was a tall man, with straight black hair and a pair of startling dark blue eyes. There were those who insisted he was a fine-looking man, and those who said that all marquesses, especially those in control of so much wealth, must necessarily be considered so. In truth, it was only when he smiled and the harsh planes of his face broke into a more pleasant cast, the piercing eyes brightened, and his chiseled mouth showed a set of gleaming white teeth, that the adjective "handsome" could be applied to him. Since attaining the title with all its attendant problems and responsibilities, he had grown into a man not given to easy smiles, and so any good looks he might have boasted were often *in absentia*.

Although he was always dressed with propriety and neatness, he shunned the extremes of fashion. He much preferred the athletic pursuits of the true Corinthian—riding, hunting, sparring, and driving a team—to the more dissolute habits of a pink of the ton. Not that he avoided parties or was averse to making up a table for whist, all the while putting away a bottle of the best burgundy, but if you had asked him he would have told you that the time he spent at his various country estates was much more enjoyable than anything London had to offer.

Now, as he paced the breakfast room, his broad shoulders and muscular, athletic build were plain to see, and although his hands were as white and elegant as any other gentleman's, they looked capable and strong. He clenched them into two hard fists before he recalled his aunt's frightened face as she cowered in her chair, and he tried to relax his expression.

The news she had given him was much worse than he had expected. Knowing the lady in question as well as he did was more than enough to make him vow that she would never, under any circumstances, join the ranks of the Vare family. All through the years of his majority he had watched Lady Pamela's progress through society as she cut such a swath of vice and wildness that even the most hardened *roués* looked at her askance. Her first husband had been an elderly man. His whole family was convinced he had succumbed to senility to be marrying such a notorious young woman who was almost forty years his junior. There had been a great deal of talk when he died so suddenly only a few months after the wedding, but nothing had ever been proved. A few years later, the widow married the Mr. Jones-Witherall, who was, at the present time, instigating divorce proceedings against her. Although she continued to reside in London, Jones-Witherall retired to the country. His friends claimed he was a broken man, his health ruined and his mind impaired. Before, during, and after her marriages there had been many

affairs with other men. The marquess remembered now
that she had even sought to attach him at one time, and he
frowned again. Although he seldom took a direct hand in
his cousin's affairs, expecting him to outgrow his capri-
ciousness as he matured, in the case of Lady Pamela
Jones-Witherall, he saw that drastic measures were clearly
demanded.

He soothed his aunt and promised he would do everything in his power to separate her son from the infamous
lady, and reminded her that until Lady Pamela's divorce
was final she was not free to marry anyone. On this
cheerful note, he took his leave.

Having laid this burden on her nephew's broad and
capable shoulders, Lady Price went upstairs much relieved to dress for a luncheon and afternoon party of silver
loo, sure that dear John—such a steady, dependable man!
—would be more than competent in detaching Archie, by
whatever means he was forced to employ, from the lady's
grasp.

Her nephew was not so sure, especially after he spent a
difficult hour in his cousin's rooms listening to him extol
Lady Pamela's unusual beauty, and, according to him,
perfectly normal high spirits that had so often been misin-
terpreted in the past. According to Archie, the lady was an
angel who had been much maligned by the vicious gossip
of mean-spirited people who were jealous of her, and she
was much too noble to sue such cats for libel, which he
was sure she should have done. It was not in her sweet
nature to be vindictive, he told his cousin, his voice
admiring. Nor could the marquess be easy when he discovered later in the day from one of his friends that the odds
in the clubs were running three to one in favor of the lady
pulling off this particular coup.

The marquess dined alone that evening, deep in thought,
and sequestered himself in his library afterward instead of
attending Lady Newcomb's ball that he had promised to
honor. It was very late before he took himself off to bed,
but Conway, his butler, noticed that his expression was
brighter and was sure he had found a solution to whatever
problem was bedeviling him.

The following morning, the marquess sent a message to

Lady Price saying that the matter they had discussed was
already in hand, and telling her he would do himself the
honor of calling on her the next day with what he hoped
would be very good news. He also dispatched a note to his
cousin, begging Archie's company at dinner, and he made
sure of his attendance by saying there was something of
import that he wished to discuss—something he was sure
would be of great interest to the younger man. Then he
closeted himself in his library with his secretary and passed
the intervening time issuing a stream of orders and dictat-
ing many letters and memorandums.

Lord Price was prompt that evening, for his cousin kept
a French chef whom it would not do to offend, the excel-
lence of his cuisine being rivaled only by the fierceness of
his temper. Until the covers had been removed, and the
decanter of port and two crystal glasses had been set
before them, and the butler and two footmen had bowed
themselves out, John kept up an easy flow of conversation.

Archie eyed his cousin with trepidation. True, John was
a good 'un, and he had always liked him, but Pamela had
warned him of the opposition they were sure to face.
Archie knew instinctively that the Marquess of Vare would
do his best to thrust a spoke in the wheel if he could. He
was sure he could win his mother's blessing eventually—
why, she had only to meet dearest Pam to see her true
worth, he told himself—but John de Mornay Philip
Haverfield was another kettle of fish entirely. It had been
his experience that marquesses, even the good 'uns—
because of their exalted rank, no doubt—tended to be
proud and full of their own worth, and devilish starched
up, to boot!

But his cousin surprised him. Raising his glass of port
and admiring its deep ruby color, he offered a toast to
Archie's approaching nuptials. Archie swallowed before he
thought, and then sputtered as he was forced to resort to
his napkin. John approved? He was dumbfounded, and
could not wait to tell Lady Pamela how wrong she had
been. He smiled, a sudden beam of such happiness that it
twisted the marquess's heart. Concealing his feelings, he
refilled his cousin's glass.

"John, you're a great gun! Pamela would have it that

you could not like her, and here I find it was all gudgeon. I cannot tell you how happy you have made me! I must toast the finest cousin a man ever had—a *nonpareil* and a real Trojan!"

He tossed off his port and the marquess tried to look suitably gratified by the compliment as he once again refilled Archie's glass. He was fully prepared to go to any lengths up to and including kidnapping to end this revolting affair, but the shifts he was forced to employ in order to do so did not make him feel any less a liar and a cad. Pushing these ignoble thoughts to the back of his mind, he introduced the part of the conversation he had been leading up to all the time.

"How unfortunate the lady is not free to marry you immediately. And I understand it may be several months before that happy day arrives, isn't that so, Archie?"

His cousin frowned, staring down into his wine. "True, very true. It is a sadness for both of us, for the case has not come up before Parliament yet. Pamela says it is all her husband's doing, from spite, you know, to keep her from marrying me. From some of the things she has told me, I can well believe it of him! I wanted to call him out, but she would not hear of it, for she dreads the gossip such an action would incur. She is really such a modest, retiring woman, cuz! I can hardly wait for you to get to know her better. And you don't think she's a bit too old for me, do you? M'mother had some silly notion that it will be different when I am fifty and in my prime, and Pamela is an elderly sixty-one, but I tell you plain, I'd rather have her than any foolish little debutante my own age. There is a great deal to be said for a mature, experienced woman. Besides, my magnificent Pamela is ageless!"

He nodded his head at this wisdom and swallowed his third glass of port while the marquess fumed and regretted that murder was still punishable by hanging. He'd give a great deal to be able to get his hands on the mature, modest, magnificent Lady Pamela, even for only a short time, if he could be assured complete privacy.

Putting aside such unpleasant fates for the lady as strangling, stabbing, drowning, and life imprisonment chained to a dungeon wall, he watched Archie carefully.

The boy had had too much port too quickly, especially after the excellent selection of wines that had been served with dinner. Now he lolled back in his chair, turning his glass this way and that on the polished mahogany table, smiling a foolish little smile. The marquess was sure he was thinking of his ladylove, his expression was so fatuous, and he made haste to speak.

"But you have not heard the proposal that I told you would be of such interest, my boy," he said. "It occurs to me that since you must wait for your bride so many more months, what better way to occupy yourself than in traveling abroad with me? I have wanted to return to the Continent for a long time, as you know, and now that we are at peace at last, this is the perfect occasion to do so. I know the war with Napoleon kept you from any grand tour you might have contemplated yourself. You must allow me to remedy the situation. What do you say, Archie, my boy? One last grand bachelor fling before the cords of matrimony bind you tight?"

For a moment the marquess thought that Archie suspected what he was up to, for his blue eyes widened and his mouth dropped open in surprise. John kept an easy smile on his face as he once more refilled their glasses and continued, "And then, after Lady Pamela has gained her freedom, we can return. But in the meantime, there are Paris and all of Italy, Austria and Belgium—perhaps even Greece—to be explored! Say you will come, Archie, for I am sure we will have a time of it you will never forget!"

To be singled out by the marquess as his traveling companion was a great honor, but Archie's face was a study in dismay. "But . . . but, John! Leave the divine Pamela for such a long time? I could not!"

"Surely you do not doubt her faithfulness, Archie?" John asked in a shocked and sober voice. "You are promised, are you not? I only thought to help you pass the time more quickly this way. Besides, it does not do to be hanging about your fiancée at this time—bad *ton*, cuz, very bad *ton!* The divorce will proceed more quickly and with less malignant gossip if you are not on the scene. Surely you would spare the lady any unnecessary anguish?"

John paused, and as Archie opened his mouth to speak,

added quickly, "And just think how much more experienced and mature you will be after a journey through Europe. There will be none then who can say you are nothing but a silly greenhead, for you will have gone where other men have seldom been. Think of the statesmen, the leaders of fashion who will hang on your every word! And surely such distinction and prominence can only please the Lady Pamela as well. Come, for your own sake—and hers!"

Archie's face flushed even more, and he gulped, his rather prominent Adam's apple sliding up and down in his distress. Vaguely he wished he had not had quite so much to drink, for his mind was confused. It was true that he felt very young next to Pamela and her friends, and that more than once she had laughed at his inexperience and naiveté before she kissed away his sullens. To be reminded of how little he had done, or seen, or experienced, was not a pleasant sensation for one who only wished to impress his betrothed. This thought, along with all the port he had drunk, and the marquess's expectant and somehow taunting glance, made him throw caution to the winds. Of course he did not doubt Pamela; the man who said that was a liar! He knew she would be here waiting for him when he returned, a more mature and world-weary traveler.

"Another toast, John, to our journey!" he cried, and the marquess drank and then threw his glass into the fireplace in exultant relief that his plot had worked so well. It was only a moment before Archie followed suit, feeling sophisticated, decisive, and the complete master of his fate as he did so.

John did not allow his cousin much time for reflection in the days that followed. When Archie protested the early starting date, the marquess reminded him that sooner gone, sooner returned. When Archie said he needed more time to assemble a wardrobe for such an extensive trip, John was quick to point out that Paris tailors were waiting for their custom, and would give them both a decided air of new fashion, not available to English gentlemen who stayed at home.

Lady Pamela proved to be difficult beyond belief when

Archie told her their plans. She created a scene that left him with his mouth ajar at her screaming invective against the marquess. It was only by the greatest persuasion that Archie was able to convince her that his journey was for the best, and still she might not have relented except she saw the little spark of doubt in his eyes at her gutter words and loss of self-control. She was forced to acquiesce at last, pardoning herself by saying that it was only that she could not bear to think of being parted from him for such a long space of time.

The Lady Pamela was rolled up and punting on tick, living on her expectations as the future Lady Price, and nothing must be allowed to overset that. She knew the marquess's purpose very well, and fully intended to surprise him by remaining faithful to her fiancé until his return. Well, *almost* faithful, but all done very discreetly, of course. And even as she smiled and let Archie kiss and caress her, she vowed to herself that the Marquess of Vare would pay, and pay dearly, for his interference in her plans.

Her dark eyes narrowed as Archie buried his face in her bright red curls, murmuring endearments. While she ruffled his blond hair, she thought with satisfaction of that time in the hopefully not too distant future when she would be able to do the arrogant marquess some great and far-reaching disservice. She would not forget. Oh, no, she would have her revenge!

# 1

---

"Not another word, Edward, until Boggins fetches my salts! I fear I shall swoon if you continue."

Lady Blake sat bolt upright on a silk sofa in the elegant drawing room of the Towers, her late husband's estate near Taunton, and stared with shocked, disbelieving eyes at the gentleman seated across from her, whom she had welcomed so cordially just a short time ago. Since this gentleman did not appear to want to argue the matter, the two sat in silence until the lady's maid had presented her mistress with not only her salts but also her vinaigrette and a large handkerchief, and curtsied and left the room.

Lady Blake took a restoring sniff before she spoke again. "I cannot have heard you correctly, Edward," she said finally, her usually cordial, though always formal tones now dripping with icicles. "As your sister, I feel I may speak freely, for although I have made no secret of the fact that I consider you slightly eccentric, I have never thought you mad! But if what you have just related to me is true, it proves you have gone beyond the pale at last and should be taken to Bedlam immediately!"

The gentleman so summarily to be disposed of did not appear to be alarmed by the prospect as he sipped his wine from the delicate crystal goblet that Lady Blake's butler had served him, and mentally thanked his late brother-in-law once again for the quality of his cellar. He was a middle-aged man of about average height, still powerful-looking with his trim and muscular frame, although his dark brown hair was now streaked with white, and there were lines on his tanned face that had not been there the last time the two had met. His sister, who was some three years his senior and could be said to have earned the title of "a lady of a certain age," still showed the remains of a conventional beauty, and as she was almost painfully thin, appeared younger than her years. She was dressed very fashionably in a blue morning gown, and on her head was a delicate confection of lace that her brother was sure was all the crack, coming as it must have from one of London's better modistes. Although he himself had scant interest in such fripperies, he had to admit that the widow's cap became Margaret very well, or it would have if she had not continued to frown at him, her blue eyes frosty with accusation and her long, narrow nose in the air. He sighed a little to himself, for although he had known this would prove to be a difficult interview, he had not imagined it would cause her such distress. He had not seen his sister for two years, and he thought her grown very proud and arrogant. She had never been so grand when she was younger, but now, as the widow of Lord Blake, the late viscount, she seemed to be overly concerned with her position and importance, and would sooner tie her garter in public than relinquish the consequence due to her.

"The very idea!" she now added, sniffing her salts again. "I am sure I do not believe you for a moment. Not even *you* would propose such an insane scheme."

M'lord raised his brows. "Then you will certainly be surprised, Margaret, when you learn of our departure." His pleasant baritone was careless, as he ignored the lady's assessment of his character. "We have stopped to visit you on our way to the coast only to bid you farewell."

Lady Blake gasped and dropped her salts. "Then it is not some ghastly hoax, some joke you have told me just to upset me? You really mean to do this terrible thing? I beg you to remember our name—why, we will all be ruined if you persist!"

Edward Lockridge sighed again. "How so, my dear? We do not intend to parade up and down St. James's Street proceeded by a crier. In fact we do not go to London at all, but directly to the coast. I think you exaggerate, for how can it be common knowledge when we will be so far away, abroad?"

Lady Blake shook her head, her face white and her lips pursed with distaste. "Of course the *beau monde* will find out; they find out everything. And the whispering! The gossip! I cannot bear it, Edward—how can you be so cruel?" She twisted her handkerchief in her delicate hands and rushed on before he had a chance to reply.

"And have you considered Rosamunde? What chance will she have to make a great match with such talk going around town about her closest relations? You must know that I mean to take her up for the Season shortly—her first Season, too! Have you no love, no concern for her? I had even intended to speak to you about Laura, for although she is just turned eighteen, I am sure I would be happy to sponsor her as well. It is a great shame that Louisa died when she did, leaving you to bring up your daughter alone, for now we see the results! And why you never married again and gave the girl a mother, I shall never know!"

She sniffed and bridled, for her niece's upbringing and her brother's refusal to consider any of the ladies she had brought to his attention as suitable replacements for his late wife had been the cause of many arguments in the past. "Louisa must be turning in her grave at what you are proposing so calmly to do, for this cannot be Laura's wish! What young girl would agree to such a mad, improvident scheme?"

Lord Lockridge wisely decided not to mention that it had been Laura's idea in the first place as he raised his hand to stem the flow that washed over him. It appeared that Lady Blake was determined to argue the matter, and was prepared to continue to do so until she had his promise to abandon his plans. Her mention of his wife had brought a momentary sadness, for she had died when Laura was only five, and he had not cared to marry again. Now he wondered if Louisa would have been horrified. Somehow he thought not, for she had been an adventurous girl, much like her daughter, and he had never known her to care very much what the *ton* thought of her doings. This had suited Lord Lockridge very well; not for him the dissolute life of a man of the town. He raised his daughter himself, he managed his estates, he traveled whenever he could, and he was exceedingly well read, having a natural scholarly bent. All this activity allowed him to avoid spending much time among the exquisites and fops of the fashionable set his sister revered and that he disliked so much.

Lady Blake tossed her head again, threatening the lace cap that sat so lightly on her blond curls. "And where is Laura, by the way? I would question my niece myself, if you please, and if I find you have coerced her into this scheme, I shall take steps to see you *are* committed, Edward!"

"She is outside on the lawn with Rosamunde even now, for we saw her there as we came up the drive," Lord Lockridge replied, waving a careless hand toward the long windows that faced the park, and ignoring Lady Blake's threat. His sister rose at once to go and see, and as she reached the nearest window, she shook her head in despair. This would have surprised anyone not privy to Lord Lockridge's revelations, for what could she find so disturbing in the charming picture before her?

Coming toward the hall across a wide lawn edged with clumps of daffodils was her diminutive blond daughter dressed in a pale green gown and a wide-brimmed leghorn hat, and she was accompanied by another girl dressed for traveling in a russet gown and matching cape. She carried her bonnet in her hand and her chestnut curls gleamed in the sunlight. As the two strolled along, they were both laughing, and altogether they made a delightful picture, worthy of being immortalized in oils by Gainsborough himself.

"So it is true!" Lady Blake whispered, grasping the brocade draperies. "Oh, I shall certainly have a spell!"

"Come and sit down, my dear, you are pale," Edward said, going to his sister to lead her back to the sofa before he went to pour her a glass of Madeira. "I am sure there is no need for you to succumb to such histrionics."

Lady Blake moaned as she took the wine he handed her. She stared before her with unseeing eyes as if she were unaware she held a glass in her hands.

"Come now, drink up, Margaret. The children will be with us soon, and—"

"But that is the problem, Edward. They are *not* children!" Lady Blake exclaimed, setting her untasted glass down on a table beside her and leaning forward to speak in a breathless, intense voice. "You think of Laura as a child, but she is not! She is a young woman now."

"Now, there I must tell you that you are wrong, sister. She may have attained the great age of eight-and-ten and be physically mature, but she is by no means a woman, with all that that implies, as yet. And for that reason I have decided to take her with me on my travels, before she begins to think of fashions and finery, men and marriage. I see no reason why Laura should not have the benefits that every young sprig considers his right. I have always regretted that I had no son—not that I would give up my dear daughter, of course—but since I was not so fortunate, I made sure Laura received a gentleman's education. She has done very well at her studies, too, I might add." He spoke proudly, for his daughter was intelligent and had shown a great desire to learn. "She knows Latin and Greek, history and science and mathematics, and by the time we return from Europe, I am sure she will be fluent in French and Italian; perhaps she may even learn German. And from our travels she will learn of antiquity and art and the customs of other lands and people. After all, why should a female be denied an education? I grant you my taking my daughter on a grand tour might be considered a trifle eccentric, but surely you exaggerate the consequences."

"Eccentric? Rather you will be thought mad! Besides, what possible use can this traveling—this learning—be to her?" Lady Blake asked scornfully. "She is a female; eventually she will marry and have children and begin to manage her household. How silly to learn Greek, or science, or German. She will have her husband to instruct her in whatever he wishes her to know beyond her wifely chores. I fear you have made her a bluestocking, Edward."

She tittered so derisively that Lord Lockridge was stung to reply, "Better that than a woman with nothing but foolishness in her head. But come, Margaret! Laura is my daughter, and I have decided that a grand tour is necessary for her to finish her education. You can be sure I will take the greatest care of her, you know."

Lady Blake had bridled at his comment about foolish women, and was about to take him severely to task for so designating both herself and her daughter, but at that moment that young lady swept into the drawing room in a swirl of skirts, her face rosy from the chill of the spring morning and her eyes sparkling with delight.

"Mama! You will never guess," she began, still holding the hand of her taller cousin, who had accompanied her into the room. "Or has Uncle Edward told you already? Good morning, uncle. How glad I am to see you after such a long time."

She dropped her uncle a curtsy that was everything that was graceful before she ran to kiss him hello. Lord Lockridge smiled down at her as she lowered her eyelashes and blushed. The Honorable Rosamunde Blake at eighteen was already a practiced coquette, and he could see she could hardly wait to reach London and her assured position as either a Diamond of the First Water, the Incomparable of Incomparables, or the Pocket Venus of the coming Season. He acknowledged her beauty even as he watched his own daughter make her curtsy to her aunt before she stooped to kiss her stiff white cheek. Lady Blake moaned again and closed her eyes for a moment in shock.

"Why, you have cut her hair, her lovely hair," she accused her brother. "How could you, Edward? 'Twas her only real claim to beauty!"

Lord Lockridge raised his brows. He knew very well that Laura was not as beautiful as her cousin, but he had always considered her a well-enough-looking girl. Now he studied her more closely, but what he saw only caused him to nod in satisfaction. She was taller than most girls, and certainly more handsome than pretty, and he thought the carefully arranged chestnut curls became her. Her face was as tanned as his own, and the dark brows above her large, wide-spaced hazel eyes were well-formed. She had a straight patrician nose and a generous mouth, and she was also long-legged and slim. Beside her cousin Rosamunde, with her china-blue eyes and rosebud mouth, her tiny waist and already voluptuous figure, she was as different as chalk from cheese. He had the sudden thought that while Rosamunde's beauty might fade early, Laura would grow more handsome with every passing year, and he nodded in satisfaction.

"I think her handsome just as she is," he said as his daughter's eyes danced in delight at the compliment.

"A father's love has made you blind," Lady Blake declared. "No one dressed in that horrible gown could be considered anything but a country dowd! Have neither of you any taste at all? She looks like a governess!"

Laurie looked down at her new russet dress. True, it was plain and simple in cut, but, more important, it was neat and serviceable and sturdy. She raised hurt eyes to her aunt's face, and the lady had the grace to look a little self-conscious.

"I am sorry, Laura, if I have hurt your feelings in speaking the truth," she said, "but even your gown pales in comparison to your hairdo, if it is possible to call that ugly crop a hairdo."

"But I had to cut my hair, Aunt Margaret," Laurie explained. "It was much too long. I wish I had done it ages ago, for I feel so free after the weight of those heavy tresses that fell almost to my waist. I simply could not be bothered with it while we were traveling, for of course I cannot take a maid."

"You will have no maid? Now, that is the outside of enough!" her aunt exclaimed, her voice so incensed that Laurie looked to her father in some surprise. "In traveling without a maid, your reputation as a young girl who has been impeccably raised and carefully chaperoned will be very much in question. And although I can see it does not matter a jot to either of you, our reputations will be ruined as well."

Lord Lockridge rubbed his hands together and said in a hearty, encouraging way, "Come, my dear, you refine on it too much. Not even the highest stickler could protest, since Laurie travels under her father's care. But let me tell you of our trip! We propose to start by seeing France, and then we will travel through the Alps to Italy. Perhaps we may visit Greece or Egypt, but in any case we plan to return via Austria and Germany. All is in train; we leave next week."

Lady Blake refused to comment on their itinerary, and Laura began to feel uneasy. She had suspected that her aunt would not be best pleased, but like her father, she had not thought that Lady Blake would take the news so badly. Now even Rosamunde was looking frightened and upset, whereas before she had thought the whole thing a wonderful lark and envied Laurie her adventure. Perhaps her aunt was right, and she would be ruined; she knew the lady was thinking of her future marriage, but she herself did not even know yet if she wished to be married. There was so much to see and do before she contemplated domesticity. When her father had told her he was going on an extended trip abroad and that he planned to send her to her Aunt Margaret for a long visit while he was away, she had been indignant at first and then she had begged to accompany him so she might see for herself all the places he had described to her over the years. Besides, to be forced to visit the Blakes, doing nothing more exciting than making afternoon calls or working on her stitchery and whispering about the neighborhood beaux, did not interest her in the slightest, although from Rosamunde's confidences this morning, it was apparent her cousin found such things fascinating—especially the beaux.

Laurie had looked her father straight in the eye and threatened to run away from the Towers and follow him before she would submit to such punishment. Edward Lockridge had finally agreed, after a long and stormy session. He loved his daughter so much, he could not bear to think of her being unhappy while he was far away. It had even been he who had the idea that she should travel as a boy, at least part of the time. The journey through the Alps, for instance, would be difficult enough without having to cope with petticoats and sidesaddles, and Laurie was accustomed to wearing boy's clothes.

He had thought of this one afternoon after a ride around the estate with his daughter. He had watched her slide off her horse and toss the reins to a groom. Standing with her hands on her hips as she explained exactly how she wanted the horse rubbed down, and his left foreleg, which she felt he had been favoring, examined, it had occurred to Lord Lockridge that it was too bad Laurie was not a boy. In her breeches and loose shirt, she looked more like his son than his daughter, especially since she had tucked her long chestnut braids up under her cap.

It was true that Laura Lockridge made a better boy than she did a young lady of fashion. Not for her an afternoon's amble, riding a gentle mare sidesaddle. Nor were there any hours spent learning to sew or play the pianoforte, arranging flowers for the drawing room, or joining another young lady on a sketching expedition. In truth, there were very few ladies for her to associate with, for Lockridge Hall was located in an isolated section of the county, and several miles from Evesham, the nearest town, and they had few visitors.

Not that Laura missed company. She was happiest donning her breeches to practice fencing, or loading her pistols to join her father in target practice. She rode a gelding as temperamental as his own, and she took every fence, every ditch, by his side without question. If her mother had lived, her life must have been different, but without any feminine influences beyond that of her old nurse, who had been pensioned off several years ago, and her father's housekeeper, who was secretly in love with Lord Lockridge and who would never have dreamed of interfering in the way he raised his daughter, she had grown up more the son than the daughter of the house.

Now Laurie stared at her aunt's angry, disapproving face, and she was glad there was no way Aunt Margaret could know of the breeches and boots and riding coats she had packed in her trunks.

"I would speak to you alone, Edward," the lady said, rising and waving a dismissing hand at her daughter and niece. "Go away, my dears, and visit. I wish this to be a private conversation."

The two girls were more than happy to obey, for they were anxious to avoid the scene they sensed was coming. Rosamunde was instructed by her mother to have the housekeeper prepare rooms for them, while Laurie wondered if her aunt would wish them to remain after further discussion with her brother. She threw Lord Lockridge a pleading look to encourage him to stand firm as she left the room, and she was glad to see the wink he gave her behind her aunt's thin, rigid back.

Rosamunde gave a little skip as soon as the drawing-room doors were closed behind them, and, taking her cousin's hand, led her toward the morning room. "How angry Mama is, Laurie," she whispered. "Almost as angry as when she caught me kissing Jeremy—Lord Brayle's son. But truly, I could not help myself. He is *so* handsome!"

Laurie smiled at this sally, but she thought Rosamunde grown very silly since the last time they had met. She sat quietly while her cousin dealt with the housekeeper and ordered some tea and cakes for her guest, but when the door closed behind this woman, she was surprised to see Rosamunde's serious stare. She raised a dark eyebrow in question.

"Laurie, are you sure you want to do this mad thing? Mama is right, you know. If you are discovered, there will be a regular scandal broth, for I have never heard of a *girl* taking the grand tour. Besides, you will be missing the Season!" Rosamunde's eyes widened and the tone of her voice was reverent as she clasped her hands and contemplated such a marvelous event. "The balls and the gowns, the parties and teas and bonnets and receptions, and . . . oh, Laurie! And the *men*! I think you must be crazy to give all that up for a silly trip."

In the drawing room, her mother was saying much the same thing, and then enumerating the vast number of things that would befall them all if her brother persisted in this insane scheme, everything from being cut by the patronesses of Almack's to having her daughter forced to accept the hand of a cit, who, according to her, would be the only man to offer for a miss from such an eccentric family. Lord Lockridge let her speak without interruption, and seeing he was unmoved by her tales of social ostracism, she was forced to speak more plainly.

"Think what she will see, Edward, for foreigners are very immoral, I believe. And think what she will be forced to hear—coarse language and lewd jokes about her. I know men—so crude!"

Lord Lockridge had a sudden vivid mental picture of

the lady's only son, Viscount Blake. A stuffier prude he
had never met; surely Margaret was not referring to that
paragon of virtue? He saw her hide her blushing face in
her handkerchief, and in the ensuing silence, he was able
to speak at last.

"My dear sister, in the first place, I intend to avoid the
more crowded routes. We will travel alone, in great state
as befits my wealth. If there is any lewd talk, I shall of
course stop it at once. Laurie is not traveling unprotected,
and she is not the kind of girl who faints at an oath or a
warm story or others' immorality. I did not raise my
daughter to be a missish prude."

"You did not raise your *daughter* at all," came Lady
Blake's quick riposte. Her voice was rich with scorn as she
added, "Well, Edward, you shall have to take the consequences on your own head for this foolish adventure, and
do not come to me and expect me to find the girl a
marriage partner when you return, for I am sure I would
find it impossible to do so. You seem to have forgotten
that men expect to marry 'missish prudes,' as you so
charmingly put it. No man wants anything but a pure,
innocent maid as a bride."

"Laurie's marriage is many years away," Lord Lockridge
said, pacing the floor in some agitation now. "And I do not
agree with you, for any man worthy of Laurie would not
be so straitlaced and conventional."

"If you can find a single soul who thinks as you do, it
will be a miracle. Come, Edward, leave Laura with me. In
six months she will have forgotten this plan and be completely happy, and I daresay when she is enthralled by the
gaiety of the Season, she will wonder why she ever agreed
to go in the first place. It is not at all impossible, you
know, that I might find her a suitable *parti* this very
spring, if you will give me the dressing of her, although
what we will do about her hair, I cannot think. Her
marriage is not as far in the future as you imagine."

"I do appreciate your concern, sister," Lord Lockridge
said in a calmer tone, "but Laurie goes with me." Then he
added in a softer, almost sad voice, "Indeed, it is most
important that I have her with me, especially after what I
have just discovered. . . ."

Lady Blake ignored the last statement as she rose to her feet and shook her finger at him. "Very well, Edward. I see you are deaf to all my arguments, and since you are just as stubborn now as when you were a child, I shall say no more on the subject."

Unfortunately, this sweeping concession did not last for very long, for whenever she thought of one, Lady Blake continued, in the days that followed the Lockridges' arrival, to call their attention to the pitfalls that lay ahead. As these pitfalls were likely to occur to her in the middle of quite another conversation, they were often bewildering.

During one dinner, when Rosamunde was telling them about the local squire, her mother interrupted her to exclaim, "*Banditti!*" leaving some question in her relatives' minds of the squire's worthiness and honesty, until she explained her fears. She also worried about sickness, accidents, and plague, as well as such trivial matters as bedbugs, fleas, wolves, and wild boars.

But the Lockridges might have been able to bear all the lady's foreboding if she had not summoned her son, the very day they arrived, to lend weight to her arguments. Dear Percival, she thought as she penned an urgent note to him, heavy with underlines. He was awake on every suit, and of course so prominent in society that her relatives were bound to heed his words. Viscount Blake hurried down from town at her summons, and he was just as stuffy as Lord Lockridge remembered. He was only twenty-five, and a handsome young man with his mother's blond hair and blue eyes, but when he opened his mouth, only the most sober and solemn words were allowed to escape. Viscount Blake thought very well of himself; he knew he had an exalted position in the nobility to maintain, and he never forgot it, or allowed anyone else to forget it either. Although he could not contradict his uncle openly, since as an older relative he deserved deference and respect, he was not slow to contribute his own mite to his mother's protests. He attempted a playful tone with the Lockridges, but from Laurie he gained only a glance of incomprehension, and from her father such a haughty glare that he retired in haste, his color high. He did not give up trying, however, being quite as horrified as his mother was, and one afternoon when he found Laurie alone in the garden, he went to stroll up and down with her.

To say that he had been very shocked to learn of her agreement to her father's scheme was surely an understatement, and he had formed the habit of addressing the air an inch or so above her chestnut curls so he would not have to look directly at such a bold, forward miss. He had never thought her a feminine girl even before this, for she had a tendency to look straight at him, her hazel eyes intent and serious, as if she considered herself his equal. What she should have done, he thought, was to blush and lower her eyelashes in the presence of his superior maleness.

Now he pointed out to her in his pedantic way how forward her behavior was, and how lacking in decorum. This was further than he had dared trespass before, and Laurie, who was not used to being reprimanded or crossed in any way, lost her always quick temper. Turning toward him with her eyes blazing, she told him that what she did was none of his concern, for she answered only to her father. Viscount Blake shook what he considered a playful finger at her.

"My dear cuz, I fear you are not thinking rationally. Your father cannot be a well man, for such a scheme as he proposes shows a lack of judgment, and even an unsound mind; I beg—"

But he was allowed to go no further, for Laurie slapped him as hard as she could for daring to insult her father, much as she had once slapped him when he had teased her as a child, and then she hurried away before she told him exactly what she thought of him.

At that, his cheek stinging, Viscount Blake washed his hands of such an unworthy branch of the family, and saying good-bye only to his mother, departed the Towers in high dudgeon that very afternoon, leaving Lady Blake alone on the field of battle.

She renewed her efforts, and both Lockridges were delighted when the day for their departure arrived at last and they could set out for Dover and the ship that would carry them to France. Laurie drew a sigh of relief as they left the gates of the Towers behind, for her aunt had been so very determined and persistent.

Slightly behind them rode m'lord's valet and general aide, Jed Simmons. He was a middle-aged man, long in Edward Lockridge's service, and he was a great favorite of Laurie's, for he had been like a second father to her. Simmons trailed a packhorse carrying such things as they would need on the road, for Lord Lockridge had sent the coach loaded with the rest of their baggage ahead of them four days ago, with two sturdy footmen from Lockridge Hall to assist his coachman.

It was early that soft spring morning when they left, and the sun was just beginning to disperse the night mist. It promised to be the kind of day that turned all of England into a garden, for the scent of flowers hung heavy in the damp air, and the fields seemed to be growing a more vibrant green right before their eyes. Lord Lockridge took a deep breath as he looked around in appreciation.

"Look well, Laurie," he told his daughter. "England never looks so fine as on the day you leave her, or on the day that you return."

Lord Lockridge set a good pace. Unhampered by the heavy, lumbering coach, they covered the miles steadily, and late in the afternoon of the fifth day's ride, they came into Dover. Laurie was exhilarated by her first glimpse of the Channel with its dark blue waves topped with whitecaps marching toward her from as far as she could see. The wind was fresh and tangy with salt, and she was delighted that they were on the brink of their adventure at last.

Rooms had been bespoken for them at The Ship, and as they rode slowly down the crowded main street, Lord Lockridge told Laurie about the town.

"I hope we do not have to remain here for long, Laurie, for it appears that no packets have sailed recently, if the crowds are anything to go by. Dover is not an interesting place for travelers, and The Ship is only one of the two inns that are at all comfortable."

When his daughter asked why they could not sail at once, he explained that it was necessary to wait for a fair wind.

"With a good stiff breeze from the west, Calais is only a three-hour sail, but without that wind it can take as long as five or six."

Laurie looked about her with interest. There seemed to be a vast number of mean, small inns in the town, and her father told her that they were, for the most part, run by old sailors retired from His Majesty's Navy or from the merchant fleet.

"Of course they like nothing better than several days' delay like this, so the packet boats' passengers are forced to remain here, paying for their meals and lodgings." He stared about him and sniffed the breeze, which his daughter thought seemed fresh enough to whisk them across the Channel in well under three hours, if only it had not been from the east. She was forced to grasp her hat to save it from being blown away in quite the opposite direction.

At The Ship, they found the landlord bowing and smiling and waiting to show them to their rooms and private parlor. The coach had arrived earlier that same afternoon, and all was in readiness. In spite of her hours in the saddle at home, and the long ride to Taunton, Laurie was glad to dismount and enter the inn. Five days of hard riding, and sidesaddle at that, had taxed her, although she would never have admitted it to her father, who did not seem to realize how tired, stiff, and sore she was.

As she prepared to follow Simmons up the narrow stairs while her father continued to chat with the landlord, she looked about with curiosity. The smoky taproom of the inn was filled with men, all talking in loud voices and all intent on their pipes and ale—most of them common seamen, from the looks of them. Laurie heard a group by the door begin to roar with laughter at a joke one of them had made, all the while sketching an hourglass with his hands, and she was glad her father had arranged for a private parlor. Suddenly she felt a tiny shiver of alarm at what she had so blithefully agreed to do, and she backed against the wall, out of sight of the taproom. As she did so, she collided with a large, well-dressed man who had just come down the stairs. She gasped as she stumbled into him, and turned quickly to apologize for her clumsiness. The gentleman was accompanied by another, younger man, who stopped behind him and raised an ornate quizzing glass.

"Kindly get out of the way, girl. You are delaying the

Marquess of Vare." He sneered in a haughty, supercilious manner.

The marquess had stopped as well and was staring at Laurie. He was frowning, and his dark blue eyes were sharply intent. Suddenly he raised one brow, and Laurie was sure her face flushed with her embarrassment, and hated herself. Before she could collect herself and speak, the younger man added, "I don't know what The Ship is coming to, John. Callow children milling about, jostling their superiors. The sooner we can take ship, the better."

Laurie was indignant. "Callow child" indeed! As she was searching for a suitable reply to such arrogance, she heard her father's voice behind her, and saw Simmons coming back down the stairs to assist her as well.

"What's amiss, sirs?" Lord Lockridge asked casually. "Ah, it's you, Lord Vare. We have not met for many a year, sir; I knew your father well at one time, when you yourself were but a 'callow child.' You have a great look of him. Allow me to present my daughter, Lady Laura Lockridge. And I, of course, to refresh your memory, am Edward, Earl of Lockridge."

"Delighted, m'lord," the marquess replied, his eyes going back to Laurie's flushed face as she tried to smooth her rumpled gray habit. "Make you known to my cousin, Lord Price."

They all bowed, and Laurie thought the whole situation ridiculous. As she curtsied and said she was honored indeed, she scowled, still angry at the sneering superiority of the London exquisites before her. She looked about fourteen as she did so, and her father took her arm and excused them both.

"We have just this moment arrived from Taunton, m'lords, but perhaps we will meet again. You are for France?"

The marquess admitted they had been waiting for a wind shift for three days, and then the parties separated. Laurie was glad her father did not ask them to dine or to join them in their private parlor. The less she had to do with such prime examples of a decadent regency, the better. Although the marquess was tall and athletic-looking, with smooth black hair and understated, elegant clothes, his cousin was slight and fair, and dressed much too elaborately for a simple seaside inn. His cravat had been arranged to a nicety, and in its folds a large diamond glittered. His blond hair was curled over his forehead and his ears in a style Laurie thought he would have trouble maintaining once he was aboard ship. She had not liked his drawling, world-weary voice, or his haughty manner either, certainly not in a man who was not much older than herself. He had been all smiles when he learned they were equals, but she thought him arrogant and proud, as if he considered himself as exalted as his stern, frowning cousin. She did not speak as she followed her father and Simmons up the stairs and along the corridor to their rooms, and she drew a sigh of relief as the door closed behind them.

Below her, Lord Price shook out his ruffles and said, "The Earl of Lockridge, eh? I do not think I have ever seen him or any of his family in town. You don't suppose he is planning on taking that young chit abroad, do you, John?"

Thus directly appealed to, the marquess recalled himself and started toward the door of the inn, saying over his shoulder, "I have no idea. Their arrival at The Ship certainly points in that direction. How very unusual if it were so. She is very young, wouldn't you say, as well as being a trifle clumsy?"

Lord Price agreed as he followed his cousin from the inn, clapping his beaver on his head and promptly forgetting the unmemorable Lady Laura. They made their way to the waterfront. The marquess wished to question the captain of their ship about the possibility of sailing on the morrow. The scowl that Laurie thought made him so stern and unapproachable deepened as he noted the strong east wind that was still blowing.

He and Archie had been stranded in Dover for three days, and more than once during that time John had wondered if he had not made a terrible mistake in concocting the scheme that involved him in taking his cousin Archie abroad. There was little enough to do in Dover, and Archie's conversation left a lot to be desired, for he was missing the divine Pamela, to whom he constantly referred. The marquess was not amused, and he found it very difficult to have to agree so constantly with Archie's lyrical descriptions of her character and beauty.

But even though Archie in love was tedious to an extreme, John never let him out of his sight, and he did not intend to relax his vigilance until the coastline of England faded from view, for he was not at all sure that the honor of being chosen as the traveling companion of a marquess would keep his cousin to the sticking point. It was entirely possible that Archie would bolt back to town and the lady's seductive arms if they were forced to remain in Dover much longer.

He foresaw an extensive journey. Archie had only responded to the flirting of the pretty maid who had served them dinner last evening with an abstracted sigh, and by his cousin's actual count, had managed to introduce Lady Pamela Jones-Witherall as a topic of conversation seventeen times. As he strode along the waterfront, remembering, John frowned even more ferociously. He had promised Lady Price that he would not return her son to London until he had fallen in love at least twice while they were on the Continent, and he could see that he must resign himself to an even longer stay abroad than he had anticipated.

# 2

The following morning, to the marquess's disgust, when he looked out his window at dawn, the wind still blew from the east. Laurie was awake early too, but she, unlike him, was delighted there was to be the delay that Simmons told her about when he brought in her breakfast tray. She watched the bustle beneath her window and smiled. "Then I shall have a chance to explore Dover. Has my father eaten?"

When she learned that Lord Lockridge had just left the inn to seek out the captain of the packet, she hastened to finish her coffee and rolls. "I shall go and meet him," she announced as Simmons prepared to leave the room. At her statement, he paused by the door.

" 'Ere now, Lady Laura! You shouldn't be roamin' the streets alone, and well you know it. You wait until I can come with you, or at least take one of the footmen, Robbie or Paul."

Laurie laughed at him. "Simmons, you do not think to turn me into a simpering miss at this late date, do you? I absolutely refuse to be hedged about with propriety. You know I am not used to being trailed by servants, and surely there is no need for it here in this little port where no one knows me. Do not worry so!"

The valet shook his head, but he did not protest again. He had loved Lady Laura since she was a little girl, and although he did not completely approve of this journey she and her father were so intent on, he had vowed to do all in his power to help. Lord Lockridge had a special reason to have his daughter with him, he knew, but he

40

tried not to think about that. Besides, he knew how anxious she was to see the sights of the waterfront and all the ships, swinging to their anchors.

Laurie dressed quickly in a simple gown of dark green that had a matching hooded cloak and impatiently brushed her chestnut curls in order before she ran down the stairs and out to the yard of the inn.

Making her way along the quay, she searched for her father, but instead of that dear, familiar figure, the first people she saw that she recognized were the Marquess of Vare and his cousin. Courtesy required her to stop and greet them.

The marquess inclined his head. "You're up early this morning, Lady Laura," he said. "But it is to no avail, I fear. The captain tells me we must wait another day. I just spoke to your father, incidentally; when finally we do sail, we shall be on the same ship."

Besides the frown that Laura was beginning to think a permanent feature of his dark, harsh face, he sounded brusque and annoyed this morning, and Laurie wondered at it. Then her attention was caught by a fishing boat that was tying up to the quay, and she watched the sailors who were opening the hold expose their catch. As two of them held up a large fish, she exclaimed, "See there, m'lord. Whatever kind of fish can that be? It must weigh four stone at least."

The marquess turned to see where she pointed, and Lord Price raised his quizzing glass and shuddered. "How excessively ugly fish are," he said in his bored voice. "And why would anyone consider them a suitable topic of conversation? How tiresome Dover is—there is no one to talk to."

Laurie's quick temper got the better of her and before she thought, she said, "I shall not detain you in that case, m'lord. However, let me tell you that I find the fish much more interesting than many human beings I have met, concerned as they are only with their exquisite attire and the tying of the cravats, and unaware of how ignorant they are."

"I say!" Lord Price exclaimed, his eyes popping in astonishment and his chin dropping into the folds of his beautifully arranged cravat. "What cheek!"

"Children, children," the marquess interrupted, a white grin splitting his rugged face, and all his annoyance gone. "Cry peace! I am afraid I have no idea what kind of fish that is, Lady Laura. I suggest you ask your father; he seems a knowledgeable man."

"Yes, he is," Laurie agreed proudly. Glancing at the stunned Lord Price, she added, "He is the most learned man I know."

Suddenly she saw him coming down the quay toward them, and she waved. "There he is now. You must excuse me, m'lords. I came out only to walk back to The Ship with him."

She curtsied and hurried away, a little uneasy that she had spoken to the beautiful Lord Price in such a way. Putting him from her mind, she called, "Father, do come and see this enormous fish!"

The marquess, thus disposed of so neatly, hid a chuckle, while Archie continued to sputter at his side. It was obvious to him that compared to the big fish, the Marquess of Vare was a very small fish indeed to the young Lady Laura. He was still smiling a little as he escorted his indignant cousin from the quay, leaving the Lockridges to examine the fishing boat's catch, with Laurie asking the fishermen innumerable questions. She did not even notice their departure.

The day did not seem long to her, for there was so much to see and do. As she strolled along the waterfront with her father sometime later, she mentioned her meeting with the Marquess of Vare and his cousin, and Lord Lockridge frowned.

"I do not wish to be overfriendly with them, Laurie, nor with any other Englishmen once we reach the Continent. We are going to learn the ways of foreigners—our own kind we can see at home. So many English band together, forgetting that the purpose of their travels is to gain knowledge of the unknown. Besides, we must hold ourselves aloof because of the deception we intend to practice at times. Remember your aunt's warning."

Laurie nodded, but instead of thinking of her Aunt Margaret, she was seeing in her mind's eye the marquess's frown and dark blue stare. She would be happy to avoid him, she told herself, and his foppish, silly cousin as well.

Simmons called her early the next morning, for the wind had swung into the west during the night, and the packet was preparing to sail at last. Laurie dressed in a hurry and gulped her breakfast so she could help Simmons with the packing. Her father was below stairs, giving his coachmen instructions. Since he had made arrangements to hire transport at Calais, their own coach was to return to Lockridge Hall after delivering the baggage to the packet. The footmen were to go abroad with the Lockridges, and Laurie thought they made an impressive entourage as she followed her father down the quay, trailed by the three servants.

Although Lord Lockridge disdained to carry much of the equipment travelers of the last century had thought indispensable to their comfort, there were still a number of trunks containing all manner of clothing. They would need warm furs for their journey over the Alps, and light-weight clothes for warmer climes. There were also pistols, maps and guidebooks, notebooks, broad-brimmed hats, and even a tea caddy. Laurie watched Paul carrying a large medicine chest up the gangplank, a brass-bound box that contained weights to measure doses, a mortar and pestle for mixing, and jar after jar of medicine. She could not help asking her father why such a box was necessary.

"I hope we never have need of it, my dear, but it is wise to be prepared. We will be traveling through sparsely inhabited, wild country in many places, and it is wise to be prepared for any emergency. On the Continent you cannot be sure there will be a doctor on hand when you need one, but both Simmons and I have some skill. And if you are not a good sailor, you may be very glad for one of the medicines I packed, and that almost at once." At her questioning look, he added with a smile, "It is a seasick remedy."

Laurie watched the sailors as they prepared the ship, feeling a bit apprehensive. She hoped she would not need the contents of that brass-bound chest, for she did not want to be a bother at the very start of their journey.

At a distance, she saw the marquess and his cousin

coming toward them from the direction of the inn, and was glad to follow Lord Lockridge up the gangplank. He had reserved a cabin for her; it seemed very tiny, with only a bunk and a small stand, both of which were bolted to the floor. The motion of the ship now that she was below made her feel a little queasy, and she was glad to climb the ladder to the deck again after she found her boat cloak. Wrapped up warmly in it, for the early morning was chilly with the fresh wind blowing, she stood at the rail with her father and watched the sailors cast off. The packet moved away from the quay, and she spared one last look back at the gulls wheeling and crying over the Dover waterfront before she turned her face to the Channel. The ship heeled over and settled down on a broad reach for France, her forefoot burying itself in the waves and then rising to shake off the water they traveled through, as if she shared Laurie's impatience to be gone.

Laurie wondered when she would see England again, but there was no sadness in her speculations. Rather she felt elated that they were off at last, and impulsively she squeezed her father's hand and smiled up at him. Lord Lockridge smiled back at her enthusiasm, and then he asked, "Are you well, my dear?"

Laurie nodded even as she explained she would rather stay with him instead of being cooped up in the stuffy little cabin. Her father's eye twinkled as he agreed.

And so for the next three hours she remained on deck, grasping the rail to keep her balance, and thoroughly enjoying her first taste of sea travel. As the coast of France came closer and closer, her excitement grew. She had not seen the marquess or Lord Price during the journey, although she had noticed the younger man staring sadly back toward Dover from the stern as the sailors cast off, his cousin by his side. She wondered if they had been seasick, but soon all thoughts of them left her mind as the packet dropped anchor. The town of Calais seemed small and mean from what she could see of it, for the packet had anchored some distance from shore.

"Why don't we go closer in, Father?" she asked, and Lord Lockridge explained that at low tide it was necessary to transfer to small rowing boats to be taken ashore. A number of these boats were nearing the packet, while back on shore there were several bare-legged porters of both sexes waiting, as well as other men who her father said where touts for the various inns, all calling and gesturing to the passengers. It was a scene of noisy confusion, and Laurie reveled in it.

When it was their turn to clamber down the ropes to a rowing boat, Laurie wished she was wearing her breeches, for it was difficult to preserve her modesty in the process. Lord Lockridge was carried to the beach first, and he was soon surrounded by touts and porters, all talking at once. By the time the waterman came back and picked Laurie up roughly to wade ashore, her father had arranged for their baggage to be carried to the customhouse and thence to the Hôtel Angleterre, where he had reserved rooms. Laurie was glad the French seemed to understand him; for herself, she found it difficult to make out their quick, garbled patois.

After the Lockridges and their servants had made their way over the sands to the customhouse, Laurie was surprised to see how thoroughly their baggage was inspected. "For contraband, my dear," her father whispered. "I see the landing fees are as exorbitant as always, but we must expect such treatment wherever we go. You'll see."

The officials seemed almost disappointed when they could find nothing to confiscate, and were finally forced to issue the Lockridges new passports and let them go.

Calais was just as mean a town as she had suspected from the deck of the packet, and she was glad they were only to remain there one night. She went to her room in the inn behind a fat woman servant, glad of the chance to rest after all the excitement of the Channel crossing, while her father went out to inspect the coach he had ordered. As the servant left her, Laurie thanked her in French, and she was delighted to see the maid break into a broad smile and call her a *"belle jeune fille."*

It seemed a significant milepost to be able to speak to a Frenchwoman in her own language and be understood.

She remembered little of their first foreign meal that evening, for she was still yawning. She told herself it must be the result of the salt air when she retired early to bed,

leaving her father and Simmons at the table discussing the
route they planned to take to Paris.

The following morning as she waited for the coach to be
brought around, Laurie looked about her with interest. It
was a clear day, slightly cool for May, and although any
number of Frenchmen were already hurrying through the
streets, there were few Englishmen in evidence this early
in the morning. Her father pointed out the diligence that
was loading for Paris, a large enough vehicle to carry
thirty passengers and all their baggage. Contributing to
the noise and confusion were some children involved in a
loud game, and beggars who seemed to know instinctively
when a foreigner was around, for they pestered him until
he was forced to give them some small coins in self-
defense. As she climbed into the coach, Lord Lockridge
threw them some money, and as they scrambled after the
coins, they cried, *"Bon voyage! Vivent les voyageurs!"*

*"Adieu, adieu,"* Laurie called back as the coach started,
with the footmen up behind and Simmons riding inside
facing them. By the lead horse rode a postilion on a pony,
his huge jackboots as big as oyster barrels, and rimmed
with iron to protect his legs from accident. Although Lord
Lockridge had deliberated carefully before hiring this
servant, Simmons was sure he was a rogue. Lord Lockridge
agreed. "They are all rogues, Simmons, as we both
remember. However, let us hope I have hired the least
rascally."

Laurie was intent on the road, although after a few
hours she would have been glad to exchange her seat in
the coach for even the postilion's pony. French roads, she
was discovering, were very bumpy, paved as they were
with large uneven stones, and in spite of the fact that their
coach was well-sprung, it was a jolting ride. As they traveled through the countryside, she was surprised to see the
vast fields that were being plowed in preparation for corn
planting, and the many rich pastures. She had not thought
France such a well-ordered, fertile country, especially
since it had been at war for so many years.

It was one hundred and eighty-three miles to Paris, but
they did not travel there directly. Instead, they paused
along the way whenever Lord Lockridge felt there was

something Laurie should see. Thus they lingered almost
three weeks in Amiens so she could practice her French
with the monks who taught the language, to improve her
accent. When they reached Rouen, so big and gray beside
the Seine that was crowded with many boats, she was
fascinated, for there Joan of Arc had been burned at the
stake, history she knew well. Her father watched her
intelligent eyes and answered all her questions, delighted
she was such a good traveler, and so interested in everything they saw.

True to his plan, Lord Lockridge avoided the other
Englishmen they saw along the way. He was always pleasant when spoken to, but he encouraged no familiarities,
nor did he seek anyone's friendship. Laurie sometimes
wondered idly what had happened to the Marquess of
Vare and Lord Price. She had not seen them since Dover,
but perhaps, unlike themselves, they were not going to
Paris, but traveling south instead. Sometimes she asked
herself why the marquess came so often to her mind.

It is because he frightened me a little, I think, she
admitted to herself. I wonder why that should be, for he
did not look cruel, just stern. I only hope we do not meet
again.

But such good fortune was not to be, and it was in
Chantilly that she quite literally ran into the marquess
again. The Lockridges had paused here so they might see
the palace of the Prince of Conde with its famous gardens.
Laurie thought the fountains and waterfalls beautiful, and
the aviaries with their exotic birds enchanting, and she
lingered behind her father so she might observe them awhile
longer. Suddenly a deep, familiar voice said from behind
her, "They are fascinating, are they not, Lady Laura?"

Startled, Laurie swung around and collided with the
marquess, who was standing close behind her. He stepped
back quickly. "You do seem to make a habit of bumping
into me, my girl," he said, the smile quivering at the
corners of his mouth at odds with his disapproving words.
Laurie swallowed and hoped her flushed face would be
attributed to the heat, for the aviary was almost tropical.

"Your pardon, sir," she managed to get out. "I apologize,
although I am sure you ran into me in Dover."

A little distraught at what she had blurted out without thinking, a bad habit of hers, she watched him carefully. The marquess, instead of being offended by her words, put back his head and laughed out loud. Before she could excuse herself, he took her arm and said lightly, "Then I must beg your pardon, too. I am sure you are right, and now we are even."

Laurie was glad when he changed the subject and began to speak of the birds.

"Do observe that handsome fellow over there in the large palm tree," he said, pointing his walking stick at a bright yellow bird with a band of black across his head, and black-and-white-tipped wings. "He almost looks dressed for a masquerade, does he not? But how disappointing to find, if he unmasked, that he was only a common sparrow. It is too bad that people too are not always what they seem, but perhaps you are too young to have noticed that."

Laurie smiled at the perky little bird, wondering what the marquess would think if he knew she was planning to travel as a boy at times. "I suppose that is true, especially among the *beau monde*. For myself, living in the country as I do, I have not noticed any such playacting or disguise."

The marquess nodded and they continued to stroll through the aviary arm in arm. She learned that he and his cousin had indeed gone straight through to Paris, where they had been for some weeks, and that they had ridden out to Chantilly for a few days expressly to see the gardens. What she did not learn was that the marquess had been anxious to remove Archie from the dissipations of Paris and that he was already planning an early departure from the capital before his cousin was completely ruined. Although Archie did not mention Lady Pamela more than ten or eleven times a day now, she was never far from his thoughts, and his sorrow at being parted from her seemed to be leading him with greater and greater frequency to the brandy decanter. John felt a rigorous journey through the Alps would do a great deal to erase the lady's image from his cousin's mind. None of this did he mention to the very young lady at his side, of course, telling her instead how much she would enjoy the French capital when she finally arrived.

By this time, they had reached the door of the aviary, and Laurie was glad to see her father some little distance away, chatting with one of the gardeners. Near him, Lord Price lounged against a wrought-iron railing, looking supremely bored, for gardens were not at all in his line. The two older men exchanged greetings and were soon deep in conversation as the four made their way back to the entrance. By necessity, Laurie was forced to walk beside Lord Price, who, in spite of an elegant bow, did not seem to have the slightest desire to renew their acquaintance. After Laurie asked him one or two questions about his travels and was rewarded by a yawn and a terse reply, she decided to ignore him.

Although no sign of it showed in his face, Edward Lockridge was not best pleased to discover that the marquess and his cousin had rooms in the same hotel where he and his daughter were putting up, and no one could have known from his manner with what reluctance he accepted the marquess's invitation to join them for dinner. He had always been a solitary man, not much given to social intercourse with his fellows, and happiest when he was alone or only in his daughter's company.

But later, after the last course had been removed, and some comfits and nuts and a decanter of port had been presented, he found himself relaxing. The Marquess of Vare was pleasant, and besides his sophistication, an intelligent man. Edward Lockridge was surprised to find that he had enjoyed their conversation. Laurie was acquitting herself well, too. He had watched her carefully, and she had contributed to the conversation in an easy manner. Lord Lockridge was proud of her.

Now the marquess began to question him about the route he intended to take through the Alps, saying that within two weeks he and his cousin planned to travel to Italy.

"You do not go to the south of France, sir?" Lord Lockridge asked. "Some travelers prefer to go from Marseilles to Italy by *feluca*, for although there is danger sailing from the Barbary pirates, it is considered preferable to the coast road at the foot of the Ligurian Alps, infested as that is by bandits."

John remarked that by land or by sea, a bandit was a bandit, and then Lord Lockridge told him that for himself, he preferred the route that led south from Grenoble into Switzerland.

"I want Laurie to see the Swiss Alps," he explained. "It is a tortuous way, and difficult, but I have always found the wildness of the mountains awe-inspiring. The only danger there is from wolves, and I would rather fight off wolves than *banditti*."

"Wolves? Bandits? Barbary pirates?" Lord Price stuttered in some distress. "Oh, I say, John, why don't we remain here in France? I have no desire to see Italy after all, and in fact would be happy to return home immediately if you wish."

He beamed at the thought of the reception he was sure to receive from Lady Pamela, even as the marquess shook his head. "No, no, dear boy, it is not to be thought of. Of course you must see Italy; the churches, the works of art, Pompeii, and of course the queen of cities, Rome herself. I should never forgive myself if our trip was curtailed."

"And remember what Samuel Johnson said, sir," Lord Lockridge added. " 'The man who has not been to Italy is always conscious of an inferiority . . . the grand object of traveling is to see the shores of the Mediterranean.' "

Lord Price subsided unhappily, thinking glumly about all the sightseeing he was going to be forced to endure, and wondering who this pompous ass of a Johnson might be. The only things that made Paris bearable were the cuisine, the wine, the pleasure of meeting other Englishmen, and the marvelous new clothes he had ordered.

He poured himself another glass of port, not seeing Laurie's disapproving glance. When she looked away, she found the marquess's clear blue eyes regarding her.

"And are you enjoying France, Lady Laura?" he asked.

Laurie began to talk easily of all the things they had seen that she had found interesting or amusing. Her description of some of the meals she and her father had eaten at the poorer inns brought a laugh from the marquess, and when she described the beds, even Lord Price roused himself from his distraction.

"There was one, sir, on a high frame that I inspected carefully," she told him with a smile. "There was a straw bed at the bottom, then a large mattress, then a feather bed, and then another large mattress with the blankets on top. I felt quite elevated, I assure you."

"Rather like 'The Princess and the Pea'?" the marquess asked idly, twirling his glass between long white fingers. "I am sure at your age you remember that fairy tale very well."

Laurie wondered how old the marquess thought she was, but she was saved from replying to this sally by the intervention of Lord Price, who was glad the conversation had left churches, monuments, and Roman ruins. "I have seen beds like that here too. A silly custom, but only to be expected from foreigners, you know. I suppose it is a good deal too much to expect them to behave as sensibly as we do." He sighed, and gulped his port while Edward Lockridge looked at him in amazement, and Laurie, after opening her mouth to speak, just as quickly closed it.

"Very wise, m'lady," the marquess murmured to her. "So much better *not* to say that, hmm?"

Laurie felt the color rising in her face. She had indeed been going to give the foppish Lord Price a setdown, but how had the marquess possibly known that that was her intent? She had no idea that her expressive eyes and the color that came and went in her cheeks gave a great many of her thoughts away, or she would have guarded her expression more carefully.

"Perhaps we might travel the Alps together, m'lord," the marquess suggested, kindly changing the subject.

Lord Lockridge denied him. "We have made no immediate plans, sir, for Laura has yet to see Paris. No, I am afraid that that is impossible, although I thank you for your kind offer. We travel alone."

"I only thought it might be safer in a group, because of the wolves, you know, and especially since you travel with your daughter," the marquess explained, somewhat taken aback by the earl's quick denial. He looked at Lady Laura. In her simple high-necked gown and with her slim figure

and short curls, he thought her no more than fifteen, and
surely no father would put such a child in any jeopardy.

"Laurie is an excellent shot," her father said, breaking
into his thoughts as he smiled across the table at her. "We
have our three servants, and I shall hire some guides to
show us the way. No, we do not fear the wolves."

Just then, his face paled and he put one hand to his
chest and bent forward over the table, choking back a cry.
John's eyes narrowed as he saw the beads of perspiration
that formed on the suddenly gray face of his guest, and the
grimace that twisted his lips.

"Father!"

"You are ill, sir!"

Both the marquess and Laurie spoke together as they
half-rose from their seats.

Lord Lockridge waved a dismissing hand, and then he
picked up his glass of port and sipped it carefully. The
marquess noted that the color was returning to his face,
and he took his seat again.

"Your pardon, sirs," Edward Lockridge said in an almost normal tone of voice. "A sudden indisposition, perhaps due to the sauce that was served on the fish. My
digestion has always been delicate."

He seemed to notice his daughter's white face and
clenched hands for the first time, and he added, "Sit
down, Laurie. There is nothing to be concerned about,
for I have had these attacks before, and I am well prepared for them. But perhaps you would excuse me now,
m'lord? There is some medicine I carry that I know would
help . . ."

The marquess said everything that was proper, and
frowned when Archie offered to escort Lord Lockridge
back to his rooms. He could see the earl did not want a
fuss made, and since the man seemed to be his normal self
again, he was willing to accede to his wishes in the matter.
After seeing the Lockridges out, he returned to the table.

"Rum thing, that, John," Archie said in wonder. "Thought
for a moment the old boy was about to stick his spoon in
the wall, 'pon my soul I did! But what a quick recover he
made."

"Yes," his cousin agreed. "Most fortunate. I am sure he

has had these 'attacks,' as he called them, before, else he would have been more frightened, for it was obvious he was in pain."

"Bit silly, don't you think, to be traveling abroad, then?" Archie remarked. "And with no one but a silly young girl along to help him. I shall never understand what made him bring her; Lord, the London tabbies would have a deal to say to her detriment if they knew. A girl on the grand tour!" He snorted and then added, "Of course, there are his servants, but what good would they be if he is taken ill in a strange country?"

The marquess stared into space, his narrowed eyes intent. "It seems most unwise, to be sure, but we must let Lord Lockridge be the best judge of that. Perhaps there is some pressing reason . . ."

His voice died away and then he added, "I shall make it a point to ask about the state of his health tomorrow."

But when the marquess questioned the hotel owner shortly after he first came down from his rooms, it was to discover that the Lockridges had already left Chantilly very early that morning, and by that time were well on the road to Paris.

# 3

Laurie spent a restless night, for although her father had said he always had trouble digesting French food, she felt there was something else wrong and could not be easy in her mind. The next morning, when she found Jed supervising the loading of the baggage in the coach, she questioned him, but she found him strangely tense and reticent.

"Now, don't you go a-worriting, Lady Laura," he commanded as he waved to the footmen to hurry with a large portmanteau. "Your father knows what 'e's about, and I'm 'ere to 'elp, so there's nothing for you to do about it. Besides, milord won't be best pleased to be fussed over—you know what 'e's like!"

Here Jed shook his head and mumbled, "And 'aven't I warned 'im time and time again? Like talking to a brick wall, 'e's that stubborn! Just as you are, Lady Laura." He turned away and called, " 'Ere you, Rob, tie on that trunk more secure-like!"

Laura knew she shared this trait with her father, along with a quick temper, but although she allowed the manservant to change the subject, she resolved to keep a close eye on Lord Lockridge, and if he suffered another spell, she was determined to make him return home and seek a doctor's opinion. She was relieved to see that when he came down to the coach he was smiling, his color good and all traces of the frightening indisposition gone.

Laurie was fascinated by Paris when they reached it at last, for it seemed so large and bustling, so crowded and noisy. She had time to look about her when their coach was stopped for customs in the Bureau du Roi by barriers that her father told her were placed before all the gates leading into the city. When at last they were allowed to pass, she was amazed at the speed of the other carriages, and the way the French seemed almost to run through the streets in their hurry. Lord Lockridge had taken rooms in the Rue Dauphin, and they proceeded there at once.

In the days that followed, they saw more Englishmen and -women than they had encountered since they left home, but although Laurie looked carefully, she did not see the marquess or Lord Price. This was hardly surprising, for the activities her father engaged in were not the sort that Archie found amusing. Not for Lord Lockridge the French tailors or the jewelry shops in the arcades beneath the Palais Royal, nor did he frequent the gardens of the Tuileries, where the quality walked in the evening, much as they did in Hyde Park, to see and be seen. He even took Laurie to visit the Louvre at an early, unfashionable hour so she would be sure to see the masterpieces there, instead of a crowd of *milord anglais* who gathered to talk in the long galleries and ignored the wealth of art around them. Nor did Lord Lockridge frequent the balls and soirees, or the gloomy *Théâtre Français* with its fantastic, outré performances, and he was never to be found lounging with his countrymen in the Café de Caveau, sipping a cup of *bavaroise*, or studying the English papers at the Cabinet Littéraire in the Rue Neuve des Petits Champs.

Laurie was not aware that there was another side to life in Paris. She admired the paintings and the works of art, the magnificent churches and the palaces of the nobility, the fine wide bridges over the Seine, and the domes, turrets, and spires of the Sorbonne and Nôtre Dame, and the windmills of Montmartre, and in spite of the filthy streets, the poverty and squalor and smells that were everywhere, she began to fall in love with the city. Although she enjoyed the children and even the street performers, called *violineux*, who carried all their belongings in large straw baskets on their backs, she could not approve the rudeness of most of the Parisians, who not only talked too much and too arrogantly, but even spit indoors, and whose women painted their faces with a white cosmetic called *fard*, which was further adorned

with heavy rogue. Above these masks, they wore masses
of frizzy false hair, and Laurie thought they looked quite
hideous.

Lord Lockridge took her to the Ecole Militaire and
Observatory, to the courts of justice and the Natural History Museum, and to the libraries of the Sorbonne and St.
Germain, as well as to Versailles, where she could not
restrain a gasp at the Gallerie des Glaces, so high and so
long with its mirrored walls reflecting the many elaborate
chandeliers.

There was so much to see and do in Paris, Laurie was
sure they would remain for some weeks, but she was
surprised one morning, only two weeks after their arrival,
to find her father planning an early departure. When she
questioned him, he gave her an evasive answer, and he
seemed so preoccupied that she swallowed her curiosity
and went away to pack. It was August now, and so hot and
summery in Paris she could hardly believe his explanation
that they must be over the Alps before the autumn snows
began. At their last dinner, Lord Lockridge told Laurie
that he intended to try the Simplon Pass, a new route that
would be a test of endurance for them all. He whiled away
the meal by describing the various routes travelers could
employ, and the methods used to transport them and their
baggage over the mountains. Laurie could not help but be
interested as he described the guides, called *coulants*, the
straw sedan chairs supported on long poles, or the *char-a-
banc*, a kind of jolting wheelbarrow. Sometimes, he said,
if there was an early snow, descent was made by sledge,
with guides at either end to brake and steer it.

Since Laurie had seen no signs in her father of further
illness, she did not connect the state of his health with this
sudden urge to be on their way, but Edward Lockridge
sensed that his condition was becoming more serious, and
he knew he did not have the luxury of endless time. As
they left Paris, Laurie vowed that someday she would
return.

Unbeknownst to them, the Marquess of Vare and Lord
Price had left the city a week earlier and were beginning
their journey through the Simplon Pass even then. Archie
thought this a great adventure, and even the wolves that

were so frequently sighted, and so bold he managed to shoot several at close range, could not dampen his boyish enthusiasm. John was glad he was having a good time at last, although he himself could have done without the wolves and the terrible inns they were forced to frequent that were so expensive, yet dirty, with their damp sheets, louse-infested mattresses, and tough peasant food.

When at last they reached the end of the pass and came out on the shores of Lake Maggiore at Domodossola, everyone in their party was relieved. Archie was suffering from a very tender arm incurred when a sledge had overturned on an icy glacier and slammed him against some rocks, and he was glad to remain in one of the inns for several days until it healed. The plains of Lombardy were green and fertile, a complete contrast to the stark peaks, the tall firs felled by so many avalanches and the frigid torrents of the Alpine streams. Both men admired the contrast of the green vineyards and vine-covered cottages where the peasants sat making silk under awnings that protected them from the hot sun. And after the poor food they had been forced to eat on their journey over the Alps, they reveled in the fresh produce and the melons, figs, and pomegranates that were so commonplace here.

The marquess saw Archie eyeing a handsome Piedmontese country girl, and he smiled in relief. Lady Pamela had been mentioned but seldom on their arduous alpine trek; perhaps Archie was recovering from his infatuation at last. The peasant girl was certainly alluring with her shiny black hair combed back in a large knot that was fastened with a foot-long hairpin. As she strolled away, the huge gold hoops she wore at her ears swung in a gentle rhythm that was echoed by rounded hips under a long full skirt.

It was almost a week before Archie's arm healed and he could control a horse again, even for short periods of time. The marquess could have hired a carriage to transport them to Milan, their next stop, but he preferred to wait until his cousin could ride. The roads were almost nonexistent and the pace so slow that traveling by carriage was sure to be a tedious experience. In the meantime, the two contented themselves by exploring the surrounding countryside.

One day, having ventured farther than they had ever gone before, they were late returning to the inn where they were staying. John had seen that Archie was tiring, although he made no mention of his discomfort, and he had slowed their pace. It was almost sunset as they rode through a deserted stretch of woods. Suddenly, shots rang out ahead of them.

The marquess pulled up his horse at once, motioning his cousin to do the same. Madame Lucia had warned him about the group of *banditti* who were currently terrorizing the neighborhood, and he had no desire to tangle with them.

"What is it, John?" Archie whispered, his blue eyes wide.

John noticed he had withdrawn his pistol from his saddlebag, and he nodded. "I imagine it is the *banditti* our hostess mentioned. Come, let us leave the main track and circle around them."

"But . . . but someone may be in trouble!" Archie exclaimed. "Should we not ride to their assistance?" He leaned forward as more shots rang out and hoarse voices could be heard yelling.

"Cowardly as it may seem, cuz, we will not. We do not know how many comprise the bandits' party, or why these travelers have been attacked. It may be just a local feud."

The marquess knew they must be very close to the fray, possibly as close as just around the next bend of the path. Suddenly he paused. "But stay . . . !"

Now it was the marquess's turn to lean forward in his saddle, his dark blue eyes intent as he raised his hand to ensure his cousin's silence.

"Don't you dare run away, you scaly rascals," an English voice cried, and then the guns rang out again, and there was a scream of pain, immediately followed by bursts of coarse laughter.

"I was mistaken, Archie," John said, his lips tightening. "It appears that it is our own countrymen who have been attacked. We will ride to help them, and if we can make it appear that we are more than just two, we might frighten the bandits away. Are you with me?"

The marquess held his own pistol now, and Archie,

although he was pale and his Adam's apple very prominent as he gulped, nodded. They both urged their horses into a gallop and raced down the track, yelling as they came.

"Follow me, men," the marquess bellowed as they came around the bend. Before him was a sight to inspire fear in anyone, no matter how brave. A gang of some eight men was attacking a large coach. They appeared to be led by a man on horseback some little distance away, for he was shouting orders and waving a sword as he urged them to further carnage. John fired at the bandit nearest him, his shot quickly echoed by Archie's pistol. Two of the robbers dropped, one howling in pain, the other dead before he hit the ground. The occupants of the coach continued to fire as the remaining bandits backed their horses away in terror. John could see the driver was dead. The frightened team was rearing in the traces, neighing in fear as a footman in livery tried to control them.

John called again, in Italian this time, as if urging a troop of men behind him to make haste.

Suddenly the leader of the bandits swore and barked an order to his men, and they turned their horses aside and dashed into the woods. Just as they had almost reached the safety of the trees, one more shot rang out from the coach, and their leader gave a hoarse cry. John saw him arch his back and then slump sideways in the saddle before his lifeless body thudded to earth. His mount continued to make good his escape, dragging the dead man, whose foot was caught in the stirrup, behind him.

When the band was out of sight, John pulled up his horse and reloaded his pistol. Archie was staring around wildly, his mouth open at the sight of the dead and dying men before them.

"Reload, man!" the marquess ordered. "We cannot be sure that they will not return!"

Archie obeyed, his hands shaking. He was more than glad to look away from the carnage.

"Hallo, the coach!" the marquess called. "Do not fire! We are friends!"

In the slanting rays of the setting sun, he could see the glint of a pistol barrel pointed at them, and he removed his riding hat and waved it. "We are Englishmen," he called again. "Do not fire!"

He waited until the pistol was withdrawn before he set his horse to a walk, Archie close beside him. When they reached the coach, the marquess bent down and peered inside. A smell of cordite assailed his nostrils, and the groans of the wounded behind him were loud in his ears as he looked into the steady hazel eyes of Lady Laura Lockridge. She was holding a pistol and it was pointed at his heart.

"M'lord, is it really you?" she asked as she lowered her weapon. Looking beyond her, the marquess saw the Earl of Lockridge, facing the other window as if on guard, and across from the two, sitting back, a middle-aged servant who spared him a sharp glance as he reloaded his own weapon.

"I have never been so glad to see anyone in my entire life," Laurie breathed, a radiant smile lighting her face. "Father, look! It is the Marquess of Vare and his cousin who saved us."

She turned toward her father, now slumped against the door of the coach, and then the pistol she was holding fell from her hands.

"Father," she cried, "you are hurt!"

As she took her father into her arms and laid him back against the squabs, the marquess dismounted and handed his reins to Archie. "Keep a sharp lookout. The bandits may yet return," he ordered, his voice brusque.

He climbed into the coach to find the servant gently removing Laurie's clutching hands. "Leave off, Lady Laura," he growled. "Let me see 'ow bad 'e is."

Laurie sank back on her seat, moving her legs to one side to give the marquess room. For the first time John noticed she was wearing boys' clothing—tight-fitting breeches, polished boots, and a twill riding coat. Her face was as white as her stock, but her eyes never left her father's still, pale face. Putting this strange attire from his mind, John watched as the servant opened the earl's coat, and he heard a half-stifled gasp Lady Laura could not suppress at the sight of the blood-stained shirt. John spared her a quick glance, afraid the gory sight might make her faint, but Laurie had compressed her lips and made fists of her hands to stop their trembling.

"Jed, how . . . how badly is he hurt?" she asked, and the marquess silently applauded her controlled, even voice.

"I'm not sure, m'lady," the servant said slowly as he felt carefully around the bullet hole that was slightly below the earl's heart. "But we must get your father to a safe place as soon as ever we can. 'And me that case!"

He jerked his head at a brass-bound box on the floor of the coach, and the marquess, seeing it was a medicine chest, reached down to get it and open it. As the servant sprinkled the wound with basilicum powder and covered it with a compress, John untied his cravat and handed it to the man. Jed nodded his thanks as he secured the bandage with it. The marquess, noting how quickly the snowy linen turned bright red, knew the earl was dying.

No sign of his knowledge showed on his face, however, as he said, "I will see if any of your men are alive, and then you must let me escort you to the inn where we are staying. It is not far."

"Thank you, m'lord," Lady Laura whispered, her eyes still on her father's face. John noticed she had taken one of his hands and was chafing it gently, and he felt his throat constrict at the loss the girl must soon face.

After he had climbed down, he told his cousin in a few soft words what had occurred. Archie remained on watch as the marquess inspected each of the fallen men, pistol in hand. One of the earl's footmen remained on the perch, holding the now quiet team, but the other lay dead beside the bandits, as did the guides who had tried to run away.

After straightening the harness and traces of the team, he returned to the door of the coach to find Lady Laura climbing down, her pistol restored to her hand. She went to kneel beside the body of her footman for a moment, her head bowed in prayer. As she rose she said, "Jed thinks it would be better if I rode. He says there will be more room and he can better support Father and ease him from the jolting of the road."

She stared around as if to find a horse in the shadowy woods.

"He is quite right," the marquess said. He kept his

voice quiet and unconcerned, for he knew she was on the brink of collapse.

"Pray God we reach a haven soon," she continued, her voice rising a little.

Noting the growing hysteria, Lord Vare said, "Ride before me, m'lady. The horses have all run off in terror, and we must be gone. Keep your pistol handy."

Laurie nodded and allowed him to give her a leg up. When she was settled, the marquess mounted behind her and put one strong arm around her waist before he nodded to the footman on the perch. "Follow me," he ordered, and then said over his shoulder to his cousin, "You bring up the rear, Archie, and keep a sharp lookout behind you. I do not want to be surprised, although I suspect the attackers won't have any heart for a further fight now their leader is dead."

Archie nodded, his thin face grim, and the little cavalcade started off at a slow pace. It was almost dusk now, and deep shadows added to the eeriness of the scene. The marquess saw how Lady Laura peered first left, then right, as they moved down the track, one of her hands grasping the horse's mane, the other moving the pistol from side to side to cover their advance. John was impressed. How had she known how to do that? he wondered, especially since he could feel the tension in her body as he held it firmly against his own. She was quivering like a coiled spring, but still she retained enough self-possession to remain on guard.

They were all relieved when the dark woods were left behind and the road began to wend past open fields and orchards and an occasional cottage shaded with mulberries.

When the marquess continued to hold his horse to a walk, Laurie spoke for the first time since they had left the scene of the ambush. "For heaven's sake, let us go faster, m'lord," she begged, her voice taut with anxiety. "I must get my father to a doctor quickly!"

John felt her trying to lean forward as if to spur the horse, and he tightened his arm. "Steady, m'lady," he said. "Your father will be safe soon enough, but he has lost a lot of blood. We cannot take the chance of aggravating his wound by moving at a faster pace on this rough road."

For a moment he thought she would protest, but then she sighed and settled back. "Yes," she said with a nod. "I know you are right, but I feel so helpless, so . . . so useless! This gentle amble is hard to bear."

"When we have your father in bed at the inn and have summoned a doctor, you can, of course, help to nurse him if that is your wish," the marquess replied. "For now, trust me to know what is best."

Laurie heard his deep, calm voice close to her ear, and for a moment she shivered before she slumped against his broad chest. Strangely, she did trust him to do all he could for her father. The quiet conviction in his voice and the calm authority that made them all obey his orders without question were soothing. How she would have liked to place all her burdens in his capable hands, she thought, and then she scolded herself. It was up to her to be strong now, not dependent on some stranger. She and Jed could take care of her father, she told herself as she straightened up and squared her shoulders.

John felt the movement and saw in profile the tilted, defiant chin. "Good girl," he said, applauding her courage. "I see you realize you must not give way now, for the earl will need you."

Laurie nodded, but she did not speak again. She was busy praying for her beloved father with the most fervent words she knew. Over and over in her mind she begged God to spare him.

Although it seemed an endless time to her, it was just a little while longer before a small village on the shores of Lake Maggiore came into sight and the marquess preceded the coach to the yard of an inn. A stablehand appeared to take his horse as Laurie threw her leg over and slid to the ground to run back to the coach. She could hear the marquess giving a number of orders to the boy, and then she heard his voice calling for the innkeeper as he mounted the shallow steps. She did not turn, but climbed once again into the coach. In the flickering light from the flambeaux, her father's face was very pale and still, and she gasped, one hand going to her mouth to hold back a cry of despair.

Jed Simmons looked up at her white face and saw the

horror in her hazel eyes, and he tried to smile. " 'E's not dead, Lady Laura," he whispered. Laurie nodded as she took her seat and picked up her father's hand, remembering to breathe a prayer of thanks.

A short time later, Jed and the marquess carried the earl into the inn and up a steep set of stairs to the marquess's own bedchamber. Laurie hovered in the background while her father was put to bed. She would have tried to help, but the marquess told Archie to take her away.

"I have ordered you both some wine, for I am sure you need it," he said, holding the earl's leg still so Jed could remove his boot without jarring him. When Laurie would have protested, he waved her away with an impatient hand. "Do not argue!" he said, and for the first time she heard a hint of steel in his voice. "There is nothing you can do now. The doctor has been summoned, and until he has made his examination, you will only be very much in the way. Simmons and I can care for your father; leave us."

Knowing the truth of his words, Laurie was forced to obey, and she allowed Archie to take her from the room.

In a private parlor, he poured them both a glass of wine with shaking hands, carefully refraining from staring at her boy's clothing, or even asking her why she was dressed that way. As he handed her a glass, Laurie looked at him for the first time. She was surprised to see his concern for her written on his face.

"I must thank you, m'lord," she said, after she had taken a sip of wine to steady her voice. "I do not know what would have happened to us if you and the marquess had not come along when you did."

Archie waved a careless hand, his brow creased in a frown. Gone completely was the mincing fop who had raised a supercilious quizzing glass to sneer at her and call her a "callow child."

"I am glad we were there," he said, his voice sober. Archie had never seen men wounded or killed; he knew the horror of the sight would remain with him always, and wondered how Lady Laura could remain so calm. He forced himself to push the bloody vision away so he could concentrate on her and her grave problems as she sat across from him at the table. He saw the unshed tears that glistened in her hazel eyes, and the little quiver of her chin, and he said, "You must not dwell on it, Lady Laura. Your father is alive, and I daresay the doctor will have him as fit as a trivet before too long. Why, he treated me for a badly bruised arm right after we arrived here, and see, it is all healed!"

He waved his arm and Laurie swallowed her retort that a sprained arm could in no way compare to a bullet hole in the chest.

She had never thought to like Lord Price, but as time progressed she was grateful for his company and conversation. He seemed determined that she would not brood, and forced her to converse about her travels, and their journey over the Alps. Even with the diversion, it seemed an age before the marquess appeared in the doorway. She sprang to her feet, leaning on the table, her knuckles white while her eyes asked the question she could not bear to put into words.

The marquess joined them and poured himself a glass of wine, saying as he did so, "The doctor is with him now, and Simmons too, of course. I came only to tell you that there is no change in his condition."

He tossed off his wine and poured another glass for them all. "Sit down, Laurie. I have ordered a meal for us."

Laurie continued to pace the room. "I cannot eat," she said quickly. "Do not bother about it for me, m'lord."

The marquess came and took her arms, forcing her to stand still and face him. She stared up into his face as he shook her a little. "You will wear yourself out to no avail, my girl! If you do not eat and keep up your strength, of what use will you be to your father? Try for a little sense!"

His voice was harsh again, and Laurie felt the color rising in her face, and she opened her lips to refuse. Even the thought of food made the bile rise in her throat. The marquess put a strong hand over her mouth. "No more. You will do as you are bade, for I have your father's permission to see to your welfare."

Laurie stopped trying to get away. "He spoke?" she asked, her eyes shining with hope.

The marquess let her go, motioning her to take her seat again. "He has come to himself, yes," he said.

And then the maid brought in a tray filled with steaming dishes, and he added, "As soon as you have finished your supper, you may go to him."

Laurie would have liked to protest this cavalier treatment, but she obeyed, afraid he might very well deny her admittance to her father's room if she refused.

The night was very long, and she was exhausted, but once she was with her father after supper, no one could make her leave him. Jed Simmons whispered in her ear, the marquess tried to order her away, and even Archie added his pleas that she get some rest, but she would listen to none of them.

When the marquess came in shortly before dawn to relieve the valet, he found her slumped over in an exhausted sleep in an old armchair drawn close to her father's side. He saw that she still held Lord Lockridge's hand, even in her sleep.

Simmons rose, his face sad and drawn. The two men were the only ones who knew that there was no chance of recovery. The doctor had shaken his head and offered no hope when he found that the bullet was lodged in a vital organ and could not be extracted. As he rebandaged the wound, he gave them instructions on how to care for milord, and he left laudanum to ease the pain. Now, before the marquess prepared to take the valet's place at his side, he whispered, "I will carry Lady Laura to her room."

He gently loosened Laurie's clasping hand, and although she stirred and murmured, she did not wake. Simmons pushed him gently aside and picked her up. "Nay, milord. I'll care for Lady Laura," he muttered, his voice possessive. "She is my charge now."

John nodded. "Put her to bed. She will need all her strength to face what we both know is coming. You and I must have a talk sometime soon, Simmons."

Jed gulped and inclined his head. A few minutes after he had left the room with the sleeping girl in his arms, the earl regained consciousness once more. Seeing the marquess beside him, he beckoned him closer. For several minutes, John bent over him, listening closely to his breathless, often labored words. At last he sank back on his pillows and John said, "Rest now, m'lord, and do not worry. You have my promise."

The earl died at noon. Laurie was beside him then. He had spoken to her only twice since the ambush, and each time she had summoned all her willpower not to show him a frightened, tearstained face. Now, however, when she knew the end had come, she gave a little choked cry and slid to the floor in a faint. Jed Simmons rushed to her and lifted her in his arms. His throat was working with his grief, and tears ran down his face, but he had promised his master and his friend to care for her, and care for her he would. The marquess held the door for him, his own face etched with the harsh lines of his concern.

When Laurie woke, it was dusk. For a moment she was perplexed, but then the memories flooded back, and she buried her face in her pillow and wept. It was a long time before she was able to rise, and she was quivering so with grief and weakness that she had to hang on to the bedpost with both hands like an old woman.

She did not leave her room that night or all the next day, and she refused to speak to anyone. When Jed brought her food, she would not eat. And when he insisted she change from her wrinkled, dirty shirt and breeches, she did not even bother to shake her head.

The valet frowned, but it was only when he told her the funeral would be held the following morning and threatened to tell the Marquess of Vare of her behavior that he was able to get her to eat and drink something, and order her a bath. He did not know that her determination to regain her strength was not from any fear of Lord Vare, but because she was determined to attend the burial, honoring her father by holding herself proudly, completely controlled as she did so.

As he started to leave her room, Jed said, "Lord Vare wants you to continue to dress as a boy, Lady Laura, at least for now."

Laurie looked at him dully and he added, "There are reasons—important reasons—but milord will tell you 'imself in due time."

He waited until she nodded, and then he went out and closed the door quietly behind him. Laurie sat and stared into the fire. What did it matter what she wore? And then she remembered all the happy hours she had spent with her father, dressed in shirt and breeches, and she thought it only fitting that she don them one more time to see him safely buried in the little churchyard of a strange village so far from home.

The hot tears began to fall, and she put her face in her hands and wept again.

# 4

Right after the funeral services for Lord Lockridge and the footman, Paul, the marquess insisted that they all leave the village at once. Laurie was given no say in the matter, and in truth, at that point, did not care very much where she went. She did not even question Simmons about this hasty departure as he helped her pack her belongings, and she climbed into the coach with Lord Price and the marquess, still dressed in her boots and breeches.

John watched her carefully, noting the violet smudges under her eyes and the droop of her mouth. It was obvious that Lady Laura mourned in private; in the church-yard she had been completely composed. And when the marquess would have put his arm around her to support her through the ordeal, she had shrugged his help away. Standing between the two cousins, she had been a slight, erect figure, but she held her head high, and not a single tear ran down her white cheeks. It was only the desolation deep in her hazel eyes that showed her grief and loss. The few villagers who had gathered whispered among themselves at the young milord's composure, and one old grandmother, tears in her eyes, had called Laurie a brave young boy. The marquess found himself relaxing somewhat.

For the rest of the day they traveled southwest, Jed Simmons driving the coach, and accompanied only by Rob, Laurie's footman, on horseback. Laurie spent most of the time staring out the window with unseeing eyes, although she roused herself to answer any direct questions from her traveling companions.

It was full dark when the coach passed through a village and pulled to a halt before an inn on its outskirts that was set somewhat apart from any close neighbors. The marquess announced that they would remain here in Cossato for a few days' rest, for his man had ridden ahead and rooms had been prepared for them. It occurred to Laurie as she followed him into the inn that she knew nothing of his plans. She reminded herself that she must make some plans of her own. It would not do to remain in Lord Vare's company; she and Jed and Rob must make their way home alone. She had her father's money belt, filled with gold coins, and although she knew she could not use his letters of credit at any foreign banks, she was sure there was enough gold to get the three of them safely back to England.

But the marquess would not hear of any such independence. When she announced during dinner that she was grateful for their help, but would delay them no longer, she thought the marquess stared at her coldly, as if he were not much interested in her decision. His cousin was quick to tell her, in almost his old haughty manner, not to be such a wet-goose.

"As if we'd let you jaunter off on your own, Laurie, after what you've been through, and you a girl and not dry behind the ears yet," he said, his blue eyes indignant that she would think them so remiss.

Laurie was about to protest, but Lord Vare was before her. "I promised your father that I would see you safely home, Lady Laura, and so I shall," he announced in a voice that brooked no opposition. "We will discuss it tomorrow, but for now I suggest you go to bed. It has been a tiring day."

Laurie hesitated, angry at being treated as if she were no more than two-and-ten, but then she caught Jed's quick nod where he stood at the sideboard, clearing away, and she rose and said good night. As she climbed the stairs, she realized the marquess was right. She was exhausted. Tomorrow would be time enough to talk about the future.

John found her the next morning in a small garden at the back of the inn, still dressed as a boy, as he had ordered. She was sitting on a rough bench, her head bowed and her face averted. There was such an air of sadness and despair in those drooping shoulders and thin white hands that gripped the edge of the bench so tightly, that it was all he could do not to go to her and take her in his arms and comfort her for her loss. If she had been aware he was watching, she would never have displayed such weakness, he knew.

He walked up to the bench slowly, and as his shadow fell across her and blocked the sun, she straightened up, wiping her eyes with the back of her sleeve, just as any boy would do.

When she made to rise and bow to him, he pressed her back down on the bench with a strong hand on her shoulder, and as she subsided, took the seat beside her.

"I beg pardon, sir," she said, her voice husky but steady. "A momentary weakness. My father would be ashamed of me."

"On the contrary, your father would be extraordinarily proud of your behavior. You have been brave and resolute, but you must never think that tears are a form of weakness, in either a man or a woman."

Laurie bowed her head, for she knew she could not look into those kind blue eyes and retain her composure. Staring straight ahead of him, he continued, "I know how much you loved your father, and it is right that you mourn him. So too did I cry when my father died, and I was many years older than you are now."

Laurie bit her full lower lip as the marquess took her hand in his and stared down at it. It was so white and slender, so defenseless. "But proud of you as he would have been, these boy's clothes that you have been wearing will not serve any longer, my dear," he said, his voice quiet. For a moment there was silence in the garden, and only the hum of bees busy in the wallflowers could be heard, and far away, some peasants calling to each other in the fields.

"What do you mean, m'lord?" Laurie asked, completely confused.

"First let me tell you that only a few hours before his death, your father, out of his love and concern for you, asked me to care for you so he could be sure you would be brought safe home."

Laurie made a little choked sound, and he pressed her hand. "I will tell you something else, Laurie. Do you remember the spell your father had in Chantilly?" At her nod, he continued, "The earl was suffering from a serious heart disease. He thought he had a year or more to live, and he wanted to spend part of that time showing you the world. But the attacks were becoming more frequent, more severe, and he knew his time was running out. He told me to tell you not to mourn the way he died, for the bandit's bullet was a quick release from ever-growing weakness and pain."

The marquess saw the tears glistening in her eyes, and before they could spill over, he said, "I will see you safely home to England, I promise you, no matter how the cards are stacked against us."

Laurie looked at him. His last words had been spoken grimly, and now she saw his familiar frown.

"I do not understand. What is wrong?" she asked, bewildered.

"I debated telling you the whole, feeling you had borne enough. Then too, I had hoped that you would be able to continue your masculine role, for it would be easier for you to travel as a boy, but I have learned that that will not be possible."

He paused and frowned again. "Now I think it better if you understand the dangers that lie ahead. You have shown me your courage and I do not think it will fail you now."

"Of course I shall try to be brave, m'lord," Laurie promised, still confused.

"You are, without a doubt, the bravest girl I have ever known," he answered, his voice admiring, and she felt her heart leap at the compliment. "But, my dear, you will need every ounce of that bravery in order to face what lies ahead. You see, I have learned that the leader of the *banditti* was the son of the Doge of Varallo. The doge has threatened reprisals for his son's death, and offered a munificent reward to anyone discovering the whereabouts of the party that was responsible. He is so bent on revenge that he has vowed to pursue us throughout Italy."

"But we did not attack them," Laurie protested. "We only fired to protect ourselves. And how can the doge hold us responsible when his son was trying to rob us and kill us, at the head of a troop of bandits?"

"He is clearly mad with his grief. I myself know the world will be a better place without this villainous prince, but I have no intention of trying to reason with his father. Somehow, we must make good our escape, and soon. By heading southwest yesterday, instead of making for Venice or Florence as most Englishmen do, I hope we have led him off our scent. This is a remote spot, but even so, where there is so much gold involved, you can be sure we are being searched for, and vigorously, right now."

Laurie looked around the peaceful garden. Peaches were ripening on an espalier against the stone wall, and colorful flowers were nodding at her feet. All was serene, but she felt a little shiver to know that even now men were drawing closer, men who would take her back to this doge so he might have his revenge.

The marquess interrupted her thoughts. "I suppose it is a shame that Simmons killed the man, although I find his death hard to regret," he said, as if speaking to himself.

Laurie corrected him. "But *I* shot him. He was getting away, and I thought my father was reloading, as Simmons was."

The marquess stared into her eyes, his own narrowed. "Make you my compliments, m'lady," he murmured. "I could wish no better man beside me in a fight."

Laurie felt her face growing warm, and said quickly, "But what can we do? Should we not travel on as fast as possible?"

"That in itself would be suspicious," the marquess pointed out. "We are English tourists. A small party tearing across the plains of Lombardy is sure to look guilty. No, we must be much cleverer than that. We will all have to play at masquerade, and I hope our traveling troupe will be consummate actors, every one. *And* actresses," he added, nodding to her.

Laurie stared at him, her hazel eyes thoughtful as he

continued, "Here is what I think it best to do, and mad a scheme though it is, I am not sure it will suffice even so. The doge is looking for a party of foreign travelers. I am sure he has been told that you were aided by two men on horseback who rode up just in time to save you, and who have been accompanying you ever since. He must also know of our stay in the inn near Lake Maggiore, and of the funerals, but he cannot know what route we took after we left. In fact, I know he does not."

"How can you be so sure?" Laurie asked.

"Because if he knew, my child, he would have taken us long before this. Since we seem to have escaped his net, at least for the moment, we are safe here. When next we reappear, we must be completely different. He is searching for two men and a boy, and that is why I insisted you continue to wear your breeches. What we will become after we leave Cossato, therefore, is one man and two women."

Laurie looked at him as if she thought him mad. "How?" she asked.

The marquess found her abruptness refreshing. "Since you are a woman—well, a girl at least—it should not be at all difficult for you to resume your normal pose. The acting must now fall on Archie's shoulders."

"*Archie?* Play a woman? He'll never do it!" Laurie exclaimed.

"He will do it when the consequences of his not doing it are explained to him," Lord Vare said grimly. He knew of the torture methods used by the doges, and would have no hesitation in describing them to his cousin as vividly and exactly as he could.

"I would volunteer for the part myself, but no one would ever believe it," he went on. "No, it must be Archie. He is shorter and slighter of build, and if he slouches . . ."

For a moment, a ghost of a smile crossed Laurie's face. No, the tall, muscled Marquess of Vare with his rugged masculine features could never pass as a woman, that was certain.

"Archie shall become your maid," John continued, ignoring her sudden choked cry of protest. "We do not have

time to initiate him into the niceties of court behavior,
flirting with fans and fluttering his eyelashes, and I am
sure that blushing is beyond him in any case. But acting a
simple, rawboned maid for a few days should not be
beyond his capabilities. Even so, you will have a great
deal to do to instruct him."

"I am not sure I can," she said, determined to be
honest. "I have not been brought up a simpering girl. My
father thought such creatures silly, and . . . well, so do I.
But perhaps if you help?"

"I cannot, at the present time. I leave almost at once for
the nearest town, Biella, so I can buy both you and Archie
some clothes." He saw the question in her eyes and went
on, "We must make haste! The longer we stay here, the
more chance we give the doge to track us down. You will
stay inside our rooms while I am gone, and neither you
nor Archie will speak to strangers. The innkeeper has
been well bribed, and Simmons will wait on both of you so
you will not have to see even the servants."

Laurie agreed, although she had a lot of questions.
Before she could voice them, he commanded, "Lady Laura,
look at me! Can you do this, do you think? Answer me
truthfully, for our lives depend on it."

"Oh, of course I can act the girl, why do you ask? But
will it not look very suspicious that we are kept hidden
away? If I were the doge, I would suspect such behavior
immediately."

His smile approved such logical thinking. "If necessary,
I will say that you are slightly indisposed, and that is why
we have broken our journey. When I return from Biella,
you will make a miraculous recovery, and we can begin
our escape."

Laurie stared at him. "You have assigned all the roles,
m'lord. May I ask what part you play in our masquerade?"

"Why, I become your bridegroom, of course, the Marquess of . . . Let me think. The Marquess of Tench. We
are on our wedding journey. I thought to play the role of
elder relative, but I do not think that would serve.
Fortunately, girls marry very young in Italy, so I will not
be suspected of cradle-snatching."

Laurie's eyes looked startled as she studied his face. It

was still and composed, the dark blue eyes steely, and the lips set in a tight line. "It is for that reason that we have avoided the more traveled routes, and often tarry in remote country inns—quite understandable and not at all unusual under the circumstances."

His words were dry and matter-of-fact, but as Laurie continued to stare at him, he coughed a little, and a tinge of red stained his cheekbones.

"Send Archie to me now, if you will, m'lady. I would make the situation known to him as well. While I am thus engaged, please write down your measurements and height, and give me a tracing of your foot. With your leave, I will take your footman with me to assist me in Biella. My man, Finch, will remain here to aid you and to keep the innkeeper from regretting his pact with me."

Laura rose from the bench. "But there is no need for you to buy clothes for me, m'lord. I have my own."

"Forgive me, Laurie, but the feminine clothes that I have seen you in would not be at all suitable for my marchioness. We must make you look older, more sophisticated . . . more like a bride. Trust me!"

She nodded, but still she felt uneasy. "How long will you be gone, m'lord?" she asked.

Her tone was subdued. John could not know how she was dreading his departure. Somehow, when he was near, she felt safe and protected. An incensed Archie, learning to curtsy and murmur "Yes, milady," was a very poor substitute for his cousin. She resolved to keep her pistols primed and loaded, and always nearby.

"I shall make all haste," Lord Vare was saying, and with that she had to be content, and she turned and hurried away. The marquess wondered as he watched her straight back and long slim legs covering the ground with such a boyish stride, if the scheme he had concocted had any chance of success at all. She was so very young, in many ways still more a child than a girl on the brink of womanhood. Could she play the blushing bride? The earl had kept her from becoming a simpering miss, but inadvertently he had delayed an important part of her growing up in doing so.

The marquess paced up and down the garden path,

deep in thought, until Archie appeared. From his sunny smile, it was obvious that Laurie had let slip no hint of the subject of their meeting. Lord Vare began to remedy this omission at once.

Laurie lingered just out of sight, unable to resist eavesdropping on Archie's first reaction to the scheme. She was not at all surprised to hear his first, bellowed words.

"You are mad, John! No, I absolutely refuse! You must find some other way."

She could not hear the marquess's quiet rejoinder, but he spoke uninterrupted for some time. At last she heard Archie say, "If what you have told me is true, I suppose it must be as you say. Egad, what horrible customs prevail in this benighted country! I cannot wait to leave it! And they actually allow people to watch the torture for sport? How barbaric!"

The murmurs of the marquess came again. At last Archie said, "Very well, but no more unless you want me to be sick at your feet! But, John, it is all very well for Lady Laura to resume her petticoats, but I do not see how I am to manage it. And by the way, why was she dressed as a boy when we found her, and why has she continued to do so? It is so strange and uncomfortable. I never know whether to address her as 'm'lady' or 'my boy.'"

Laurie edged a little closer to hear the marquess's reply. "She is used to dressing as a boy at home, I gather, and she was wearing her breeches because it was easier to travel the Alps that way. And thank heaven she did! Her masquerade may be the very thing that will save us all from the doge's torture chambers."

Laurie hurried away then without waiting to hear any more, to write down the measurements the marquess required. She did not see him again, for he sent Simmons to her room to get her note.

When Archie came in to luncheon, he was in high dudgeon. He barely spoke to her, and as he was accepting a serving of veal from Simmons, he muttered, "Madness! This is all insane madness, and your part in it, Laurie, deplorable!"

Simmons coughed, and Archie looked up in surprise at this little sign of disapproval. From the look in the servant's eyes, he saw the man would allow no discourtesies to his mistress, and Archie subsided.

Right after the meal was over, Laurie announced it was time to begin instructing him in the ways of femininity and how he should behave as her maid. The rest of the afternoon was spent with Archie mincing about, learning to bob a curtsy, and speaking his part in high-pitched tones. Laurie tried very hard not to laugh. She did not know what the marquess had told him, and she did not want to know, but it was obvious that it had been enough to make him try his hardest to master what was, to him, a repulsive role. She decided that to laugh at him would be most unkind.

In spite of her good intentions, they quarreled several times, and once Archie taunted her for her boyishness.

"I am sure you will have as hard a time of it as I, m'lady," he said. "Just look at you! Ladies do not sprawl in chairs, neither do they cover the room in three long strides. Perhaps it would be more to the point if we attended to your reeducation, else you give the game away in a trice!"

Laurie looked down at herself. She was so used to her breeches that she had leaned back at her ease in the chair, draping one knit-covered leg over the arm to swing her polished boot to and fro.

Hastily she faced front, putting her legs primly together while Archie sneered at her. "Do not worry about me, m'lord," she said, her voice gruff. "I promise you will be absolutely amazed at my transformation when your cousin tells me to resume my proper role."

It was a long two days later before that happy moment occurred, and by that time it was all Simmons and Finch could do to keep Archie and Laurie from each other's throats. They were both bored by their confinement in the inn, and tired of talking to each other, and Archie was sick of playing the woman, his best efforts derided under a constant stream of instructions. John found them silent, glowering at each other from opposite sides of the hearth in his private parlor.

Archie jumped to his feet. "Cuz, at last! Thank the Lord! I began to fear some ill had befallen you . . ."

Laurie rose more slowly, but her smile told him how glad she was to see him. "Your quest was successful, m'lord?" she asked, going to pour him a glass of wine.

"Yes, but it took much longer than I thought. Rob has taken my purchases to your rooms. While I change, may I suggest you both do the same? We will meet here for dinner in an hour's time."

Laurie nodded and bowed, and Archie pointed an accusatory finger at her. "There she goes again! John, wait until I tell you . . ."

Laurie left the room, her head high. She would not remain and listen to that insufferable fop enumerate her deficiencies for another second.

It was much longer than the hour the marquess had named before she returned to the parlor. The clothes he had bought her were a perfect fit, and richly made. It had taken a long time to decide which of her new dresses she wanted to wear, and then she had to struggle to arrange her chestnut curls in a more feminine style. She began to agree with her aunt that cutting them so short had been madness, as she threaded a ribbon through.

The marquess had thought of everything: lacy underthings and petticoats, nightrobes and powder, even a small vial of scent and sets of beads and ear bobs. There was one small package that contained a wide gold band studded with diamonds. As she slipped it on her left hand, she marveled. Everything must have cost him a fortune, she thought as she tied on her petticoat and admired her slippers of pale green satin. The gown she had chosen was of the same shade of green, with tiny puffed sleeves and a low, round neckline. It was caught above the waist by a satin ribbon, and fell to her ankles in slim folds. After the modest gowns and the white shirts and cravats she was used to wearing, it seemed very flimsy and revealing. As she studied her reflection in the cloudy glass over the dressing table, she wondered what the marquess would think of her. Her hazel eyes grew wide as she contemplated what seemed to be a vast expanse of white skin, and when she felt herself flushing, she tried to pull the neckline higher. The satin band was tight and it flattened her breasts and made it hard to breathe, and she had to pull the gown down again. As she did so, she reminded herself that the marquess had selected the gown as suitable, and it was the most fashionable one she had ever owned. As a married woman, and the legendary Marchioness of Tench, she should not blink an eyelash at revealing her slender neck, her soft shoulders, and even the gentle swelling of her breasts. Still, she threw a soft white shawl over her shoulders before she left the room.

When she entered the parlor, both men rose from the table where they had been sitting waiting for her. Feeling shy, Laurie looked first at Archie. He was dressed in a simple long-sleeved stuff gown of navy blue that was buttoned to the neck and completed with a large apron and an old-fashioned mobcap that was pulled down to cover his short blond hair. His eyebrows had disappeared under the ruffle of the cap, and his pale blue eyes were popping in astonishment. He looked so comical and gawky, she could not help smiling. Turning away before she disgraced herself, she found the marquess regarding her intently.

Suddenly she could not think of a single thing to say, and she felt quite as tongue-tied and idiotic as Archie.

"How lovely you look this evening, my lady. My compliments," John said, his voice warm with approval as he came to her side and bowed.

Thus recalled to her manners, Laurie sank into a curtsy, remembering to keep her head high and her back straight, and praying she would execute it with style and grace. John extended his hand and she took it, allowing him to draw her up beside him. Before he released her, he raised her hand and kissed it in tribute. Laurie felt her heart jump as his firm lips touched her skin. When he straightened up, his dark blue eyes were sparkling with appreciation, and Laurie tried an answering smile.

"I simply cannot believe it," Archie mumbled, finding his voice at last. "Whoever would have thought it possible? And how could I have missed such femininity, even dressed as you were in those old-fashioned, childish gowns? I have been blind!"

Silently the marquess concurred.

The masculine, educated voice coming from the tall,

ungainly maid caused Laurie to forget his insults about her clothes as she began to laugh. Archie frowned, his hands on his hips and his legs spread wide.

"So, you think I'm amusing, do you, Laurie? I'll thank you to try for nicer conduct, m'lady. It is too bad your manners did not change along with your fine new clothes!"

Suddenly he looked down at his outfit and his stance, and he scowled. "And why is it I who have to be the butt of this joke? If my friends should ever hear a whisper of this, I'll never be able to show my face in town again."

Laurie stifled her laughter, very much aware of the marquess standing so close beside her, still holding her arm.

"I beg your pardon, m'lord," she said, her voice shaking only a little bit. "You may be sure your secret is safe with me. It was just the sound of your voice and the way you are standing that made me laugh. And haven't I told you, time and time again, to pitch your voice higher, and try to stand more demurely, Archie?"

Suddenly she turned to the marquess. "But we cannot call him 'Archie' anymore, m'lord. What shall we call him?"

The marquess led her to the table, and she was glad that the narrow cut of her skirt made tiny steps imperative. "How do you like 'Betsy' or 'Maggie'?" he asked as he seated her.

Archie's face grew even redder. "I say, I'll not be called either of them; how common and loathsome!"

"Perhaps we should choose a name as near to his own as we can find," Laurie pondered. "That way, if we start to forget and call him 'Archie,' we can change it to 'Ar . . . Arlene.' "

"Well thought on, Laurie. 'Arlene' it shall be," the marquess agreed. Archie opened his mouth to say he didn't like "Arlene" either, but he closed it with a snap at the look in his cousin's eye.

Just then Simmons and John's valet came in with large trays. Jed smiled his approval that this mistress was correctly attired once again, and outside of a faint quiver of his lips, Finch acted as if he had never seen her dressed any other way. They both ignored Archie-Arlene.

The marquess took the seat at the head of the table and signaled the servants to begin. Archie sank into his chair across from Laurie, muttering as he twitched at his awkward skirts.

"Surely Arlene should assist in the serving of the meal, m'lord?" Laurie asked the marquess, keeping her eyes carefully away from Archie's face. "Who would believe the Marquess and Marchioness of Tench would allow a maid to take her dinner with them?"

John saw that she was teasing, and held up a deterring hand when Archie would have protested. "And so she shall, Laurie, after this evening. But I think in dressing as he has, Archie has suffered enough for one day. Time enough tomorrow for him to assume his regular duties."

"Very well, but it is not what I am used to," Laurie said, making a small pout and lowering her lashes. "However, if you say so, John, I suppose I must agree. . . ."

Her voice died away in gentle resignation to her lord's wishes, and Archie snorted. "Look at her! Butter wouldn't melt in her mouth. Why, all she needs is a fan, and she'd be flirting and playing the coquette all over us! Coming it much too thick, Laurie!"

He snorted again, and Laurie suddenly grinned at him. "I'm praticing, Arch . . . Arlene," she explained in her normal tone of voice. She had been trying to think how her cousin Rosamunde would behave in like circumstances, and patterning her behavior accordingly.

The marquess nodded as he took a serving of pasta. "Very well thought on, m'lady. There may come a time when you will be glad to see Lady Laura simper and blush, Archie, for her femininity may save us all."

While dinner progressed, the marquess kept up an easy conversation about Italy, his trip to Biella, which he said he could not recommend to anyone in search of culture and refinement, and the bad cooking of the innkeeper's wife. Laurie took her cue from him, although she wondered what his plans were for their escape. Surely they could not remain here so close to the scene of the ambush without being detected.

When the covers had been removed and another bottle of the local wine opened, Laurie rose to leave the men,

but the marquess caught her by the wrist. "I would ask
you to remain seated, m'lady," he ordered. "We have a
great many things to discuss."

Obediently Laurie sank back into her chair, and nodded
to Simmons to pour her some more coffee.

"Finch, fetch young Rob, and Simmons, pull up some
chairs, and pour yourself a glass of wine," the marquess
ordered next.

Now Archie looked somewhat surprised that he was
to sit at table with real servants, and John explained, "Do
not forget that we are all in this together, cuz. What we
decide to do must be unanimous, and we must have any
story we invent down pat. Ah, there you are, Rob. Come
in, my boy, and sit down."

The sturdy footman with his open English face and
straw-colored hair looked astonished at the order and at
Lord Price's attire, and his eyes slid over to Lady Laura.
She nodded to him, noting the fright and misery in his
eyes. She remembered that he and Paul, the other footman,
had been very close friends, and he must be missing him,
even as she was missing her father. Before such a thought
could make her sad, she said, "Do as the marquess orders,
Rob. We must all of us make plans to get away from here.
I'm sure that you will be glad to see England again, won't
you?"

"Aye, milady," he whispered, sitting on the edge of his
chair. "That I will!"

"I propose that we leave here tomorrow, as early as we
can," the marquess began. "Finch tells me the landlord is
getting restless, and we cannot risk his sending a message
to the doge."

"But won't he send for him right after we leave, in any
case?" Archie asked. "How can we then escape certain
capture?"

His voice was sober, and Rob looked frightened. "Listen
to the plan I have made, and then tell me what you think
of it," John replied. "We shall leave here at dawn, you and
Lady Laura dressed once again as young men. When we
are some distance away, we shall stop in some secluded
spot so you can change into your new garments. Rob must
also change into some of Archie's clothes. He was on the

perch of the coach, and the doge may have a description of the earl's livery. From the moment you all assume your new roles, the masquerade we play will begin in earnest. The innkeeper will tell any pursuers that two men and a boy stayed here, but those Englishmen will disappear. In their place we will become a honeymooning couple attended by the lady's maid and three menservants. Does everyone agree so far?"

He waited until they all nodded—all but Laura. He saw she was frowning and tracing an absent pattern on the tablecloth with her fork. "Yes, m'lady? You have some objection?" he asked.

"No, I am sure that is the only avenue of escape we have," Laurie replied, raising serious hazel eyes to his. "But we are probably the only English in the neighborhood, and therefore our disguise will be quickly suspect. But . . . but I'm afraid I have no suggestions as to how to avoid it."

Finch coughed and raised his hand. "M'lord, if I may?"

At the marquess's nod, he continued, "What if we told the innkeeper we were going in one direction, while actually we went somewhere else? That might take the doge off our trail."

Jed Simmons clapped him on the back, and the thin, elegant gentleman's gentleman tried to look pleased at the familiarity. "Good idea, Finch," Jed said. "That might well work. I was thinkin' perhaps it might be best if we split the party, but I'd feel a deal better if Lady Laura 'ad as many men around 'er as possible."

The marquess saw her indignant look and nodded to Rob, who had been shyly trying to get his attention. "Milord, wot if we don't tell 'im, not outright, I mean. Wot if we wuz to let it slip where 'e could 'ear? Say, I'm talkin' to Simmons about this place we're a-goin' to, but quiet like, as if I don't want 'im to rumble it?"

"Good thinking, Rob!" The marquess smiled, and then he added, "What a devious group of good intriguers I have in hand here. Perhaps our escape is not going to be as difficult as I imagined."

He stood up and added, "Hand me that map case just behind you, Finch. Let us decide right now where we shall *say* we are going and where we will actually *go* instead."

He spread out the map of Italy on the table, and willing hands weighted down the corners.

"Where in heaven's name are we now, cuz?" Archie asked, leaning forward to study the map.

"Here, in Cossato," the marquess said, pointing a long finger at the spot. "As you can see, we are a long way from any border or the sea." He traced a southwest route and then stabbed at another point on the map. "If we say we are making for Turin and the Cottian Alps, the doge will assume we are trying to escape to France. Therefore, before we reach the next town, Buranzo, we will head east."

He showed them all the route he proposed, and continued, "I hope we can reach Milan before the doge or his agents suspect the trick. In Milan we can disappear amid the other Englishmen making their way to the south of Italy and Florence and Rome."

He paused, a frown darkening his blue eyes. "It might be best to divide our party there. Archie and I could continue to Rome, while Lady Laura, with Simmons and Rob, could make for Genoa and a ship to England. But I cannot say now what would be best. I dislike abandoning you, Laurie, especially since I promised the earl to see to your safekeeping."

He looked at her, his eyes somber, and she returned a steady gaze. How lovely she is this evening, so slim and yet with such gentle curves, he thought. In the slender green gown she reminded him of a budding flower that was just about to burst into luxuriant bloom. The tousled chestnut curls made her appear very young, but there were dignity and composure in her eyes and demeanor. How brave she was as well! Most girls would have fainted long ago at merely the thought of the mad dash across Italy that he was proposing, the only woman in a company of men. But such missishness was not for the Lady Laura Lockridge, oh no. He noticed a faint tinge of color come into her cheeks as he continued to stare at her, and he forced his mind back to the problem at hand.

He went over the plan again, searching for flaws and

making sure the servants memorized the name "Turin."
To make sure the innkeeper understood, he coached Rob
to say it in Italian.

"You can mutter something about what a funny name
'Torino' is, and how glad you'll be to hear good English
names again," he said as Rob mumbled "Torino, Torino"
over and over again. "And if one of you can mention the
Cottian Alps as well, it can do nothing but good."

As he folded the map, the marquess smiled. "It is time
for me to dismiss the company. Try to get as much sleep
as you can. Tomorrow will be a long, hard day, for I
intend to put as much distance between us and Cossato as
I can. Finch, wake everyone at dawn. Before I go to bed,
I shall see the innkeeper and pay our shot, and you may
trust me to be very reticent about the direction we plan to
travel."

The servants rose and bowed themselves out, and Archie stood as well, to stretch and yawn. "How glad I am to
be able to take off these ridiculous clothes, if only for a
short while," he remarked. "I'm off to bed. Good night,
Laurie . . . er, m'lady. Good night, cuz!"

"A curtsy, if you please, Arlene," Laurie demanded,
and he sighed, but the awkward bob he gave them both
looked better performed in a skirt than it ever had in his
riding breeches, and Laurie was satisfied.

When she would have followed him, John said softly,
"Stay a moment if you would, Laurie."

She looked surprised, but she waited by the table until
Archie closed the door behind him before she asked,
"There was something else, m'lord?"

The marquess fiddled with the straps of the map case
before he answered. Laurie wondered at his sudden silence,
imagining she had done something to displease him until
he dropped the case and came to stand close to her.

"I just wanted to tell you that I will do everything in my
power to see you safe out of this imbroglio, Lady Laura.
We are in for a difficult time, and it will require all your
fortitude, but I have seen how courageous you are."

His dark blue eyes seemed to burn into hers as she
faced him, and once again he raised her hand to kiss it in
tribute.

She wanted to answer him, but her throat was tight and she could not think of the words to say.

"Do you know, I do not even know how old you are," he said.

Surprised, she whispered, "Why, I am eighteen."

"Eighteen? Then you are past your girlhood, and all this time I thought of you as a child. I have never known anyone remotely like you. No wonder your father was so proud of you."

Laurie pulled her hand from his and stepped back. "Please, m'lord, you must not speak of my father. Until we are safe, I cannot allow myself to think of him, for to do so would make me sad and weak. I will have all my life to mourn him after we escape the doge."

"Of course," John agreed. "And will you believe me when I tell you that although you will never forget him, the ache you feel now will diminish in time?"

Laurie nodded, lowering her head so he could not see the tears come into her eyes. He took her chin in his hand and raised her head, and in spite of her efforts to control herself, a single tear escaped and ran down her cheek. He wiped it away with a gentle finger.

"Go to bed, my dear," he said into the silence that lengthened between them. His deep voice was soft and full of his concern for her, and she shivered.

As she walked to the door, she remembered she had not thanked him for her new wardrobe.

"M'lord, the clothes you bought me are beautiful. Thank you. When we are safe, you must present the bill, for I cannot be your debtor. Of course I will return the diamond band."

She held up her left hand and was startled by his suddenly haughty expression.

"But naturally the Marchioness of Tench must have an appropriate wardrobe," he said, his eyes narrowed. "Do not regard it; it was nothing."

Laurie bit her full lower lip. Now he sounded bored, his voice cold and stern, almost as if she had displeased him somehow. She wished there was something she could do to bring back his soft, intimate tones, and then she whirled and left the room without another word, furious at herself for such a silly thought.

John remained where he was, staring at the door she had closed so hastily behind her. It was several long minutes later before he went to see the innkeeper to pay the bill.

# 5

It was barely light when Laurie came down the stairs of the inn the next morning and nodded to the fat innkeeper. Signore Bianco was all smiles, rubbing his hands together and looking thoroughly pleased to be ridding his inn of these strange English gentlemen. Laurie strode into the coffee room. Dressed once again in her breeches and riding coat, with her chestnut curls brushed smooth, she looked the complete young man. As she entered the coffee room, she greeted Archie with a husky good-morning, and then turned a chair around so she could straddle it and lean on the back. No one, she was convinced, could possibly guess from her posture and demeanor that she was not a brash stripling.

Archie eyed her cynically from where he sat at the table, and he only nodded his greetings. Laurie jumped up to go to the small window, as if to see what kind of day they would have for traveling.

"The marquess has not come down, m'lord?" she asked next, coming to take a seat and pour herself some coffee.

"He has come and gone," Archie said curtly. "He must have been up for ages, for even now he is seeing to the team and the coach. What a ghastly thing for gentlemen! I must beg you to keep your tongue between your teeth, boy. I do not care to converse at this ungodly hour."

He tore off a piece of bread and glowered at it, and Laurie applied herself to her breakfast. In the hall she could hear Jed Simmons directing Rob in loading the baggage, but although she strained her ears, she could not hear their conversation. Saying a small prayer that Rob would remember his lines and speak them convincingly, she drank her coffee.

It was only a short time later that Finch came to summon them to the coach. Laurie's face took on a look of petulance as she came outside to find the marquess waiting for them. "But I still don't see why I cannot ride," she whined. "How tame to sit in this old coach all day. Do say I may ride beside it, uncle!"

John raised an eyebrow at his sudden descent to the role of elderly, spoilsport relative, and then he motioned her to take her seat. "You forget you have been ill, my boy. Perhaps tomorrow. Archie? Do you join us in the coach, or will you take the footman's horse?"

Archie shook his head and climbed into the coach. "It is much too early to ride," he pronounced, his voice almost as annoyed as Laurie's had been. "And why we have to set off at this ungodly hour I shall never know. Why, my friends would be astounded to see me, not only up but dressed as well, when surely only peasants—"

The marquess cut off this tirade by entering the coach, followed by Finch, who shut the door firmly behind him. The innkeeper, bowing and smiling, called "*Addio, addio! Sicuro viaggio!*" until the coach, tooled by Jed and accompanied by Rob on horseback, left the yard.

Laurie leaned back in her seat, and Archie dropped his petulant pose to say, "Whew! I'm glad we are away, and I don't think the innkeeper suspects anything, do you?"

The marquess smiled at them both. "No, I am sure he did not, such good actors as you both are. Well, that is one hurdle we have overcome. But I would not care to wager a ha'penny that our oh-so-genial and trustworthy host is not even now preparing a message for the doge."

He banged on the roof of the coach, and Simmons could be heard urging the team to a faster pace.

"If I may, m'lord?" Finch murmured from where he was sitting back beside Laurie. "Rob whispered to me that the landlord heard him complaining that our destination was Torino. He said Simmons scowled at him and nodded toward Signore Bianco as if he wanted to keep Rob quiet. Furthermore, as Rob was getting ready to mount, he asked the innkeeper what he knew about the Cottian Alps, claiming he had no heart for a journey as treacherous as the one we had coming over the Simplon Pass."

"Excellent!" John exclaimed. "That may buy us the time we need."

A hour later, Simmons pulled the team to a halt beside a run-down shed set beside a lonely wood. When Laurie climbed down, she shivered a little. Even in the bright morning light, the shadows under the trees and the heavy underbrush reminded her of the ambush. For a moment she clung to the handle of the coach, her face white and strained. John noticed her expression, and guessing she was remembering her father's death, ordered her to make haste in a harsh, authoritative voice.

His words broke the spell, and although she was hurt by his unfeeling tones, she knew he was right. Archie handed her the bag she had prepared, and offered to let her use the shed. She saw that Rob and Finch were following him into the wood as she made her way to her impromptu dressing room.

Fifteen minutes later, the coach was once more under way. Laurie was now wearing a pale blue muslin gown and matching bonnet, complete with stole and reticule and gloves. When she looked at her new maid, she had to cover her mouth, although her hazel eyes still danced above her fingers. Somehow, Archie had acquired a buxom figure along with his dress, apron, and cap. As Laurie settled her skirts in her place beside the marquess, Archie eyed her with loathing from where he sat opposite with Finch.

"I'll thank you to wipe that silly grin from your face, Laurie," he growled. "This was all Finch's idea."

The valet inclined his head. "Just so, m'lord," he said primly. "It seemed to me that Lord Price was not as . . . er, *convincing* as he might be. Now he looks the part."

He sounded proud of his ingenuity, and Laurie swallowed her laughter, to congratulate him in shaking tones. Archie-Arlene stared pointedly out the window, arms crossed under a large bosom.

"Where do we turn off this road, m'lo . . . John?" Laurie asked, to change the subject. She was busy tucking up some errant curls that had escaped her bonnet. John watched her, his eyes distant. When he did not answer immediately, she looked at him in surprise, and he forced his mind back to their escape.

"In about a mile, if the map is accurate. We have not made the time I would have liked, but it cannot be helped. This route we take around Buranzo will slow us even further, for it is only a farm track. When we reach the main roads again, we must make better speed."

He sounded so concerned and worried that Archie stared at him. Catching his cousin's eye, the marquess began to chat of other things. It would do no good to upset Laurie or his cousin. Somehow he must get them both safe out of this, but it was hard to sit in a jolting coach that lumbered along at a crawl when all his senses cried out for the speed that would take them to safety. Perhaps he had been wrong. Perhaps it would have been better to abandon the baggage and ride cross-country to Milan.

Everyone soon grew weary and sore from the jouncing. The marquess would not allow a halt until they were some miles away from Buranzo, and even then, they were allowed only a few minutes to eat some bread and cheese and swallow a glass of the harsh country wine before he insisted they take their places again. Laurie began to think him overly cautious. They had seen no one all morning, with the exception of a few peasants plodding along the road or working in the olive groves and fields; certainly they had not been chased by a group of men intent on their capture. But John knew that the sight of a huge coach traveling at what was a dangerous pace on the narrow, rutted roads was sure to attract attention in the quiet countryside. He breathed a sigh of relief when they crossed the Sesia River and made their way through the town late that afternoon. He could see that Laurie was tired, for her face was white with strain and her hand grasped the leather loop at the side of the coach to stop herself from swaying, but she did not ask him to stop. It was Archie who suggested that they spend the night in Sesia.

"I say, John, there's what appears to be a decent inn! Surely you do not expect to find another out there in the countryside. And soon it will be dark. Besides, putting aside our own weariness, there are the horses to consider."

Laurie tried not to look hopeful as the marquess appeared to reflect. "We cannot take the chance of changing the team here," he said at last. "We are still too close to Cossato. No, we must go on. I intend to spend the night in Caltignaga. It is only twenty-one miles from Cossato, but who would believe we could travel that far, especially with women in the party? No, Archie, I am sorry, for I know how exhausted we all are, but it must be Caltignaga."

It was after ten that night before Simmons pulled the weary horses to a stop before the inn John chose. Laurie was sure she would always ache from the top of her head to the tips of her toes, and as she prepared to step down from the coach, she swayed a little. She was furious at her weakness, but more furious when the marquess, without a word, swept her up into his arms and carried her inside.

The innkeeper and his wife were both bowing and smiling, but when that woman saw the burden in the marquess's arms, she exclaimed and hurried forward.

"My wife is not well, and she is very tired. Show us to your best rooms at once, if you please," the marquess ordered in Italian.

"Ah, *la povera signora! Venga, signore.*" The good woman beckoned as she led them to the stairs, issuing a stream of orders at the top of her lungs as she toiled up the narrow steps.

"Why did you do that?" Laurie whispered, very much aware of John's broad chest and strong arms.

"Why, Laurie, it is what any new bridegroom would do," he teased her, his blue eyes blazing into hers. "Put your arms around my neck, if you please."

Laurie did as she was bade, but she was glad when the landlady threw open a door. The rooms she showed them were mean and none too clean, but Laurie was too tired to notice. As John set her on her feet, she was forced to cling to him for a moment, until her head stopped swimming. The marquess put arm around her and hugged her close, dropping a light kiss on her cheek as he did so. "You will soon feel better, my dearest," he murmured, to the great delight of the landlady. "Come and sit down."

He led her to the one armchair the room possessed. Laurie stared up into his harsh-featured face, her hazel

eyes wide at the soft, intimate tones he had used. He
winked at her, and then, turning to the landlady, who still
hovered in the doorway beaming at them, he spoke rapidly in Italian.

Laurie leaned back in the chair and closed her eyes. So
she was to be the helpless little bride, was she? Vaguely
she heard the woman exclaim, and the marquess's words
of confirmation.

"Ah, *la luna di miele, sì, sì,*" she said, curtsying and
taking her leave, all smiles at the thought of a honeymoon.

As the door closed behind her, Laurie opened her eyes
and sat up straight. She had no time to question the
marquess, however, for just then Rob appeared with the
baggage, followed by a red-faced lady's maid carrying her
mistress's stole and reticule. Rob put the portmanteaus
down in the middle of the room. Laurie wondered why his
eyes were full of laughter, and why he was almost as red
as Archie, who had dropped her belongings on the table
and who now stood arms akimbo, glaring at them all.

"What's amiss, cuz?" the marquess asked.

"You ask what's amiss, John?" Archie hissed in an out-
raged whisper. "Do you realize how I have been insulted?
'Buxom armful' indeed! Why, I have even been pinched!"

John's lips were twitching, but he sent a warning glance
to Laurie and the footman. "Then you should be applauded!
Our scheme has definitely succeeded if you have already
captivated the men below."

"Hummph!" Archie said, and would have continued to
protest except that Finch came in, followed by Simmons
with more baggage. The valet drew himself up and said,
"Don't stand about there, girl! Busy yourself unpacking for
the marchioness! And as for you, Rob, some hot water at
once. Put the cases over here, Jed."

In a moment, order was restored, Hot water appeared,
bottles of wine and glasses were presented by the innkeeper,
and trays of hot food were brought in. At last the inn
servants disappeared and they all sat down to eat and drink.

When the meal was over, the marquess dismissed the
servants. Simmons was sent to sleep in the coach to guard
their possessions from thieves, and Finch followed him
from the room.

"We shall not require your services any longer, Arlene," the marquess said as he poured himself another glass of wine. "I have told the landlady that you are Rob's wife, so you will share his room."

"You did what?" Archie asked, as if he couldn't believe his ears. "Sleep with a footman? I say!"

"But I only did it to spare you from unwanted attentions, cuz," John replied, his voice meek, but a devil in his blue eyes. "As you have discovered, it would be unsafe for such a fine, robust figure of a woman to be alone. I am sure you can do without the fondling that you would be subjected to otherwise."

Laurie frowned at Rob's grin, and he stiffened to attention.

"Be on your guard, both of you," the marquess ordered, his voice serious again. "We are being watched carefully—in fact, there is a man in the taproom who appeared very interested in us. He could be in the doge's employ, or have heard about the reward. We must do nothing to feed his suspicions."

The two young men nodded and took their leave, Rob bowing and Archie bobbing a curtsy, and for the first time in what seemed like hours, the room was quiet. Laurie stifled a yawn, her eyes half-closed as she stared into the fire.

"Get into bed, Laurie," the marquess said as he came to pull her to her feet. "You are asleep on your feet."

"Where will you sleep, John?" she asked.

"Do not worry about me. Even though I must remain in this room to belay suspicion, I doubt I shall be able to sleep tonight," he said, as if the subject bored him.

"But you are tired too! You must have some rest!" she protested.

"There is that dubious armchair if I feel the need," the marquess pointed out, and before she could protest further, he added, "Enough! I am going out to confer with Simmons about the team. Sleep well."

He bowed and left the room. Laurie unbuttoned her gown with slow, tired fingers. The marquess had looked different after everyone else had left, and yes, he had behaved differently as well. He had been so stiff and formal and cold! She pulled the gown over her head and hung it on a hook on the wall. Was he angry with her? Was he annoyed at all the trouble she had caused by shooting the leader of the *banditti*? Was he perhaps regretting the promise he had made to her father, and wishing he had never come up with their coach? For a moment she felt like weeping, and then she took the nightrobe he had bought for her and went behind the screen in the corner, where the washbasin and a chamber pot were set.

When John returned, she was fast asleep. She looked very slight in the big bed, and very young in the cotton gown that buttoned to the chin and was trimmed with embroidery and satin ribbons. In the firelight, her chestnut curls were touched with gold, and her thick lashes glinted against her soft cheek. John studied her quietly, his hands clenched by his sides. She was so lovely, so vulnerable. He realized that even if he had not made that promise to the earl, he would still have made sure she reached England safely. As he watched, she smiled a little in her sleep, and both hands went up to cradle her cheek. Whom was she dreaming of? he wondered; and then, ashamed to be spying on her while she slept, he went and sat by the dying fire.

When Laurie woke the next morning, she was alone. She sat up in bed, clutching the covers as a knock came at the door, and then Archie came in with a pitcher of hot water and a pot of chocolate.

"Good morning, Archie," she said in a normal voice. "I hope you slept well?"

"Yes, thank you, milady," Archie said, his voice as high-pitched as anyone could wish. He put his tray down on the table and sidled up to the bed, and as he pretended to plump her pillows, he hissed, " 'Ware your words, Laurie! That man in the taproom is still hanging about, and John says he suspects us!"

The landlady bustled in then, carrying a breakfast tray, and he backed away and coughed.

"Get away from me, you stupid creature," Laurie commanded, making shooing motions with her hands. "How many times have I told you I cannot have you near me when you have such a cold?"

Obediently Archie coughed again, burying his face in his apron as Laurie thanked the landlady and wished her good morning. This good woman would have liked to stay and ask the young English wife about her travels, but the marquess came in, followed by his valet, and she was forced to curtsy and move away from the bed.

Laurie noticed that John had changed his clothes and shaved while she slept. He was as immaculate as if he had been dressed at home, instead of in a tiny room in an Italian inn. His shirt and cravat shone white below his dark, harsh-featured face. In contrast, she felt tousled and sleepy-eyed and lazy.

"My darling!" she cried, raising both her arms to him for the benefit of the slow-to-leave landlady.

John sat beside her on the bed and pulled her into his arms. He buried his face in her curls, caressing her arms and back as he did so. Laurie was very much aware that beneath the thin cotton gown she wore, she was completely naked. She wondered if he could tell, and then chided herself for such an irrelevant thought.

The landlady sighed at his ardor. She would not have done so if she could have heard John's hurried whispers of instruction. As he raised his head, Laurie kissed his cheek, her own hand pressing his arm to let him know she understood.

As he rose, the marquess said, "Finch, some coffee please, and then, after the marchioness has dressed, I will take her for a stroll before we must take coach again. You and Arlene pack the bags and see them safely stowed. I am anxious to be on our way."

"Certainly, m'lord," the valet said, handing Laurie her tray before he poured his master a steaming cup.

The landlady tried to protest, saying that the young lady needed to rest, and a day spent at the inn would be of great benefit to her. Laurie could not resist showing off her Italian as she thanked the woman for her concern, but said she was as anxious as her husband to be on their way. "There is so much of your beautiful country to see, *signora*," she explained, while the marquess stared at her. As the door closed behind the landlady, Laurie wrinkled her nose at him and tucked into her breakfast.

"I hope that was wise, Laurie," John said, finding his voice at last. At her surprised glance, he added, "Admitting you can speak Italian, I mean. Now, where did you learn, I wonder."

"My father taught me, after I had mastered Latin, of course," Laurie confessed, and then, remembering his first remark, she asked, "But why wouldn't it be wise?"

"It might have been better if everyone thought that English was your only language. Then, if you should be questioned, you could pretend not to understand," the marquess explained as he set his cup down and beckoned to Finch. "I shall leave you now to dress. Be as quick as you can, for I want to be away from here in short order."

As soon as the door closed behind the two men, Laurie slid out of bed. She decided the blue muslin that she had worn yesterday would do, although it was creased from the long hours in the coach. Since it appeared that the marquess had another such day in mind for them, what did it matter? She sighed a little, for the big bed had not been very comfortable, and she had spent a restless night. As she washed and dressed, she hoped they would reach a place of safety soon. Their escape was not only tiring, but frightening as well. They were all on edge, playing a desperate part, never able to forget that they could be taken up anytime and detained and questioned. Laurie shivered as she combed her hair and arranged the blue bonnet on her curls, and then she tried to put on a bright smile as she went down to join the marquess.

As they strolled the streets of the town while the servants loaded the coach, the marquess seemed preoccupied. Although he answered all her questions, she could see his mind was elsewhere, and she was glad when they began to make their way back to the inn. Finch had made sure she had her parasol, for even this early the sun was strong, and now she tilted it at a defiant angle over her shoulder and stared straight ahead. I must be boring him, she thought miserably. Of course he is not interested in my inane schoolgirl remarks, accustomed as he must be to sophisticated, witty women of the world.

When they reached the inn yard, all was in readiness, and they climbed into the coach. Laurie waved good-bye to the landlady as Simmons clucked the team into motion once again.

Archie stared out one window and Finch the other as the coach threaded its way through the crowded streets of the town. Laurie had no desire to speak either, nor, did it appear, did the marquess. It was not until the open countryside was reached, and a faster pace possible, that the marquess broke their silence.

"I hope to reach Magenta by nightfall, my friends. It will not be as long a journey as we had yesterday—in fact we can stop for a luncheon in Galliate, to break the trip, if you wish. And from Magenta it is only a short distance to Milan, where we can fade into the crowds of tourists and become quite unexceptional."

He tried to make his smile warm and reassuring, but after his conversation with Simmons early that morning, he was not sure his effort was successful. The earl's valet had reported that the man in the taproom who had asked so many questions and who had watched them so closely had left the inn shortly before.

"And on as good a piece of 'orseflesh as I've seen in this country, m'lord," he had said. "I watched which way he went, and it seemed to me he was bent on retracing our path. It worries me."

It worried the marquess as well, but John was determined to keep it from Laurie and Archie. If the man was a paid informer for the doge, there was nothing they could do about it. Having set the masquerade in motion, they must all continue to play their parts.

Some of his concern must have communicated itself to the others, for when they reached Galliate, no one professed any interest in stopping for more than a quick meal. John did nothing to dissuade them, and in a short time they were on their way again. As the afternoon wore on, however, the atmosphere in the coach lightened. Perhaps it was knowing that they would reach Magenta in a short while; perhaps because so far their escape had been flawless; in any case, they all began to feel better. The afternoon was sunny and pleasant and not too warm, and Laurie and Archie were soon in a spirited argument about the merits of country living as opposed to spending one's time on the myriad delights to be found in town. Finch looked disapproving as their voices rose, but when Laurie sat forward on her seat, her eyes flashing at being called a "country bumpkin," and accused Archie of being a worthless dilettante, and Archie's only reply was an indignant "I say!" the marquess laughed out loud. He was well aware that Archie could not refute her statement, not having the slightest idea what a dilettante was.

"It is not helpful of you to laugh, cousin, for it only encourages her to go on to even greater insults," Archie informed him, his offended dignity more than slightly ridiculous, dressed, as he was, as the buxom Arlene. "And let me tell you, my girl, such pertness in one who is a positive greenhead is most unbecoming. Be careful you do not get so puffed up with conceit at your wit that you forget the proprieties. Who would want you in that case?" He sneered.

Stung, Laurie tossed her head. "What do I care?" she asked, her tone airy. "I have no interest in fops and exquisites."

"Well, that's a good thing, at any rate," Archie snarled. "For I can tell you, no man of any sensibility would want such a bookish, unfeminine girl!"

Laurie caught her breath, and would have replied, except the marquess put an elegant hand over her mouth. "Children, if you please! Cry peace!"

Laurie twisted her face to get away, and his fingers closed over her chin. "Yes, it is too bad of me not to allow you to have the last word, is it not? But I must insist there will be no more, Laurie. What began as an amusing diversion is fast turning into an alehouse brawl."

Laurie thought the marquess sounded annoyed, and she settled back, trying to look dignified and aloof. Just then there was a loud snapping sound and the coach tilted alarmingly to one side. She could hear Simmons calling for the team to halt as she slid down the seat on top of the marquess, helpless to stop herself. Across from them, Finch was trying to extricate himself from Archie, who had landed in like manner.

When the coach stopped at last, they all climbed down into the road, thankful that no one had been injured. The reason for the accident was quickly discerned. One of the wheels of the coach had broken away from the axle and was now lying some little distance away. Simmons ordered Rob to the horses' heads and came back to confer with the marquess.

"Well, 'ere's a mess, m'lord," he said, shaking his head. Finch had gone to get the wheel and was rolling it back to the coach, and Laurie could not stifle a gurgle of laughter at the sight. The elegant gentleman's gentleman, dressed all in spotless black, reminded her of an elderly child playing with a huge hoop.

"I fail to see what you can find amusing about this situation, Laurie," Archie reprimanded her in his most lofty manner.

Simmons took the wheel from Finch, and he and the marquess inspected it carefully. "We're in luck, m'lord," he said at last. " 'Tis not damaged too badly, although we will need a new pin. Rob can ride back to Galliate for one."

The marquess stood in the dusty road, his face grim as he rubbed his strong jaw in thought. "No, do not go back, Rob," he said. "There should be a good-sized village a mile or so ahead; you may be able to find the pin there."

Rob pulled his forelock, and putting the pieces of the part they had to replace in his jacket pocket, and taking some money from the marquess, was soon on his way. As he mounted his horse, the marquess ordered him to make all speed, and he nodded before he galloped away.

Simmons and Finch began to unload the coach to lighten it, while Archie stood nearby making suggestions. The marquess came up to Laurie and offered his arm.

"Let us repair to the shade of that tree over there, Laurie," he said. "There is nothing to do until Rob returns."

"But shouldn't we help with the unloading?" she asked, looking back over her shoulder.

"There is no need; besides, I think it best to separate you from my cousin for a bit. You are a little firebrand, aren't you?"

Laurie was sure from his tone that she had lost his esteem with her hoydenish ways, and she was surprised at how sorry that made her. Trying to explain, she said,

"Yes, I admit I have a very quick temper. But I could not just sit there and let him insult me, could I? 'Country bumpkin' indeed! Why is it that men who live in town think themselves so superior to those who pass their time happily in the country, engaged in healthy pursuits, and reading, and rational thought? Archie, on the other hand, is silly! He hasn't a serious thought in his head, and yet he criticizes me. It is too bad!"

The marquess released her hand, and she sank down on the soft grass under the olive tree. John removed his hat and joined her.

"Since there is little likelihood of your ever agreeing with each other on the subject, why not substitute some other topic of conversation?" he asked, his eyes half-closed as he leaned back on his elbows. "For example, the weather. It is a beautiful day, is it not? If only we were not in flight, how pleasant this journey through the countryside would be."

Laurie looked around. The olive grove behind them was pleasantly shady, and somewhere nearby she could hear the ripple of a brook. Overhead, some puffy clouds moved slowly across the sky. She sighed as she picked a blade of grass to chew. "But we are in flight, sir. Until we are sure we have escaped capture, our travels can be nothing but frightening."

"I will not let anything happen to you, you know," the marquess said conversationally.

Laurie turned to look down into his half-closed eyes. "A rash promise to make, don't you think, m'lord? Better to say you will try, for no man is infallible, as I have discovered to my sorrow."

The marquess heard the sadness in her voice and knew she was thinking about her father. He could think of nothing to say, and after a moment of silence she continued, "I . . . I would thank you for your concern, however, and for everything you have done for me. I had no idea how to get home, and although Simmons has been abroad many times, it was just as my father's *aide-de-camp*. What bothers me is that by accepting your help, I have drawn you into danger too."

John waved a careless hand. "Do not refine on it too

much, Lady Laura. Since we rode up when we did, we are all in this together. The doge would settle for any one of us, I think. He will not care who actually pulled the trigger of the gun that killed his son."

He watched Laurie throw the blade of grass away and prop up both her elbows on her knees to support her chin. She was scowling now, and in his eyes looked very young. "If he finds us, I will not let anything happen to you either, m'lord," she vowed, her voice stiff.

"Whatever do you mean?" he asked idly, noticing the way the slight breeze stirred in her curls and rustled the hem of her blue gown. He thought her cheek looked so soft and glowing as a ripe peach, but he forgot the comparison at once at her next words.

"Why, I shall tell him that I shot his son, of course. Even such a great villain as the doge would not harm a girl, would he?"

She sounded so determined on this course that the marquess sat up abruptly. "You shall do no such thing!" he ordered. Laurie started, for she had never heard that particular tone in his voice before. "I have never heard such a bacon-brained scheme," he went on. "If we should be taken up by the doge, you will play the part I have assigned, and none other, no matter what happens to any of the rest of us."

He took hold of her shoulders and held them tightly, forcing her to face him. "I'll have your promise on it, Laurie," he said, his voice still stern.

For a moment she sat silently, her chin lifted in defiance and her lips tightening with denial. John shook her a little. "Your promise, I said, and I meant every word of it."

"And what will you do if I refuse m'lord?" she asked, her voice haughty. "Beat me?"

The marquess made a growling sound deep in his throat. "I am beginning to think that that is what you need most. First the scene with Archie—and you deliberately provoked him, as you are well aware—and now this . . . this defiance of me! You will give me your promise, Laurie, and at once!"

Laurie was caught on the horns of a dilemma. She could

not give the marquess that promise, but she found herself a little frightened of him. There was a line of white around his mouth, and his jaw was set hard. Above the rigid planes of his face, his blue eyes seemed to have darkened with his anger at her stubbornness and her refusal to do as he bid her. His hands tightened on her shoulders, and she stifled a gasp of pain.

"I shall be bruised there tomorrow," she said in a breathy whisper.

John loosened his grip at once, but he did not let her go, nor did he take his burning eyes from hers.

"I am waiting, Laurie," he said evenly, and somehow the quiet words frightened her more than his angry ones had done.

"I will promise to tell him only as a last resort," she got out through stiff lips, and the marquess let her go.

"There is no need for this melodrama in any case," he said, trying to ease the tension that almost crackled between them. "Even if we are taken, we have only to play our parts, There is no way the doge can connect us with the death of his son if we all keep our heads."

Laurie thought to point out that Archie was the weak link in his plan. If it should be discovered that he was not a woman, no amount of acting or denial would serve, but wisely, she forbore to remind him of it. She seemed to sense that the marquess had had about all he could stand, and she did not want to upset him further. She peeked at him under the brim of her bonnet, and found him staring at her, looking perplexed and uneasy. Lowering her lashes, she smiled a little, not knowing why she did so.

"Minx!" he exclaimed, his voice amused now, as if he found her a delightful child. "You play the boy so convincingly, and yet the moment you put on your petticoats, you become completely feminine again."

He shook his head and added, as if to himself, "Women are amazing creatures. I doubt there has ever been a man who could really understand them!"

# 6

Rob returned from the village shortly thereafter, waving the new pin triumphantly over his head as he came. He had managed to accomplish his errand by sign language and by paying a great deal more than the part was worth, and he was feeling very proud of himself. The others, who had had nothing to do but wait for his return, were not so sanguine. The marquess, who had fallen asleep for only a few minutes under the olive tree, worn out from his uncomfortable night in the lumpy armchair, was pacing the road. His anxiety, especially the way he kept checking the sun and his pocket watch, soon communicated itself to the others. Simmons was looking grim, Archie impatient, and even the imperturbable Finch a trifle worn. Laurie congratulated her footman, and then, as the men began to repair the coach, she wandered off into the nearby grove. They would all be cooped up together shortly, perhaps for a long time, and she had to prepare for it, as well as give the men the opportunity to do so as well. The marquess, his coat off as he helped lift the coach so Simmons could slide the wheel back on the axle, saw her go, and he divined her purpose and silently applauded her tact. It was not the first time she had shown herself sensitive to others' needs, and he found it an amazing trait in one so young.

The grove was shady and cooler than the dusty road, and she lingered there, out of sight behind a slight dip in the terrain. She could hear the crisp orders of Lord Vare, and the voices of the others, and when she heard Simmons call to Rob to hand him the medicine chest, she knew the coach had been repaired and even then was being reloaded. She knelt to wash her face and hands in the little stream, drying them on her handkerchief, before she picked up her skirts to head back to the road.

And then she heard something else, something that caused her to pause, one hand grasping a tree trunk to still its trembling. The thunder of many horses pounding along the road from Galliate grew louder and louder. From where she stood, half-hidden in the grove, she could not see them, but she could tell by the tenseness of the men beside the coach that their good luck had run out. She could not hear the words, but she could see the marquess quickly instructing the others.

She drew a deep breath as a troop of horsemen, resplendent in black livery with gold-trimmed hats and slashes set in their wide sleeves, surrounded the coach. One of them held aloft a standard of gold on a black ground that fluttered in the breeze.

Laurie made herself move forward, not hurrying, and trying to look as cool and unconcerned as it was possible to do with her heart pounding in her throat.

One of the soldiers, dressed more elaborately than the rest, had reined in his horse at the marquess's feet. John stood his ground, his coat slung over one shoulder. Laurie was not close enough to read the expression on his face, but she heard the leader ask in a loud voice, "You are English travelers, are you not?"

The marquess nodded. "There was something you wanted, my good man?" he asked, his voice cool.

"I am Capitano Rossetti, the Doge of Varallo's man, *signore*, I have come to escort you and your party to my master."

The marquess was shrugging into his coat, assisted by Finch, but at these words he paused. "Indeed? Whatever for? I do not know your doge."

"His highness has a great desire to . . . er, to *speak* to you, *signore*. To you and to all the others in your party," the captain said, and Laurie heard the thinly veiled insolence in his voice.

She saw that Simmons was eyeing the perch of the coach, where he had left his pistols, and she prayed that he would do nothing to endanger them all or give the game away. Rob had taken a position beside Archie, his arm around him as if to protect his wife from harm, and she applauded his cool thinking. Finch was, as usual, looking superior and collected. As she strolled toward them, she hoped she could perform her part as well.

"You must thank this doge of yours, and say everything that is proper, but I am afraid that that will be impossible. We have been much delayed by an accident to our coach and we must continue or we will not reach our destination before dark," the marquess said.

Laurie heard the captain snap an order to his men, and when she saw them raise their pistols, she knew she could delay no longer.

Running forward now, she called, "John, who are these men? Why are they here?"

The marquess whirled, the look of disappointment on his face quickly shuttered, and Laurie knew he had hoped she would remain hidden. He brushed past the captain's horse to come and take her arm and lead her forward. Laurie could feel the tenseness in the muscles under her hand. She pressed his arm as she made herself smile at the troop of men.

"This is the Doge of Varallo's guard, my dear," the marquess said. "And this is their captain . . . ah, Rossetti, was it not?"

The captain removed his plumed cap and bowed over his saddle. "I am honored, *signora*," he said, his rising inflection making the salutation a question. His eyes were insolent as he stared intently at her slight figure in its blue muslin gown.

"This is my wife, the Marchioness of Tench," the marquess introduced her.

"I am sure the doge will be delighted to meet the *signora* as well," the captain purred, his dark eyes never leaving Laurie.

"You must make our regrets, as I have told you. We cannot accept the doge's kind invitation," Lord Vare repeated.

Laurie saw the captain's frown and his quick glance around to make sure his men were armed and ready, and she made herself laugh. At that gay, girlish sound, the captain swung back to stare at her again.

"Oh, please, darling John, must we hurry on?" she asked the marquess, hanging on his arm. "I should love to see a real Italian *palazzo,* and meet the doge and his family. You know no one has been at all friendly on our journey, and I did so hope to meet some of the Italian nobility while we were here. Please, dearest," she begged, smiling up into his dark, disapproving face. When he did not reply, she made a little *moue,* and sighed. "I am so tired of this confining, jolting coach! Please say we can accept the doge's hospitality, if you love me?"

"But, my dear, you are not thinking . . ." The marquess found his voice at last. Laurie was glad he was following her lead. "No doubt this doge's palace is many leagues distant, and we would not make Milan for many more days. You do remember that we are to meet Lord Willoughby and his wife there, do you not?"

"There is no need for you to travel to the doge's *palazzo,*" the captain interrupted. "The doge has come south and is even now at his sister's estate, the Villa d'Emillio. It is only a short distance from here; you will not be . . . er, *inconvenienced.*"

Again his voice sneered at them, and he laughed, as if at some private joke. Laurie saw a muscle tighten beside John's mouth and hurried into speech. "How wonderful! What is the noble lady's name, sir? It is most kind of her to receive us, total strangers that we are."

"She is the Principessa Isabella, *signora,* wife of the Principe d'Magenta."

"Why, John, isn't that the town where we planned to stay tonight? So you see, there is no reason at all not to accept the hospitality of these nobles. I am thrilled to think I shall have the opportunity to converse with them, and discuss their customs and their country."

The marquess did not reply, and she tapped his arm playfully, laughing as she did so. "You must admit defeat, dear sir," she said, beckoning to her maid as she climbed into the coach.

The captain gave them all a mocking bow as they took their places, and then he slammed the door of the coach behind them. Laurie could see him telling his men where to position themselves so as to cut off any escape attempt, and then he rode forward to confer with one of the guard privately. She gasped a little and whispered to the marquess, "Isn't that soldier the man who was spying on us in the inn last night, m'lord?"

The marquess nodded, not even bothering to look, for he had recognized the man earlier. "It is indeed," he said, his voice stiff.

Laurie made herself smile at the soldier stationed nearest the coach door as they began to move. "I can see you are angry with me, m'lord, but what else was there to do? He was going to take us to his doge whether we agreed to it or not. I only thought to stay his suspicions and prevent bloodshed."

Her voice was disappointed, and the marquess made himself smile at her. "Your performance was excellent, Laurie! But still I wish you had remained in the wood. It was such a perfect opportunity for you to escape this coil."

"If I may, sir?" Finch asked, and Lord Vare nodded. "You cannot be thinking clearly, m'lord. How could Lady Laura escape, alone, without money or a conveyance, and in a strange country? It is much better to have her safe beside us."

Archie, who had turned away from the window and the peering eyes of the guard trotting beside them, said, "Safe? Not quite the word I would use, Finch. I have never felt less safe!"

"Enough!" the marquess interrupted, his voice firm. "What's done is done. I do not know how far it is to this Villa d'Emillio, but we must go over our story and be sure we are all agreed on it. Finch, I charge you with telling Simmons and Rob what we decide. I know that they do not speak Italian, but you can be sure this doge will have translators so he can question all of us."

For the next several miles they went over their story. John and Laurie were the Marquess and Marchioness of Tench, which was located in a remote section of the English Lake Country. They memorized the details of their fictional estate, the name of the nearest village, and what crops were grown there. The honeymoon couple were on their way to Milan, but they also planned to see Venice, Florence, and Rome before sailing on to Greece.

Laurie's eyes were serious as she digested this information; then she asked, "Where have we stayed since we arrived in Italy, John? He is sure to ask that, and we cannot tell him the truth."

The marquess nodded. "We shall say we stayed with friends, English friends who are renting a villa near Lake Como. That is some distance away from his lands—he would not know that we tell a lie. The night before last, we stayed in a small country inn. He knows we were in Galliate last night, and we can confirm that."

"What is the name of these English friends?" Laurie persisted. At the marquess's surprised look, she added, "If they question us separately, we must tell the same story."

"Let them be . . . oh, Lord and Lady Dock. That is easy to recall. George is a cousin of mine, and his wife's name is Helen."

"Helen and George," Laurie repeated, committing the names to memory, and then she looked at Archie and she frowned. Even in the mobcap and gown, and with a voluptuous figure, there was that about his face, slim as it was, that proclaimed the man. He stared back at her, and the grim cast of his face as he contemplated their danger made her fearful.

"Archie, you must not look so stern, so masculine! But stay! I said last evening that you had a bad cold. Try to keep your face hidden in a handkerchief as much as possible, and cough often. That will confirm the story, and perhaps draw their attention from you."

Finch agreed. "Very well thought on, m'lady, and not a moment too soon."

He indicated the window, and they saw that they were passing through a pair of black iron gates that were heavily decorated with gilding. Immediately the coach settled down to a smooth glide as they made their way up a well-raked drive lined with tall dark cypress trees.

Laurie gasped as the Villa d'Emillio appeared before them. A huge four-story stone block, it glowed golden in the afternoon light, and yet it seemed stark and unwelcoming, perhaps because of the narrow windows of the front, or the formal arrangement of the pillars, or the ivy that grew in dark green profusion in neat, formal beds. The coach circled a large fountain where nymphs and cupids poured endless streams of water to a pool below and stopped before a set of shallow steps. In a moment, the captain of the guard was there to open the door and bow them out. Laurie thanked him prettily in his own language as he handed her down. As he reached to assist Archie, she said, "Do not put yourself to the trouble, *capitano*. My maid has caught a wretched, contagious cold, the stupid thing!"

As she took the marquess's arm to climb the steps, she cried, "Oh, John, isn't this impressive? And the fountain, how lovely! I am so glad we came. How old is the building, Capitano Rossetti?"

The captain seemed somewhat confused, especially since he had been expecting to escort cringing, frightened captives to his doge. This English lady with her constant prattle that made her seem so childlike was an unwelcome surprise. He had hoped to gain his doge's esteem as well as the reward for capturing the party he sought so fiercely, but now it appeared that he had made a mistake. And yet, how could that be? he asked himself, giving the knocker of the villa a mighty clang. This was the only English party in the neighborhood who remotely resembled those he sought. But the doge will get the truth from them, one way or the other, he told himself, grinning in anticipation as an elderly *maggiordomo* bowed them welcome.

As Laurie entered, she looked around in awe. The hall they stood in could have accommodated the doge's entire guard, and on horseback at that. The floor was made of white marble streaked with gold, and the pillars that lined the walls and formed niches for various statuary rose three stories to a domed roof made entirely of stained glass. She clung for a moment to the marquess's arm, and for the first time, seemed speechless at such splendor. Behind her, the captain was giving orders to his troops, but she did not listen. She was surprised when she stole a look at the marquess to see that he was smiling, for the captain had ordered his men to be ready to continue the search at any time.

"What is it, m'lord? What did he say?" she whispered.

The marquess pressed her arm in warning, as two muscular servants dressed all in black livery trimmed with gold bowed before them and indicated that they were to follow.

John turned and nodded to the others behind him, and the little procession, led by the *maggiordomo* and guarded by the footmen, crossed the huge hall, their footsteps ringing on the marble floor. They were taken to a drawing room, the butler indicating that they were to wait.

The marquess spoke to the man in Italian, and the butler's face brightened as he explained in his own language that the doge and the principessa would be with them shortly. He offered wine, and the marquess agreed it would be very welcome.

Laurie had removed her bonnet and shawl and handed them to Archie. She noticed that one of the footmen was staring at him, and was glad when Archie pretended to sneeze. "Cover your face, you useless wench!" she exclaimed, retreating in horror. "Do you think we all want to catch your cold? Stand over there, away from me."

Archie, his face covered by his handkerchief, retreated, accompanied by Rob, while Finch and Simmons stood at attention behind the marquess and his bride as they sat down together on a narrow sofa.

"What a charming room, John, don't you agree?" Laurie asked, and the doge's servants transferred their attention from the buxom lady's maid to her. "I have always loved blue and gray, and I have never seen a finer Oriental."

She sipped her wine, and the marquess said, "Most grand, but I beg you, my dear, not to think to decorate the hall at Tench in like manner. If you did, we would need an entire ship to transport your purchases."

Laurie thought he was trying to warn her of something, and she made a little face at him. "I know that you are teasing me, dear sir," she said gaily. "I did not buy all that much in Paris, did I?"

John took her hand and kissed it. "You have made a great many French merchants happy, my love, but I will say no more. You know that you may buy whatever you wish."

She wondered at the fatuous look of a besotted bridegroom that accompanied this statement, and wished he had saved it for the doge. Why waste it on these sullen, suspicious servants, who, after all, could not understand a word of English? The marquess, however, was sure at least one of them did, and it was for his sake that he had acted as he had.

The door opened, and Capitano Rossetti came in, stripping off his gauntlets as he moved to stand before them. "Ah, I see the *maggiordomo* has seen fit to serve refreshments. Enjoy the wine while you can." He sneered, his dark eyes intent on their faces. John released Laurie's hand as he settled back at his ease.

"Would you care for a glass, *capitano*?" Laurie asked innocently.

"My dear! How very unsuitable," the marquess drawled. "One does not ask a servant, even the captain of the guard, to drink with one. What can you be thinking of?"

"I beg your pardon, m'lord. 'Twas just that he looked so hot and dusty, but of course you are right." She smiled her regrets to the suddenly furious captain, and wondered why John had chosen to anger him. Surely it was very dangerous!

The doors of the drawing room were both thrown open then, and in ringing tones the butler announced the Doge of Varallo and the Principessa Isabella d'Magenta. Laurie leapt to her feet to see them enter, as John rose leisurely beside her.

The couple were attended by several others, but they themselves drew all eyes at first. The doge, a thin, wiry man dressed all in black, was completely bald, but he sported a luxuriant black goatee and mustache. In his drawn, colorless face, his black eyes burned like two chips of jet.

His sister, the *principessa*, was a voluptuous woman in her early forties. She was also dressed in black, a lustrous satin embroidered all over with silver thread and bugle beads. On her dark brown hair she wore a matching cap, and she held a fan in one bejeweled hand as she moved languidly into the room.

Behind her were three other women—ladies-in-waiting, by the look of them, Laurie thought—who were also dressed in black. The absence of any color made her uneasy somehow, and as she looked back to the doge and saw him regarding her intently, a *frisson* of fear ran down her spine. Still, she tried to smile, lowering her lashes so he could not see the terror there.

"You, there!" the doge thundered suddenly in English, pointing a long white finger at Finch. "Refill Lord Vare's glass at once!"

Laurie tried not to gasp, but Finch was more than equal to the occasion. He did not move a muscle, nor even look in John's direction. "Sir?" he asked, as if confused by the barked order.

The doge shrugged and turned to Rossetti.

"May I present the Marquess and Marchioness of . . . er, of *Tench*, your Highness?" his captain said.

John bowed, and Laurie sank into a deep curtsy.

The doge moved forward and held out his hand. Reluctantly Laurie took it, her hazel eyes wide at the touch of his cold, dry fingers. Lord Vare smiled at the handsome *principessa*, and she smiled in return as she settled herself on a stiff brocade sofa.

"So you are the Marchioness of Tench, are you, my dear?" the doge asked, his high-pitched voice holding an undertone of disbelief.

"Indeed I am, your Highness," Laurie said. "Not that I have been so for very long, however."

Her blush at these ingenuous words caused the *principessa* to smile as she moved her fan gently to and fro.

"Do be seated, m'lady, m'lord." The doge's words were courteous, but still they sounded very much an order. Laurie took her seat beside the marquess once again.

"It is very kind of your highness to receive us," John began, and the doge waved an impatient hand. "M'lady has often remarked how difficult it is to meet any of the nobility while traveling, so this is a memorable occasion for us. And may I say how impressed we are with the Villa d'Emillio, *principessa*? A truly noble home."

The princess inclined her head, her glance speculative. John had seen that selfsame glance before. He could tell the princess was attracted to him as a man. There was a warmth in her brown eyes and in the way she teased him with her fan, now disclosing, now hiding the deep cleavage of her gown, that he knew very well from past experience. His knowing, answering grin was very white in his dark face.

Laurie had no idea what this exchange was all about, but for some reason she did not care for it. Switching to Italian, she said, "I agree that it is most impressive, ma'am. I quite long to explore it, and the gardens, which I am sure must be a delight, if that charming fountain in the forecourt is any indication of them. Cellini, is it not?"

The doge had not taken a seat, nor had he taken his eyes from his guests. Now he interrupted this artless prattle to say, "So, you speak our language. Have you been traveling through Italy long, m'lady?"

"Not so very long. We came through the Alps via the Simplon Pass—I have never been so frightened in my life!—and then we made a stay with a relative of my husband's who has a villa near Lake Como. I cannot tell you how glad I was to rest after what was a most terrifying experience!"

The princess spoke for the first time. "You have visited our cities, m'lady?" she asked idly, her light voice almost bored.

"No, not as yet, ma'am. We intend to travel to Venice and Florence, and of course eventually to Rome. I am so excited!"

The princess ignored her enthusiasm as she pursed her full lips. "The only reason I ask," she said, "is that I wonder where you purchased your gown. It is Italian, is it not? I am sure I could not be mistaken."

Laurie saw the doge leaning forward eagerly, and was horrified to find herself at a loss for words. They had not discussed what she was to say about her new clothes, and she did not know what to reply.

"M'lady has nothing but Italian clothes," John said carelessly. "Her own were lost during an accident in the Alps when two of the packhorses lost their footing high above a gorge. At the time, she was most distraught, but new folderols soon brought the smiles back to her face, didn't they, my dear?"

"Yes, for I so adore shopping! And Helen was so kind

about helping me. She had found the most clever dress-maker near where she is staying. Wasn't that fortunate?" Laurie breathed, relieved that that particular hurdle had been overcome.

"Helen?" the doge asked, his black eyebrows meeting in a frown.

"Lady Dock," both Laurie and the marquess answered together, and then they smiled at each other. Laurie settled back as John continued, "My cousin George's wife. You do remember we told you we stayed with them when we first arrived?"

The doge looked disappointed, and he turned his attention back to Laurie. "I understand you have been ill, *signora*. Not a serious malady, I trust?"

Laurie's brain was working feverishly. No sooner did they escape one trap than they were precipitated into another! She remembered that she had pretended to be ill at the inn at Cossato; did he mean to trick her by mentioning that?

As she hesitated, the doge looked to Captain Rossetti, and the man moved forward. "You do not care to reply, for some reason, *signora*?" the captain asked, his voice menacing. "But that is to be discourteous to the doge. I must insist!"

Laurie buried her face in her hands as inspiration struck. "I . . . I would rather not, your Highness," she said, her voice prim.

"But I will hear your answer!" the doge demanded. "Come, we cannot have such a lovely visitor ill in our land. What was the nature of your sickness?"

Laurie hesitated, and then she rose and went to the *principessa* to whisper in her ear. Every eye in the room was on her as she did so. The *principessa*'s eyebrows rose. "It is true?" she asked, her voice incredulous. "You are with child?"

Laurie nodded, not daring to look at the marquess, and her flush as she thought of what he must be thinking would have convinced the most doubting person that she spoke the truth. The *principessa* made room beside her on the sofa. "Sit down at once, my dear," she said.

She put her arm around Laurie's slender shoulders and

fixed the marquess with an indignant stare from which all seduction was gone as her maternal instincts were aroused. "Why, she is naught but a babe herself! I wonder you dared to bring her abroad on such a strenuous journey in her condition, m'lord," she snapped, her eyes accusing.

"I have only recently learned of it, Highness," John said, his voice wry. "I intend to take her home as soon as I can, for of course we must curtail the rest of our trip under the circumstances. I am sure you need not doubt my care of my wife, not when she is perhaps carrying my heir."

The doge crossed his arms over his chest. He was not to be diverted by news of the coming happy event. "And how long have you been married, *signora?*" he asked. The marquess held his breath.

"Since last April, your Highness. We were married on my eighteenth birthday."

She dared to look at John then, and when she saw the rigid cast to his face, she cried, "Oh, dearest, was it wrong of me to tell them? But . . . but you know how delighted I am—why, I want to tell the whole world. Imagine, me having a baby!"

The *principessa* chuckled. "You will discover it is not such a delight, before much longer, my child," she warned, and then she beckoned to her ladies-in-waiting. "Take the marchioness to her room," she ordered. At her brother's frown, she shook her finger at him. "I must insist, Guido. The child must have her rest."

She drew Laurie up beside her and gave her into the care of her smiling ladies. Laurie saw the approval in John's eyes and thanked her hostess in a small voice. "I shall be glad to retire, your Highness. It has been a long day."

"Perhaps a bath would be welcome, after the dust of the road," the doge purred. Laurie turned to see him staring at his sister, as if to convey some hidden meaning.

"*Sì,* of course! You may leave it to me, Guido. It shall be brought to her at once," the lady agreed. She spoke rapidly to one of her women in an undertone.

As Laurie was leaving the room, she beckoned to Archie and Rob, who were still standing quietly at the side of the room. They came forward, Archie coughing into his handkerchief. "Bring me the large portmanteau and my dressing case from the coach," Laurie ordered as she swept past them. Archie bobbed a curtsy and hurried after her, Rob close behind.

The room she was shown into up the marble stairs was at the back of the villa, overlooking the sunken gardens. It was decorated in ashes-of-roses and silver, and although it was extremely formal, the huge canopied bed looked comfortable, and there was a chaise covered with silk pillows set before some French doors leading to a small balcony.

"How lovely, your Highness," Laurie said, her voice admiring.

"I am sorry we did not have more warning of your coming, child, or I would have had it filled with flowers," the princess said, sitting down in a chair near the empty fireplace and fixing her dark eyes on her guest. "Would you care to undress? Loosen your laces, perhaps?"

Laurie laughed. "I will wait for my baggage, ma'am. Besides, I do not wear corsets or lacings."

The princess eyed her lithe, slender waist. "After the *bambino* comes, you will," she warned her. "I myself once had a waist like yours, but after nine children . . ." She sighed and shrugged in resignation.

The two talked of Italy and the villa until Rob appeared with her portmanteau, and pulled his forelock before he retired. Laurie braced herself as Archie came in with the dressing case and the rest of her belongings.

The princess rose and went into an adjoining room. "Yes, I thought I heard the maids. Your bath is being readied now, my dear. You, there," she ordered, pointing an imperious finger at Archie, "help your mistress to undress!"

Archie stopped opening the portmanteau to stare at Laurie, his eyes popping with dismay. Then the heavy scent of lily of the valley wafted from the next room as one of the princess's maids added oil to the hot water, and he sneezed.

"I cannot have the woman anywhere near me, your Highness," Laurie said quickly. "She has a terrible cold and has been useless for days. Do go away, Arlene!"

"What an ugly, ungainly creature. I wonder you can bear to have her near you even when she is healthy," the princess drawled, little knowing she was striking fear into Laurie's heart, and indignation into Archie's. "I suggest you turn her off; to have to see one so grotesque every day cannot be good for the *bambino*."

"Why, I could not do that, ma'am! Abandon her without money in a strange country? It would be cruel."

The princess shrugged. "What can her fate matter? She is only a maid."

Laurie waved to the hovering, indignant Archie. "I shall call you if I need you, Arlene. Go, go!"

"I shall have one of my maids attend you," the princess said, sinking into her chair again. "Tell me, my dear, how long have you known of your pregnancy?"

Laurie saw that she meant to remain, and although she was not used to being naked before others, she steeled herself to unbutton her gown. She talked about her fictional pregnancy as she removed her clothes, wondering why the princess stared at her so closely. As she slipped out of her last lacy undergarment, she could not help but notice the lady's satisfied nod. As Laurie put on her dressing gown, she heard her murmur, "So much for your suspicious mind, Guido."

"I shall leave you now, child," the princess said, rising and clapping her hands. The ladies-in-waiting appeared at the door. "Enjoy your bath, and then I pray you rest until dinner. If you want anything, Maria is here to serve you."

Laurie curtsied as the princess went languidly to the door. Turning, she said, "I have put your delightful and oh-so-virile husband next to you." Her dark eyes were full of hidden meanings as she added, "There is a connecting door."

When she had gone, Laurie went and climbed into a gilded tub, sinking down into the scented water and saying a fervent thanks that so far they had not been discovered. She felt exhausted from the tension of the experience she had just undergone, but the soothing water revived her as she washed. The maid, Maria, stood nearby holding a large soft towel, and Laurie allowed herself to be dried and helped back into her dressing gown before she was led to the chaise. Maria arranged the pillows and covered her with a silk throw, and adjusted the curtains to dim the room. At last Laurie was left alone with her thoughts.

She had not imagined that she would be able to even doze, but when she woke it was to voices in the adjoining room, and it was twilight. She sat up, straining her ears, and was reassured to hear the marquess's deep tones, and the answering ones of Finch. Swinging her legs over the side of the chaise, she went to the door and called. She knew it was probably time to dress for dinner, and she should summon the maid, but first she had to speak to the marquess and find out what had happened after she had left the drawing room, and where the others were.

The marquess opened the door and came in. He was dressed only in his breeches and an open-necked shirt, and his blue eyes flashed a warning. Looking behind him, Laurie could see a strange Italian manservant hovering near Finch as he laid out m'lord's evening dress. Finch looked disdainful.

"My dearest, have you had a good nap?" Lord Vare asked, putting an arm around her and hugging her before he shut the door behind him.

"It was delightful," Laurie replied, her gay voice in complete contrast to the worry in her eyes. "Where are the others?" she whispered.

"All safe, do not worry. Come away from the door to that chair near the window and sit with me in case someone comes in."

After he had taken his seat, he pulled her onto his knees, putting both arms around her. For a moment, Laurie sat bolt upright, her hands folded in her lap.

"A little more affection, if you please, my bride," the marquess ordered quietly. She sighed and relaxed against him, one hand stealing up to grasp the collar of his shirt. The marquess looked down at the chestnut curls tickling his chest. He could smell the heady scent of the bath oil she had used, and for a fleeting moment had the irrelevant thought that in any other circumstances, holding the Lady Laura would be nothing less than enchanting.

"Archie has gone to bed," he said quietly, forcing this foolishness from his mind. "That cold you invented was the perfect solution to get him out of the way, for Rob will be the only one to see him. I think the Italians are afraid of the strange diseases we might have brought with us. Finch remains in my rooms next door, and Simmons sleeps over the stables."

"What happened after I left the drawing room?" Laurie asked. "Do you think the doge believes our story?"

"I am sure he is beginning to have doubts about us, and yet, being the only birds he has in hand, is reluctant to dismiss us from his list of suspects. He questioned me further, mostly about our Italian travels, and I am sure my answers were satisfactory. It was a stroke of genius, by the way, to mention your pregnancy, although when you did so, I was hard put to control my expression. What, after all, do you know about such things? Did the *principessa* question you about it when you were alone? Were you able to answer her?"

"Yes. Strange, I did not even think that my ignorance of that state might be a stumbling block, I was so worried about Archie. She was staring at him and suggesting I turn him away because he was so ugly and ungainly. I thought she would never leave me! Why, do you know, m'lord, she even stayed until I had undressed for my bath? And then she murmured something about her brother's suspicions. I wonder what she meant?"

John chuckled at her innocence. "He sent her with you to be sure you were not the boy he sought, in disguise. What better way to observe you than . . . um, ready for your bath?"

Laurie felt the heat rising above the neck of her gown, and wondered she had been so stupid as not to understand immediately.

"What a fool I am," she chastised herself. "Of course!"

"A delightful fool, my dear," John assured her. She looked up to see his dark blue eyes sparkling with appreciation. "Such innocence is very rare—and very endearing."

# 7

Laurie felt his arms tighten, and then he said in a completely different tone of voice, "A delightful place, the Villa d'Emillio, is it not, my love?" His blue eyes blazed a warning, and he was glad to feel her stiffen in his arms.

"I could stay here forever, John, except I expect you will insist we be on our way soon. But the *principessa*—"

"There was something you wanted?" John interrupted in Italian, looking past her. Laurie sat up and turned to see the maid, Maria, bobbing a curtsy in the doorway to the dressing room.

"*Scusi, signore, signora,*" she began, and then told them both the dinner hour was near.

The marquess rose and set Laurie on her feet, keeping one arm around her waist. "Why is it that whenever I am with you, love, I lose all track of time?" he asked. "Very well, I will leave you to dress now, but I will be back in half an hour to escort you downstairs."

Laurie smiled up at him, and then John caught up her hand and kissed it, still holding her locked against his side. Maria smiled and sighed. So fervent, so much in love, the dark English milord!

When the marquess came back, Laurie was dressed in the green gown she had worn the first evening at the inn in Cossato, but tonight she had no shawl draped over her shoulders to mask her figure. Maria had brushed her hair for a long time, clucking her disapproval at its length, but she had arranged it in a becoming style with white rosebuds tucked here and there among the curls.

The marquess took Laurie's arm and led her down the

broad marble stairs to the drawing room, where they had been received on their arrival. Both the doge and his sister were waiting for them, and Laurie was quick to apologize for any delay. She thought the doge looked very grave, as if he were disappointed somehow, although his bow was elegant when he kissed her hand. The *principessa*, dressed in another black satin gown that was cut very low, waved away her excuses, never taking her eyes from the marquess in his form-fitting evening clothes, snowy-white cravat, and the silk stockings that showed off his muscular legs. Laurie saw the little smile in John's eyes as he bowed to the lady, and wondered at it, but then the doge was offering his arm, and together the two couples went into the dining salon.

Later, Laurie could not remember what she had eaten or drunk during the long formal meal that followed, although she was very much on her guard throughout. At one point, when the fish course was being removed, the doge asked John about his family, saying that he himself was slightly acquainted with some of the English nobility.

"Indeed, sir?" John asked, sipping his wine. "Have you the felicity to know the Duke of Wellington perhaps? He is a distant relation of mine; in fact, it is to meet one of his aides that I travel to Milano. Lord Willoughby is pledged to me there. Much as we have enjoyed your hospitality, we must be on our way tomorrow. No, no, dearest, do not pout," he said, smiling a little at Laurie, who tried to look terribly disappointed at this marvelous news. "You know how important my meeting with Lord Willoughby is."

"State business on your honeymoon, m'lord?" the *principessa* asked, her dark eyes teasing. "You English are so restrained! I shall never understand you."

"But you must remember that we have been married since April, your Highness," John reminded her, and they both laughed. Laurie felt more than a little angry to be excluded from this repartee, especially when John leaned closer to the *principessa* to say something in an undertone. Piqued, she turned toward the doge, to find him regarding her with his black, unblinking eyes. His pallor tonight was more marked, and above the black beard his lips were almost colorless. He would look dead, Laurie thought, trying to hide a shudder, if it were not for those burning eyes. How glad I shall be to get away from here!

"Have you seen other English on your travels through Italy, m'lady?" he asked now, nodding to his *maggiordomo* to approve the wine for the next course.

"I'm afraid I did not notice, your highness," Laurie murmured, and then she blushed as the *principessa* gurgled with laughter and shook her finger at her brother.

"How should she, Guido? Especially since there is evidence that she was much too involved with her husband to care?"

Laurie sat up straighter, trying to ignore her. "Was there some special reason you asked, your Highness?" she said, her voice stiff with offended dignity.

The doge's face grew even colder as he told her about his son, shot in the back by villainous foreigners. He did not mention the band of *banditti* the prince had led, nor the fact that it was they who had attacked the coach; to hear him tell it, it was his son who had been set upon and murdered. John could tell Laurie was indignant, and he was glad to see that the anger she was feeling made her eyes widen and her color fade. She looked suitably horrified at the tale, but the marquess did not trust her to speak. When the doge finished, he said, "Our sincere sympathies on your great loss, Highness. But are you sure the men were English? I find it hard to believe that there is such a band, so far from their own shores."

"*Sì*, I am positive! Three men and a boy and their attendants. One of the villains and a servant were killed by my son's men, but their deaths do not slake my thirst for revenge. Not at all! I shall have them, every one, and they shall pay with their own lives for the murder of my son . . . eventually. I am sure they will be glad when death finally comes."

He smiled, as if in anticipation, and Laurie swallowed hard.

"What a shame you let your temper get the best of you, Guido," the *principessa* remarked. "It would have been so much easier to identify the villains if you had been a little more restrained; perhaps, I should even say, more *inglese* in your approach to the men who brought you the news?"

She gave the marquess a sultry smile and raised her wineglass to him, but Laurie did not see, for she was staring at the doge. His thin face was taut with emotion, and his black eyes burned as if with fever.

"I admit to uncontrollable rage in my grief, Isabella, but what else was I to do to the cowards who brought back my son's body? Thank them? They should have protected him with their lives!"

The *principessa* shrugged, looking bored, but Laurie could not help asking in a tight little voice, "What happened to them?"

"I had them beheaded," the doge announced in a conversational tone. "After, of course, they had told me all they knew of the attackers." He snapped his fingers at a footman hovering nearby. "More wine, at once! And serve me some more of the *aragosta fra diavolo*."

Laurie put down her fork, her face pale. She drew on every ounce of courage and self-control that she possessed to calm herself. The doge did not appear to notice her distress as he turned to the marquess and said, "I would ask you, m'lord, to be on the lookout for these infamous Englishmen, and if they cross your path, to send me word. They shall not escape Italy, or my justice—that I have pledged!"

Laurie pretended to sip her wine, aware the *principessa* was looking idly from her face to John's.

"Of course I should be delighted to assist you, sir, but how to get word to your highness . . ." the marquess replied, his voice dying away as if he were perplexed.

"Never fear, you shall be watched," the doge announced.

"Watched?" John drawled, one black eyebrow raised.

"Perhaps you used too strong a word, *mio fratello*," the *principessa* remarked.

Her brother shrugged as he speared a piece of lobster. "Let us say you will be watched *over*, m'lord. As guests of my country I would not have you come to harm, and as you see, the countryside is not safe. My captain and some of the guard will escort you to Milan to ensure that you escape my son's misfortune."

"How kind of your highness," Laurie said, feeling it was time she contributed something to the conversation. "John has told me of the danger from bandits, but we have never seen any, thank the Lord. I shall be much more comfortable in Capitano Rossetti's care, won't you, my dear?"

John agreed, his voice mild, as if he were but little interested, and then, as the servants presented the next course, he changed the subject.

Laurie felt she had been sitting at table for hours before the princess signaled her to rise and leave the men to their port. When the two reached the salon, the princess went to the doors that led to the terrace and beckoned. "Shall we go out, m'lady? It is a warm night; I am sure you will not be uncomfortable."

Laurie was glad to agree, for she had not been looking forward to sitting on the stiff chairs of the drawing room smiling and conversing. The *principessa*, for all her languid ways, would be quick to catch her in a fault, and those sleepy brown eyes were keen beneath their heavy lids.

As she stepped outside, Laurie saw there were flambeaux lit in the wrought-iron brackets set against the wall, and many more burned in stands in the sunken garden. Their brilliance seemed unnecessary when bright moonlight flooded the scene.

Until the men joined them, the two women strolled up and down, enjoying the heady scent of the flowers that wafted toward them in the slight breeze. There was little conversation, although the *principessa* did mention her nephew once again.

Leaning against the balustrade, she said, "I could see that you were upset at the fate of my newphew's retainers. Do not waste a moment's pity on them. They were not his servants, they were *banditti*."

"*Banditti, principessa?*" Laurie asked, her voice suitably confused.

The princess shrugged. "My nephew Arnolpho, noble heir of my brother that he was, was never one of my favorites. Indeed, it is hard for me even to grieve for him. He was always cruel, almost sadistic, ever since his childhood. He was the leader of a band of cutthroats because it amused him to see others suffer. *Il mio fratello* cannot see that our noble line will be better off without him. He would have brought the name of Varallo to disgrace after Guido's death. Besides"—and here she shrugged again, as if it were of no importance—"Guido has three other sons. Italian men are virile—perhaps your husband even has some Italian blood, m'lady? Aye, how you are fortunate! I admit I envy you. He is so masculine, so handsome, so tall . . . so compelling." She turned to Laurie then, her dark eyes teasing. "But of course I tell you nothing you have not already discovered, do I, my child? All those wonderful, long passionate nights since your wedding that you have shared with him! Tell me, does he please you? Is he a good *amante*?"

Laurie tried not to stiffen, but she was relieved to see the doge and the marquess joining them, so she was not forced to reply.

The marquess came to her side and took her arm, smiling down at her, and Laurie gave him her most caressing smile in return, well aware that the *principessa* was watching them with her dark, intent eyes.

"Why don't the two of you walk in the gardens, m'lord, since you will not have time to see them tomorrow?" this lady asked now as she arranged the lace shawl she wore over her bare white shoulders. "There is a full moon and the air is almost balmy, is it not? Not, I am sure, that you need such a setting to inspire you to romance." The husky chuckle that accompanied this statement was warm and seductive.

Laurie noticed that the doge had drawn slightly apart from them and was leaning on the balustrade, staring into the night, as if he had forgotten his guests. She was sure he was planning his revenge on his son's killers, and she wondered that even the fondest parent could be so blind and so cruel.

The *principessa*'s next words drove the doge from her mind. "Of course," the lady was saying, "if you are too tired, child, we shall excuse you. The early days of a pregnancy require much sleep. I myself was always tired when I was in that state. And you need not fear that your handsome husband shall lack for . . . mmm, entertainment. I shall be delighted to show him the gardens myself."

Her voice was rich with meaning, and Laurie found it

hard to keep from bridling. Before the marquess could answer, she said, "You are kindness itself, Highness, but it will not be necessary for you to bestir yourself. I am not in the least tired, not after the long rest I had this afternoon. Come, John, let us explore! I could not bear to leave Villa d'Emillio without seeing more of its wonders."

John tucked her hand in his arm as they excused themselves and went down the steps to the grass. They had not gone very far before Laurie heard the *principessa*'s amused laughter. "That . . . that woman is disgraceful!" she whispered to the marquess.

Lord Vare looked down at her profile, the straight little nose, the prim set of her mouth, and her determined round chin, and he smiled. He wondered what the *principessa* had been asking his bride, to upset her so. "Thank you for saving me from her clutches, m'lady," he said meekly, and Laurie was sure she heard a quiver of laughter in his voice.

She stopped and stared up at him, her hazel eyes dark pools in the moonlight. "You are teasing me, aren't you? I suppose you would have enjoyed her company!"

The marquess grinned openly now as he escorted her down a set of stone steps to an enclosed garden. Against the far wall there was a small pool filled by streams of water descending from some statuary above. The sound of the fall as it trickled over the rough stones and splashed into the pool below was liquid enchantment, as was the nightingale singing some little distance away, but Laurie did not notice.

"It would be difficult not to," the marquess said in reply, his voice mild. "The *principessa* is a beautiful woman, don't you agree?"

Laurie tossed her head. "If you care for that sort of obvious, overblown charm," she said before she thought. "How ridiculous for her to flirt with you at her age—why, she is quite old."

Lord Vare put back his head and laughed out loud, and she pulled away from him and went to sit on a marble bench placed before the cascade. She scowled at the beautiful sight, wondering why his laughter made her so angry. The marquess took the seat beside her.

"I will grant you that she is somewhat obvious in her intentions," he said after a moment's silence. "However, I am surprised that someone as unsophisticated as you noticed it."

"I would have to be both blind and deaf not to," Laurie said hotly, feeling a pang of disappointment that he thought of her still as a naive young girl. To change the subject, she asked, "Where are her husband and children, do you suppose?"

"The *principe* is in Rome on business, or so the doge informs me. As for her abundance of offspring, I thought she might take you to the nursery so you could admire them."

"I am sure they outgrew the nursery long ago," Laurie retorted, and then she rubbed her arms as if she were chilled. "Oh, I cannot wait to leave here, m'lord," she said, her voice shaking a little. "The look on the doge's face at dinner when he talked about dealing with his son's killers frightened me. What if he—?"

She was allowed to say no more, for suddenly Lord Vare pulled her into his arms. Startled, Laurie had no time to close her lips before he bent his head and kissed her. He held her close to him, one of his hands caressing her back while the other was tangled in the curls at the nape of her neck. A strange wave of delight coursed through her at his sure strength and the firm, warm lips that possessed hers so completely. She wished their embrace never had to end.

All too soon he lifted his mouth from hers an inch or so and whispered, " 'Ware what you say! We may be spied on!"

For a moment, Laurie was confused, still lost in the emotions he had aroused. Then she put her cheek against his and mumured in his ear, "In the garden? I don't believe it!"

The marquess kissed her eyelids, her cheeks, and the little curls that clustered on her brow as he explained, "Why are there so many flambeaux, then, on such a bright moonlit night? Put your arms around me," he ordered, and then added in a louder voice, "my darling!"

Trying to control her breathing and the sensations she

felt as she obeyed him, she whispered, "But I . . . I feel ridiculous!" All unbidden, her hands crept up to caress his shoulders and his neck.

"It is not a situation I have ever found myself in before either, m'lady," Lord Vare murmured. "Patience! We will be gone tomorrow." He drew away from her a little then, and it was all Laurie could do not to tighten her arms around his neck and beg him to kiss her again.

"How beautiful the gardens are tonight, John," she said in what she hoped was a normal tone of voice, trying desperately to hide the disappointment she felt.

"The gardens can't compare with you, my beauty," he told her, his voice intimate and husky, and then he rose and drew her to her feet. Laurie leaned against him for a moment, her knees weak. Almost reluctantly he held her close again until she stopped trembling, and then he said, "But enchanting as the setting is, I cannot be easy. It will soon grow cool, and you should not be out at night in your condition. Let us go in to bed. I want to make an early start tomorrow."

Laurie picked up the skirt of her gown to climb the steps. "Do you expect Lord Willoughby to be before us in Milan, John?" she asked, proud that her voice was so even. She wondered at his self-control, the coolness of his tone.

Behind them, Captain Rossetti drew back from the peephole in the wall where he had been watching them. His face was dark with disappointment. He had been so sure these English were the party his master sought! Crestfallen, he went to the doge to report his failure to hear anything incriminating to support his theory.

The marquess and Laurie made their way back to the terrace, deep in conversation about the mythical lord who was supposedly bringing messages from the Iron Duke. Laurie was glad there was no sign of the doge or the *principessa* when they entered the villa, and that they saw no one but footmen until they reached her room. She could not have stood the *principessa*'s knowing smiles just then.

As they entered, Maria came from the dressing room, and the marquess bent to kiss Laurie's hand. She stared down at his smooth black hair, glad she had a moment to school her expression. When he rose, he patted her cheek and said, "You are tired, my love. Go to bed. I will not come to you tonight, for we have a long day ahead of us tomorrow."

Laurie nodded, and then, to his surprise, she reached up and put her arms around his neck. Standing on tiptoe, she shyly kissed his lips. "Sleep well," she said, her voice shaky with emotion, and then she slipped out of his arms and ran to join the maid. Somewhat stunned, Lord Vare retreated to his room next door.

As Finch and the Italian manservant helped him undress, he tried to forget how soft and sweet her lips had been under his, and how her slim, pliant body had felt so close to his own. But when the servants left him and he climbed into bed, he stared up at the canopy over his head, all thoughts of sleep forgotten. He pondered her voluntary good-night kiss. Why had she done it? At last he sighed. She is still more a child than a woman, he told himself, and so she is not aware of what she does. To her, that kiss was just part of the masquerade she must play to ensure our escape from the doge, and nothing more. If the maid had not been there she would never have behaved so. Then he remembered her jealousy of the *principessa*, and a frown creased his brow. She would not have reacted like that unless she was beginning to care for him. He told himself that from now on he must be very circumspect where the Lady Laura was concerned. She did not have the sophistication that would permit her to treat the situation lightly, as an older girl who had been about the world a little would have. There had been an astonished innocence about her kiss in the garden that told him he was the first man to take her in his arms.

Then why did you kiss her so passionately? his conscience inquired.

Lord Vare turned over and punched his pillow, feeling guilty that he had enjoyed the embrace so much. He knew he had been at fault in prolonging it. After all, he could have laughed and put a hand over her mouth, or given her a short brotherly kiss to stop those dangerous words.

But you had no intention of being brotherly, now, did

you? his conscience stabbed again. Did you really think there was someone hidden in the garden . . . or was that just an excuse?

Lord Vare told himself coldly that these were the ravings of an insomniac as he straightened his rumpled covers. He would see to it that there was no repeat of tonight's folly, for he would put a wall between them from now on. He would treat her formally; adopt an air of uncle-like propriety, a distant stiffness that would serve to remind him how dependent she was on his maturity and wisdom to keep her safe. Her reputation was already in jeopardy, traveling alone with him and the other men, and he must do nothing to bring harm to her. When they reached England again, he would find some way to ensure she was not touched by scandal. The loss of her father was more than enough for her to have to bear.

Simmons had told him of her aunt, Lady Blake—perhaps she would have some ideas on how to handle the situation. He had sent an express to this lady, telling her of her brother's death and promising to bring the Lady Laura safely home to her. Perhaps he should write again and ask her to join them somewhere in France? If she were seen to accompany her niece on the packet to England, there could be no gossip.

It was a long time before the marquess fell asleep, and even longer before Laurie dropped into an uneasy slumber in her big bed next door.

She was so busy calling herself every kind of fool that she did not even think about sleep. Whatever had possessed her to kiss Lord Vare like that? What must he think of her? Although she had fled to the dressing room at once, she could still see only too clearly the disbelieving look on his lean, aristocratic face under the cap of shining black hair, and the eyebrow he had raised at her boldness. She groaned a little. Why, why did I behave so? she asked herself. And then she drew a deep breath. I had to see if it was still as wonderful as it had been in the garden, she admitted, determined to be honest with herself. After all, I did not know that kissing a man would feel like that. I wonder if it is always that way? And yet, I cannot imagine feeling so breathless, so warm, in anyone else's arms.

For a moment she let herself remember how gentle and yet how all-consuming John's lips had been in the garden, and how the slight roughness of his face where the dark beard was beginning to grow had served to emphasize his manhood. And she could still smell the heady scent of his warm skin and feel the compelling pressure of his strong arms and hands that had held her so closely to him, and yet as carefully as if she were fragile and precious. She moved her head restlessly, trying to find a cool spot on her pillow as she wondered why, deep inside, she still felt a tingle that was almost an ache when she remembered his embrace.

She was fast asleep when Finch knocked on her door early the next morning. As she rang for the maid, she heard Lord Vare's voice, and suddenly all the events of the previous evening came flooding back. She prayed he would not come in, for it would be so much easier to meet him when they were surrounded by others and she was dressed for the journey. But still, a perverse part of her waited eagerly, her eyes often straying to the connecting doors.

Lord Vare did not open those doors.

After breakfast in bed, as she let the maid button her into an aqua traveling gown, she decided that she would act as if nothing had happened between them at all, since he obviously did not think it at all important. As soon as they were safely away, she would be cool and distant, and a perfect lady.

When she came downstairs, she found the *principessa* dressed in her customary black, waiting to bid her guests good-bye. She was talking to the marquess, and Laurie was annoyed to see how close she was standing to him, one hand caressing his arm. Still, she made herself stroll slowly down the last few steps.

"Good morning, your Highness," she said, sinking into a curtsy. Then she held out her hand to Lord Vare. "I trust I did not delay you, John? I did try to hurry."

The marquess smiled at her and she lowered her eyes as if intent on the buttons of her glove. She hoped the tumult of her thoughts was not obvious to everyone. Looking around, she saw Archie standing near the door beside

Finch. He was holding her parasol and shawl, and she waved her hand. "Take my things to the coach, Arlene, and await me there."

Archie bobbed a curtsy and hurried away, and the *principessa* said, "I beg you to convince your little bride to discharge her maid, m'lord. For the *bambino's* sake, she should not have to have someone so ugly near her at this time."

As they walked slowly to the coach, she continued to expound on the subject until she caught sight of the five soldiers mounted and waiting beside the coach.

"And here is the faithful Capitano Rossetti to see you safely to Milan. You need not fear *banditti* today, m'lady. The *capitano* is quite *feroce*—how do you say it?—ah, *fierce* in the execution of his duty, are you not, *capitano?*"

The leader of the guard smiled as he bowed over his saddle, sweeping his gold plumed hat before him as he did so. The *principessa* did not notice for she was offering Laurie a cool cheek to kiss. And then she gave her hand to the marquess. Laurie saw him raise it to his lips and kiss it slowly, and when she saw him whisper something to the lady, she turned away.

Motioning Archie to precede her, she climbed into the coach, assisted by Finch. She could not restrain a mutter of distaste for the noble lady's behavior, and Archie whispered, "What's amiss? Is something wrong?"

"That woman is no better than she should be," Laurie told him in a sharp undertone as she arranged her skirts, carefully refraining from looking to where the *principessa* still lingered, talking and laughing with the marquess.

"Just as well," Archie answered, bending down as if to help her, as one of the guard edged closer and peered inside. "She is so hot for John, she hasn't had many glances to spare for me, and that, thank you, is just to my liking!"

Laurie saw the guard staring at them and turned away, hissing to Archie to cover his face with his handkerchief as she did so. It seemed an age before the marquess took his seat beside her and Finch closed the door of the carriage and signaled Simmons, on the box above them, to let 'em go.

Everyone was strangely quiet on the journey down the drive, and it was not until they turned out of the gates on the road to Milan that the atmosphere lightened.

"Whew!" Laurie said as she settled back and tried to relax her tense muscles. "I was so afraid that something would happen to prevent our escape, right up to the last moment."

"But we are safely away now, and I do not foresee any more problems," the marquess informed them. "It will just be a matter of continuing the masquerade until the *capitano* grows weary of shadowing us. You heard or saw nothing to the contary, Finch?"

His valet shook his head. "Nothing, m'lord. I venture to say we have convinced them we are just who we pretend to be."

Laurie noticed that Archie had nothing to contribute to this heartening review of the situation, and she looked across at him, somewhat surprised. She had been sure he would crow over their escape, but now she saw he was looking troubled as he bit a thumbnail, deep in thought.

"What is wrong, Archie?" she asked, unable to still the quiver of alarm she felt.

"It is probably nothing, and yet I cannot be easy," Lord Price admitted slowly. "You see, when I was getting dressed this morning, one of the maids came into my room."

Abruptly the marquess leaned forward, his dark blue eyes intent. "What?" he asked in disbelief. "She saw you without your clothes?"

Archie held up his hands. "No, no, John, it was not as bad as that! I was dressed, except for that ridiculous mobcap. But . . . but she seemed startled, and I saw her staring at my hair before I could cover it."

Laurie groaned. "Why?" she asked no one in particular. "Why did it have to happen, after everything else went so well?"

Lord Vare seemed to be thinking hard. "It is certain she has not told anyone, for otherwise they would never have let us go. Perhaps she did not see you clearly?"

He sounded dubious, and Laurie added, "Maybe she thinks all Englishwomen have short hair. After all, I do."

"I do not think we can count on her forbearance in the

matter," the marquess went on, almost as if she had not spoken. "She is bound to gossip, if only to the other servants. And when word of it gets to the doge . . ."

The pounding of the horses' hooves and the jangle of their harness were plainly heard in the silence that followed these words. Everyone was frightened as they all contemplated what was sure to result when he learned of their deception.

"But what are we to do?" Archie asked, his face white and strained. "There are the captain and the guard riding beside us. If the doge sends someone after us . . ."

His voice had risen higher and higher, and he stopped, ashamed of this loss of manhood. Laurie tried to smile at him. "If we can just reach Milan, perhaps we will have a chance to make our escape."

Lord Vare nodded. "We must hope that the maid does not mention it to anyone just yet. Perhaps knowing how cruel the doge is may stay her tongue. After all, she cannot know whether he will reward her for the information or order her killed because she did not sound the alarm at once. The longer she vacillates, the better off we are."

Finch inclined his head. "You are most certainly right, m'lord. Any servant who worked in the Villa d'Emillio would think twice before calling attention to herself. A very lower-class establishment," he added in scornful assessment.

The marquess leaned back in his corner, his eyes deeply thoughtful. They all waited, holding their breath, until he said at last, "Here is what I think we must do. When we reach Milan—and pray God we do!—Archie must disappear. If the *capitano* inquires for him, we will say that the Lady Laura took the *principessa*'s advice and turned her maid away. If he persists with his questions, we can say that we think Arlene found a position with a traveling Englishwoman. Unfortunately, we will have no idea of this lady's destination, for she will leave Milan shortly after we arrive. The first thing I shall do there is hire a house. It will be more difficult for the *capitano* to keep an eye on us that way. In a hotel or an inn, he could have us watched more carefully. And every hour the maid remains silent will make our new deception easier."

"But . . . but where will I be?" Archie asked. He did not even try to hide the terror he felt at being alone in a strange country in danger of being caught by the doge—alone, without his cousin's support and expert conniving.

For the first time since he had heard Archie's confession, the marquess smiled. "Why, cuz, you will be with us, of course."

Laurie turned to stare at him in amazement, and even the imperturbable Finch widened his eyes a little.

"You become Lord Willoughby, who else? You have arrived with my messages from the Duke of Wellington, and you will honor our hired establishment as our guest. I am sure I will be able to convince you to continue your travels with us, especially since dear Lady Willoughby has returned home with a lingering fever." Lord Vare grinned at his openmouthed cousin. "You'd rather play a high-and-mighty lord from the Foreign Office than a lowly maid in the second act, wouldn't you, my boy? It is so much more in your line. Now you can be as pompous or manly as you like. I think we should change you a trifle, however. Perhaps a mustache would do it, or we can dye your hair. Finch will take care of it."

His valet nodded, his face serene again. He looked as if he were used to disguising gentlemen this way every day of the week.

Feeling much more lighthearted, Laurie said in a carefully colorless voice, "May I suggest he become a more *portly* gentleman? It will make him look so much older."

"I'll thank you to keep your helpful suggestions to yourself, Laurie," Archie growled, looking down at his voluptuous figure with distaste. "I'll have no more padding!"

Laurie turned away before she laughed out loud at his indignant expression, to find Lord Vare regarding her, his face unsmiling. Impulsively she took his hand in both of hers.

"You are nothing short of magnificent, John," she said. "No matter what the problem, you always know just how to handle it. If I had any doubts before, they are gone now. I know we will all be safe, thanks to you."

Her hazel eyes shone with admiration and her lips curled in a smile as she leaned toward him and pressed his hand.

"Why, thank you, m'lady," the marquess said coolly as he removed his hand from hers. Then he turned to the others. "Still, may I suggest we all occupy ourselves in fervent prayer until Milan is reached? We are not safe yet! Finch, Archie, can you think of anything else that we must do? Anything I have forgotten?"

Laurie flushed and turned away to stare out the window of the coach. She felt as if she had been slapped. If he had spoken his thoughts out loud, Lord Vare could not have shown more clearly how bored he was by her girlish enthusiasm and impulsive behavior. A mental picture of him bending over the *principessa*'s hand, his dark blue eyes sparkling as he whispered to her, came to her mind, and her lips tightened. Remembering her vow to be cool and ladylike, she told herself she would take care not to bother him again.

# 8

It was early afternoon before the outskirts of Milan were reached. By that time they were all very tense, for there had been little conversation during the drive. Laurie did not know what the others were imagining, but she herself seemed to have been straining for hours to hear a galloping rider come up behind them. She had watched the guards fearfully to see if any of them turned their heads and pointed until the *capitano* ordered Simmons to halt the coach. She envied Jed and Rob, riding outside and ignorant of this new threat.

She barely saw Milan as they drove to a hotel on one of the busiest thoroughfares. The marquess jumped down almost before the coach came to a halt, to climb the steps, calling for the landlord as he went. Finch assisted Laurie, who was followed by Archie, his head bent over her belongings as if frightened he might lose them.

Seeing the *capitano* coming toward them, Laurie waved Archie into the inn, and then she tried to smile at the dark, disgruntled face before her.

"I thank you for your escort, Capitano Rossetti," she said, glad her voice did not quiver as she lied to him. "I have seldom enjoyed a more peaceful journey, knowing you and your men were there to protect us."

The *capitano* bowed a little. Laurie thought he seemed very disappointed, as if he had been sure the doge would find them out, and he himself would be lionized and rewarded for his astuteness. And somehow she knew that even if the doge had let them go, his captain did not really believe that they were the English innocents that they claimed, even now.

The marquess returned to escort her into the hotel. "I have procured a private parlor for you, dearest," he said. "As we discussed, I am off to hire a house for the duration of our stay."

The *capitano*, openly eavesdropping, brightened. "You remain here, milord? For how long?"

Lord Vare stared at the man, his hauteur plain to see in a pair of cold blue eyes. "Naturally we stay here until the arrival of Lord Willoughby and his wife. Dispatches from the Duke of Wellington cannot be disregarded; we shall remain in Milan until I have studied them and replied. Not that this is any of *your* concern," he concluded.

He offered his arm to Laurie. "Come, my dear. You shall have a luncheon while I am gone. And do not forget what you promised me you would do. I know your soft heart, but you must tell your maid at once that . . ."

He shut the door of the hotel behind them, leaving a furious captain outside. How he would love to have this haughty English milord at his mercy for several hours, he thought as he went to tell his guard that they might dismount and rest.

The marquess did not speak to Laurie as he ushered her into the parlor where Finch and Archie were waiting. "Archie, you will remain here with Lady Laura," he said when the door was safely closed. "Finch, somehow you must get word to Rob and Simmons of the new state of our affairs. Be as inconspicuous as you can. The captain has not left us, and I suspect will not do so for some time. I will be back as soon as I can."

He nodded and hurried away. Laurie sank into a chair and let Archie pour her a glass of wine. The luncheon that was served shortly therafter was not very good, but even if it had been ambrosia, she knew she would have had no appetite. "Hurry, John, hurry!" she kept saying over and over in her mind. She tried not to think of the maid at the villa who right now might be confiding in one of her friends, or even standing before the doge confessing her suspicions in a halting voice. And then she pictured the lone rider galloping furiously toward Milan, the *capitano*'s triumphant smile, the doge . . .

She rose from the table abruptly, leaving Archie in mid-sentence. He frowned at her rudeness until Finch shook his head and put his finger to his lips as Laurie began to pace the room.

It was over two hours before the marquess came back, and by that time even Finch was looking a trifle worried. As Lord Vare led them from the hotel, he told them he had hired a suitable house in one of the better sections of town. There was also the added plus of other English in the same neighborhood.

As Laurie climbed into the carriage, Jed Simmons gave her a look of encouragement. She noticed that the guard was already mounted, waiting to follow them. Catching a glimpse of Rob's set, concerned face, she knew Finch had told him what had happened. As the coach drove out of the yard, she tried to take deep breaths to steady herself. They had escaped capture this far; surely it would be only a little while longer before they were safe at last. Beside her, the marquess was giving his cousin quick, terse instructions.

"There are some Italian servants in the house, Archie. Go to your room at once, as if you were still ill. Rob will bring your own clothes to you, and Finch will get the dye for your hair. After dark, slip away and make your way to an inn on the northern outskirts of the town. Stay there tonight, and then, early in the afternoon tomorrow, hire a horse and return here. You must change yourself as much as possible. Walk with a longer stride, deepen the tone of your voice, make it boom a bit if you can, cultivate a frown. In other words, become Lord Willoughby. Can you do it?"

Archie seemed uncertain for a minute, and then he smiled. He had just remembered a friend of his mother's. If he based his performance on that middle-aged popinjay, he did not think he would have any trouble at all. "I understand, John. And when you see me next, although you may call me Lord Willoughby, in reality I will be Sir Reginald Gately-Wood."

He laughed triumphantly, and the marquess echoed him. Laurie looked from one to the other as if she thought them both gone mad. She saw that although Finch was shaking his head, a trace of a smile lingered on his prim lips. Obviously she was the only one who did not know this Sir Reginald, and no one was going to bother to tell her why he was such a perfect model for Archie. She felt left out and forlorn.

The house the marquess had rented was in a quiet street, not too far removed from the center of the city. Laurie could see there were several streets and alleys that Archie could use to make his escape, as she climbed the steps to be welcomed by a smiling butler.

Although she remained on edge, everything went exactly as planned. Archie went upstairs, coughing and sneezing, Finch bowed himself away on his shopping expedition, and Rob and Simmons repaired to the stables. After inspecting the ground floor with a casual eye, very conscious she was alone with the marquess again, Laurie excused herself.

"I find I am tired, m'lord, and with your permission would retire," she said. She did not meet his eye as she spoke, and her voice was stiff and cold. The marquess felt a pang of regret, although he knew he should be delighted at her coolness, and he nodded.

"Of course, m'lady. Rest well. I shall see you later, at dinner."

Laurie curtsied and left the room, her head held high. The marquess pretended to busy himself with his maps and papers, ignoring the guard who paced up and down the street outside.

When Laurie came back to the salon, it was dusk. Lord Vare waited for her there, immaculate as always in his well-tailored evening dress. Laurie's eyes were shadowed and tired; he knew she had not been able to rest. As he bowed to her, he whispered, "So far, so good, Laurie. In a little while, Archie will disappear, and then, I think, we can all relax at last."

A strange butler announced dinner before she could reply, and she made herself smile as she took the marquess's arm. He could feel her tremble, and could not help pressing her hand where it rested on his arm, for reassurance. He wished he might have taken her in his arms to comfort her.

Laurie gave no sign that she noticed his concern. "Who is this servant, m'lord?" she asked, staring at the fat, elderly butler who was beaming at her as he held her chair. "He is not the *maggiordomo* I saw before."

"The *capitano* procured him. He told me we would find his services superior to those of the man whom we hired with the house. So kind of him, was it not, my dear, to be so concerned with our well-being?"

Laurie nodded, his point well taken. There was no doubt the butler spoke English and would report everything they said or did. "I shall certainly reprove all our acquaintance when we return home, John," she said calmly. "You remember how they told us that we would not find the Italians friendly? Such fustian when you consider all the doge and his sister have done, to say nothing of the *capitano* . . . well!"

Switching to Italian, she asked the butler his name, and smiled as he offered her some soup. "Thank you, Antonio, that looks delicious."

The meal seemed endless. Although she knew the marquess was right, she could not relax until Archie had left the house. If the messenger from the villa should arrive now, and he were surprised in his preparations, there would be nothing they could do or say to save themselves. Lord Vare seemed to sense her uneasiness, and kept up a light chatter about their travels and the delights that still lay ahead of them. Laurie was glad she was required to contribute very little.

At last, as the butler served them fruit and ices, there was a knock on the door, and at the marquess's command, Finch came in.

"I took the liberty of disturbing you, m'lord, to inform you that I have attended to the commission you gave me. I venture to think you will be pleased with the results."

"Thank you, Finch, excellent!"

The marquess dismissed him and smiled at Laurie sitting opposite. "Finch is an excellent servant, is he not, my dear? Imagine being so concerned about finding a good laundress for my cravats! But stay! I forgot to ask you. Did you turn the maid away as we agreed?"

His tone was light, and although Laurie knew he spoke

for the butler's benefit, she was reassured at last. She made herself frown a little in spite of her elation. "Indeed I did, John. I know you and the *principessa* are right, but it tore my heart to do it. You may be sure I gave her enough money so she will not be in want until she finds another post."

"I am glad. You must not worry about it further, dearest. There are many English parties here in Milan, about to head for home. She will have no trouble finding a place with one of them. We really could not risk having her near you with that terrible cold. And her husband agreed so quickly, I do not think their marriage is anywhere near as happy as ours, my love."

Laurie looked up to find him regarding her with an intimate smile, but she was not fooled. Behind her, she could hear the butler, still busy at the sideboard, and she lowered her eyes to toy with her dessert.

In the drawing room after dinner, the marquess was firm as he dismissed the butler. The man left reluctantly and Laurie watched Lord Vare's face. Was it safe to talk here? There was so much she wanted to ask him, but she would take her cue from him. He pointed to the piano, as if asking her if she could play, and she shook her head.

"What a pity you never learned to play, love," he said then, his eyes twinkling. "But what say you to a game of cards? It is early yet; let us see if I can win back some of those guineas you have taken from me on our trip."

Laurie joined him at the card table. "Piquet," she whispered, and then added in a louder voice, "I accept your challenge, sir. But know I am intent on taking as much of your money as I can. You must concentrate more, my dear. I cannot believe you play so badly with your friends."

John shuffled the pack. "Somehow my friends are not as distracting as you are, love," he said calmly, looking across at her in her gown of primrose silk. The tight-fitting bodice clung to her young curves, and the low-cut neckline showed smooth, glowing skin. "Not anywhere near as distracting," he added as if to himself. Laurie pretended she had not heard as she picked up her hand.

They were deep in play when the doors to the drawing

room were thrown open and a furious Capitano Rossetti strode in, followed by the butler. "So!" he bellowed. "I have you now, *assassini inglesi!*"

Laurie gave a shriek and dropped her cards, while John rose from the table, his face as darkly furious as the captain's.

"You will have the goodness to explain why you have forced yourself in here this way, *capitano*," he ordered, his voice harsh. "And I demand you apologize to the marchioness for startling her so, in her condition."

"You are in no position to demand anything," the captain told him, waving two of the guard into the room. He strode back to the door and ordered the others to search the house.

"As soon as you find him, bring him to me," he concluded, and then he came back to stand before a frowning marquess. The two men glared at each other, and when Laurie saw Lord Vare clench his fists, and heard the soldiers cocking their pistols, she put a slim hand to her face.

"Whatever is the matter?" she asked, her voice plaintive. "Oh, how you frightened me, *capitano!*"

Rossetti's bow was ironic. "Unfortunately, there is worse to come, milady. Much, much worse."

He rubbed his hands together in anticipation, and the marquess's voice spoke coldly in the sudden silence. "There had better be some very good explanantion for this extraordinary behavior, Capitano Rossetti, or you shall be made to regret it. Who is it you search for? There is no stranger here."

The captain lounged against an ornate gilded table. "I seek no 'stranger.' It is one of your own party that I require, milord. And of course the reason why you saw fit to engage a man to serve as your wife's maid." He chuckled, good humor restored. "But I doubt you can explain that."

"A man?" Laurie asked, her eyes wide. "Oh, no, no, you are mistaken, Captain. Arlene is not a man!"

"I have it from an excellent witness, milady," he said. "You have fooled us all, have you not? But in doing so, you made a grave error. The Doge of Varallo does not like to be made the fool. It makes him even crueler and more vindictive than ever. I think you will come to regret your clever deceit shortly."

The marquess drew himself up to his full height and stared down at the lounging captain. "This ranting is to insult us, Rossetti. You have either overstepped all bounds or else gone raving mad. Naturally my wife's maid is a female."

"We shall see, milord. The 'maid,' as you call him, will be stripped right here in the salon as soon as my men find him."

Laurie gasped, both hands to her face. There was no need for her to pretend horror anymore.

The marquess surprised her with a deep chuckle. "Then it is just as well she is not here, is it not, my dear? So upsetting for the poor girl! I cannot believe, as ugly as she is, that she has driven you to such desperate straits of ardor, *capitano*. But then, there is no accounting for tastes."

"Jesting will make things go even harder for you, milord," the captain said through gritted teeth. "But what do you mean, she is not here? Where is she?"

Laurie took courage from the marquess's slow smile. He was so cool, so brave! "The marchioness discharged Arlene this afternoon," he said casually. "I persuaded her to take the *principessa*'s advice and let the woman go as soon as we arrived. She was worthless with that endless cold of hers, and I did not wish Lady Tench to risk catching the infection. No, Arlene is long gone. Search where you will, you will not find her here."

The furious captain put his hand on his sword as if he wished he could draw it and run Lord Vare through, and then the two soldiers who had been searching the house came to make their report. They assured their leader the maid was nowhere to be found. Rossetti whirled to question the butler. Antonio shrugged his shoulders and declaimed any knowledge of her whereabouts. No, he said, he had not seen her leave. He whined that he had not known that she was his responsibility, not with the doge's guard watching the house.

John took advantage of this lengthy discussion to pour Laurie and himself a snifter of brandy. "Drink this, my dear. It will steady you," he said as he handed her the glass. His eyes were calm and reassuring, and Laurie did not look away from them as she sipped. She knew she would draw more strength from his serene blue gaze than she could from the fiery liquid.

"Where has he gone? Where have you hidden him?" Rossetti demanded, turning again to his English captives.

"Still he persists," the marquess remarked, managing to sound bored. "Perhaps it is the burning sun in these southern climes that makes men mad, my love. Once more I tell you, there is no 'he,' *capitano*. There was only a poor English wench, not very attractive or skilled, and sick in the bargain. She is gone—where, I cannot say. The marchioness saw that she had enough money to make her way home, if she did not find another position with some traveling English party. No doubt she is still somewhere in Milan. If you must speak to her, I suggest you search the inns and hotels."

The *capitano* stared at Lord Vare. "Bring me milord's footman and coachman, and his valet as well," he ordered the soldiers on guard at the door. He did not take his eyes from the marquess's face as he said, "We will question this footman. He is, or so you *claimed*, the maid's husband. Surely he would object to her dismissal if what you say is true."

The marquess laughed again. "How can you think so, you who have seen his wife? They were not a happy couple—he is delighted to be rid of her, or so he tells me. I pity the poor man, myself. What a dreadful thing to be bound for life to such a gawky, plain woman."

"You are much too harsh, m'lord," Laurie broke in, her glance reproving. "You know Arlene was much more attractive before I made her cut off her hair."

Capitano Rossetti transferred his attention to the marchioness. "Now, why would you do that, milady," he said, his voice silken.

Laurie made a little *moue* of distaste. "She had lice, *capitano*. Some of the inns we have stayed at were positively filthy! Oh—of course I refer to Swiss inns, not any in Italy," she added, as if she were afraid she had hurt his national pride. "There was nothing for it but to cut her hair very short so it could be washed every day with harsh soap. I do so hate lice, don't you? And in one's personal servant, such an affliction could not be endured."

"I wonder you did not turn her off weeks ago," the captain snarled.

"Lady Tench is ever tenderhearted," the marquess remarked, raising his snifter to the lady in a toast. Above the brim, his blue eyes glowed and Laurie looked away. Even with the danger they faced, she felt her heart jump at this sign of his approval.

There was an uneasy silence in the salon until Rob and Simmons, their hands tied behind their backs, were shoved into the room. They were accompanied by the guards and an erect, disapproving Finch.

"You wished to see us, m'lord?" he asked, looking only at the marquess.

Capitano Rossetti rose from where he had been lounging against the table. "*I* wished to see you, *cameriere*. You will answer *my* questions now."

"Sir?" Finch inquired, still looking to his master.

As Rossetti flushed red with anger, the marquess waved his hand. "Do as he says, Finch. This farce grows wearisome; the sooner we can conclude it, the better."

The valet nodded and turned to face the captain. Behind him, Rob and Simmons were held helpless by the guards.

"Now, you will tell me about milady's maid—all about her, and at once!" the captain ordered. Slapping his heavy gauntlet with its buckles and studded brass design against one hand, he strode to where Finch stood at attention.

"Tell you about Arlene, sir?" Finch asked, as if bewildered. "What would you know? She was milady's maid, although she was only employed as such just before we left England. When Lady Tench's regular dresser took ill at the last moment, it was thought easier to bring Arlene, since she is Robert Bogle's wife. He is the footman," he added, as if he spoke to a backward child.

"I know who he is," Rossetti snarled, thrusting his face toward Finch. The valet did not stir or retreat. Suddenly the captain turned back to Laurie. "You have had the most unusual bad luck with your servants, have you not, milady?"

Laurie only looked at him, her expression haughty as

she inclined her head. The captain seemed confused for a moment by that direct hazel stare, and then he turned to Finch again.

"Would you have said she was a good maid?" he asked.

Finch looked uncomfortable. "Well, as to that, sir, I hardly like to venture an opinion." He moved his eyes as if to remind Rossetti that Rob stood behind him.

"Answer me!" Rossetti commanded.

Finch stared past the captain's gold-trimmed shoulder. "In my opinion, and you will excuse me for saying so, Rob, Mrs. Bogle was not very competent. She was clumsy, and my mistress was often turned out in only ordinary style." The valet sniffed. "Not at all what the Marchioness of Tench requires."

"That's all right, Mr. Finch," Rob piped up. "Arlene wasn't trained up to be a lady's maid. But coo-er! She is a 'and in the dairy!"

Abandoning Finch, the captain marched toward the helpless footman. "And you did not protest when your wife was discharged so far from home?"

Rob shrugged. "Wot's it matter then?" he asked carelessly. "We'll all be going 'ome sooner or later. And Arlene 'ated the travel, she was glad to leave. And, to tell you the truth, I was glad to see the back of 'er. Nothing but whine, whine, whine about the weather, you foreigners, the food, the coach, and her cold. Be a real treat not to 'ave to listen to 'er complaining. Good as a 'oliday, it'll be!" He grinned then and winked at the captain, man to man.

The wink seemed to push Capitano Rossetti past the limits of his short patience, and he raised his leather glove and struck Rob hard across the face. Laurie half-rose to her feet as the heavy welt, already seeping blood, turned color on the fair skin beneath the straw-colored hair. Rob gasped, but he did not cry out.

"There will be no more insolence, no more lies!" Rossetti screamed. "There are ways to get the truth from you—all of you, including the little bride and mother-to-be! In fact, I—we—will start with her!"

In the sudden silence, Lord Vare's voice rang clear and cold. "For threatening my wife and striking my servant,

Rossetti, you will answer not only to me, but to your doge and the English ambassador as well. I do not think the authorities will look kindly on your actions toward guests in your country—especially guests who are relatives of the Duke of Wellington. This may well precipitate an international incident for which the Doge of Varallo will be blamed."

For a moment Rossetti stared around as if perplexed. Not a single one of his prisoners looked frightened, as surely they must if they were indeed guilty. Finch held himself stiffly, his thin, austere face showing his disgust. Then Simmons shook himself loose from his guard, who retreated in confusion as the bound man only stood to attention as well. Rob's eyes burned with defiance and pain as the blood dripped over his shirt, and Laurie kept her head high and her hands clasped tightly so he would not see them tremble. But it was the demeanor and words of the marquess that decided the issue.

"You will leave this house at once, taking your soldiers and your lackey with you," he said, nodding toward the fat butler. "Of course you may continue to guard the house, if you insist. What does that matter? But you will not enter it again until I have communicated with your master, not unless you wish to court the direst consequences. I trust I have made myself clear? You are excused!"

His voice was cold, as cold as ice, and steely with determination. The captain still looked confused, and for the first time unsure of himself. He had heard of the Duke of Wellington and the English ambassador, of course, but what convinced him to retreat was the threat of a complaint to his doge. True, his master had ordered him to investigate this maid, but he had not said he could use force. If he had overstepped his bounds, and only on the evidence of a green girl, he would be punished for it. He bowed to the inevitable.

"You will be guarded, of that you may be sure, milord," he said stiffly. "This affair is not concluded yet, by any means. When I find the maid, I will have all the evidence I need, and then we shall see. And you, *especially* you, will suffer for it."

He stared at Laurie for a pregnant moment, and then

he beckoned to his men and left the room, holding himself erect as if to salvage the remnants of his pride. No one spoke or moved until the heavy footsteps clattered down the steps and the front door slammed.

Laurie was the first to move, rising to run to Rob, who, now that the danger was past, had slumped against the wall. Finch busied himself untying the two men as she snatched up a cloth from one of the tables and pressed it to the wound. "Jed, quickly! The medicine chest," she ordered.

The marquess waited until Simmons left the room, and then he spoke quietly to his valet. "Go and bar the doors, Finch. We may have vanquished the captain for now, but he will be back."

As Finch left on his errand, Lord Vale poured out a generous tot of brandy and gave it to Rob. The footman was seated now, with Laurie kneeling before him, still trying to stanch the wound. "Drink this, Rob," he said, his eyes concerned.

"Oh, Rob, I would not have had this happen to you for the world," Laurie mourned. "You were so brave! And your poor face—does it hurt very badly?"

Rob managed to gulp some brandy between her ministrations. "Aye, it burns like the devil, m'lady," he said cheerfully. "But I've 'ad worse accidents than this. Don't you fret, now."

"Let me see," the marquess said, bending and taking the cloth from Laurie's hand. Kneeling beside her, he inspected the cut. "You will have an interesting scar for a long time, Rob, but thank heaven he missed your eye. It is not a deep cut, either—we won't have to stitch it."

Simmons came in then with a basin of water and the medicine chest. As he set his equipment down on a nearby table, he said, "Hope it won't put your wife off, Rob my boy. Why, you're as ugly as she is now."

Laurie looked on in amazement as all three men broke into hearty laughter. She failed to see what they could find amusing about the situation. She moved aside as Simmons, still chuckling, came to dress the wound. The marquess smiled down at her.

"Pour out some brandy for Simmons and Finch, that's a

good girl," he ordered. His face was still alive with amusement, and although she did not realize it, relief as well. As he watched Simmons clean the cut, he made his plans. Tonight he would write a stern, disapproving letter to the doge and send it to the villa first thing in the morning. He would also contact the English ambassador and any other notables he could locate in Milan. Then he must remember to engage another butler, and a lady's maid for Laurie as well, he thought as he handed Simmons the basilicum powder and a compress. It was too bad he could not invite some of his English neighbors to a reception tomorrow night, for if the house were crowded with the English nobility, the captain could not threaten them, and Archie's reappearance would be less noticeable as well. But with the deception they practiced, that was not possible. Lady Laura could not play his wife before their own countrymen, not and preserve a shred of her reputation in the process.

Laurie had poured the brandy as ordered, and now she walked slowly down the length of the salon. She was still on edge, and so frightened that it was all she could do not to burst into tears. The maid had talked, and if she had done so only a few hours earlier . . . But she must not dwell on it! There were still dangers to be faced ahead of them. What if Archie's new disguise did not convince the captain that he was an English lord from the Foreign Office? What if there were some slip? The plan seemed insane now, and she shivered as she sank down into a chair and covered her face with both hands. They were still, every one of them, living on the edge of a sharp-bladed sword. She wanted to scream at the three men who had laughed so carelessly at a silly joke. Didn't they realize their peril?

Hearing their voices, she raised her head. The marquess was holding a branch of candles high so Jed could see more clearly, and the light illuminated them as if they were actors on a stage. There was Rob seated in one of the stiff chairs, his head thrown back so his wound could be bandaged and his blond hair white in the candles' glare. Bending over him was Jed Simmons. She felt her eyes misting as she watched him. He was so confident and efficient, and yet she knew how gentle he was being, for he had bandaged many a cut for her when she was a child. Now his curly, grizzled head was close to the young footman's, and although she could not make out his words, she knew he was reassuring Rob as his square tanned hands bound up the wound.

And there, standing above them both, was the Marquess of Vare. In the candlelight his sleek hair gleamed like black satin above his strong-planed face. He was in profile to her, and she stared as if mesmerized at his broad, high forehead, sculptured nose, and determined jaw. His black brows were contracted as if his thoughts were far away.

Laurie felt something deep inside her stir and glow.

Once again he had saved them. It seemed to be almost second nature to him to take command of every situation, no matter how dangerous, and bring them safe out of it. Her gaze went to where his white hand held the candelabrum steady. White and aristocratic—a complete contrast to Jed's. And yet she knew she would trust herself to him as quickly as she would to her old friend. Lord and servant—so different and yet so much alike in their quiet strength and competence. Watching them, she was reminded of the hills at home she knew so well. No matter how cloud-covered or storm-lashed, you knew they were there; unchangeable, firm.

The marquess turned slightly then and stared down the room to where she sat so quietly. His dark blue eyes burned on her face as if he wished to read her thoughts. Suddenly she was glad she was in shadow as she stared back at him, her heart in her eyes.

"Why, my lord," she whispered, "I do believe I am in love with you."

And the feeling deep inside her began to swell and run like quicksilver through her veins, leaving her helpless before the truth of what she had just discovered.

# 9

Lord Vare wrote his letter to the doge before he went to bed, and into it he put all the anger and scorn he had so readily to hand after the scene just passed. When Rossetti had threatened Laurie, he had had all he could do not to throw himself at the man, unarmed as he was, and throttle him, he was so furious.

Now, as he sanded his note, he wondered at the sudden change that had come over them all after Rob's bandage had been secured. For a few brief minutes there had been no lord, no servants—only a group of Englishmen intent on saving their lives by whatever means and courage and wit they could each bring to the problem. In calling attention to himself and talking brashly, Rob had taken the blow for all of them. The marquess knew everyone had suffered when that heavy studded glove had struck Rob's cheek. And he remembered Simmons's quip about Rob's wife—the laughter had been just what they needed to break the tension. What had happened to change that camaraderie so shortly thereafter?

Was it possible that Laurie had been responsible? He remembered that she had sat apart from them for some time, and had only come back to the group when Finch went to ask her if there was anything she required. At the time, he had applauded her ever-present tact and consideration for others. If she had been hovering over Rob, he would not have felt free to curse or cry out if Simmons's ministrations had been too painful. Lord Vare remembered he had thought once again how remarkable a girl she was.

And how could Laurie have altered the mood? She had gone to her room almost at once, after bidding each of them good night. The marquess recalled that she had not met his eye, and he frowned. Then he rubbed his forehead. How silly he was to regret her coolness when it was just how he intended her to behave.

He snuffed out the candles in the salon and went up to bed. He had dismissed Finch with the others when he saw how tired and worn the valet had looked standing behind Laurie's fresh young beauty. As he climbed the stairs, he made himself think of Archie, hoping he had reached an inn safely, and was fast asleep in preparation for the role he must assume tomorrow.

When Laurie came down the next morning, she found the marquess had already left the house. As Finch served her some fruit, rolls, and coffee in the walled garden at the back of the house, he told her of the marquess's early departure.

For a moment Laurie was concerned. "But, Finch! Is it safe for him to go out? And why did Capitano Rossetti let him go?"

She looked up from her melon to see a little smile on the valet's prim lips. "I rather think the good captain was so stunned, he did not dare to protest. You see, m'lady, Lord Vare took Rob with him. I daresay you wouldn't have known him, so swathed in bandages as he was."

Finch bowed and turned to the serving table, and Laurie could have sworn she heard a muffled chuckle, and she smiled a little in return.

As Finch refilled her coffee cup, he said, "Lord Vare asked me to tell you he will return in time for luncheon, m'lady. Until then, he suggests that you rest this morning, and try to forget last evening's *contretemps*. M'lord is confident there will be no repeat of such a distasteful scene."

He waited until Laurie nodded, and then he added, "Do not worry if any of the neighbors should come to call, m'lady. I shall tell them, of course, that you are not receiving."

Laurie lowered her cup. "But why not, Finch? I should enjoy meeting some English people, and surely if the house is filled with visitors coming and going, the captain would never dare to force his way in."

Finch coughed a little. "Unfortunately, visitors are not possible at this time, m'lady. Remember, when you return home, the Marchioness of Tench becomes the Lady Laura Lockridge once more."

He bowed, and after asking if there was anything more that she required, left her to her thoughts. She felt a little sad as she pondered his last words. If only the Doge of Varallo and his vicious *capitano* would disappear, how happy she would be to play John's marchioness indefinitely. Then, firmly, she told herself she was being silly.

When she had wakened that morning, she had been content just to lie in bed and think about the marquess. Still drowsy and warm, she had remembered all the things she loved about him—his dark blue eyes that could blaze or soften or twinkle, his ready wit, his power, and all the lean hard length of him, so straight and noble and dear. And she had recalled their kiss in the garden. She knew she would always remember it, but still, she wished she might kiss him like that again, not once, but many times.

Reality returned while she was dressing. She might be in love with the marquess, but it was obvious that he was not in love with her. She was too young, too immature, too unsophisticated. His close attention to the *principessa* had shown the type of woman he preferred. Laurie knew there was no way she could compete with beautiful, voluptuous, and worldly women like that. She sighed and wished there was someone—anyone!—she could talk to about this truly unsolvable problem.

After her breakfast, Laurie wandered restlessly around the house. When she looked out the front windows of the salon, she saw the doge's soldiers, still on guard. Then Capitano Rossetti turned to stare in her direction, and she drew back out of sight. For a while, she returned to the garden, trying to enjoy the sunny September morning, but the heavy scent of the flowers and the drone of the insects did not suit her mood. She wondered why she did not seem able to sit still.

At last she went out to the stables at the back of the house. Jed Simmons was there mending a bridle, and without a word she went up to him and hugged him. Jed looked down at the shining curls that rested on his broad chest, and hugged her back. How he loved this girl! She was the daughter he had never had, and he knew he would give his life for her without a moment's regret. He heard her sigh, and thinking she was missing her father, tried to turn her thoughts.

" 'Ere now, Lady Laura, none of that! Your father wouldn't want you to be so sad. And it won't be long now, you'll see, before we're safe 'ome again."

"I know, Jed," Laurie agreed. "But it has been so different, so hard. So much has happened . . ."

Jed hugged her again, and then he put her aside and picked up the bridle he had been working on. "I tell you, Lady Laura, it was a good thing for us that Lord Vare caught us up when 'e did. I could ask no finer man to 'elp you, for just see all that 'e has done for us." Simmons shook his grizzled head. "Don't know what would 'ave 'appened to us if 'e 'adn't come along. And Lord Price too, although at first I thought 'e was as silly a young man as I've ever seen—'e's done 'is share. But whoever would 'ave thought we'd find ourselves in such danger?"

"You like Lord Vare a lot, don't you, Jed?" Laurie asked, her voice careless. The valet shot her a suspicious glance and saw she was not looking at him. "Aye, that I do," he said slowly. "Your father would 'ave liked 'im too. 'E's a real man, not one of those London good-for-nothings. A man like 'im, now . . ."

He paused and then he went to hang the bridle on the wall and take down a cloth to polish the brass of the coach, and Laurie waited somewhat breathlessly to hear what he would say next.

Instead, she saw him straighten up, his good-natured face stern and forbidding, and she turned to see one of the *capitano*'s men lounging in the stable doorway. Jed came forward at once to bow to her and lead her past the guard, talking all the while. "Don't worry, m'lady. I'll see to the springs before we travel on, and 'ave the coach cleaned as well."

When they reached the house, he added in a harsh whisper, "Go back inside, Lady Laura, and don't come out 'ere again! These foreigners, sneaking around to eavesdrop! We'll talk again soon, when we're safe away."

He tugged his forelock and bowed, and Laurie was left alone.

Luncheon was served in the garden by Finch. As they ate, the marquess told her about the new butler and lady's maid he had engaged, and Laurie tried to keep her tumultuous thoughts in order and her eyes on her plate. Fortunately, there was plenty to discuss. He told her of his visit to the English ambassador, with a heavily bandaged Rob as proof of the *capitano*'s cruelty, and the ambassador had promised to write a firm letter of protest to the doge. Lord Vare had also seen two other highly ranked English lords and explained his plight to them, and they had promised to use all their influence with the Italian nobility to ensure that such an incident did not recur. Laurie told him about her morning—the guards in the street, and the one who had come into the stable while she was talking to Jed—and the marquess begged her to stay inside the house unless he was with her.

It was all very ordinary, but after they returned to the salon to wait for Archie, a silence fell between them. John had brought his notecase and books with him, and he pretended to interest himself in their contents, while Laurie tried to read a book about Italy her father had recommended. She found it hard to concentrate on the pages with the marquess just across the room. And then, every time a horse went by in the street outside, she would start up. Several times she could not stop herself from running to see if Lord Price had arrived at last. John watched her with an indulgent eye.

"Sit down, Lady Laura," he said at last. "You will wear yourself out to no purpose. Archie will come in his own good time."

Laurie sank back down on the sofa. "But it is almost three! You are not worried, Joh . . . m'lord?" she asked, carefully avoiding his eyes.

John wondered at her stiffness. Today she was only a shadow of the companion he had come to know and enjoy, and he had no idea why she was looking so self-conscious.

He smiled at her a little, to ease her tension, little knowing how it stabbed her heart.

"No, I am not worried. Archie has never been one to do things by the book. He will be here, of that I am sure, if only to avoid being left alone in a strange country. Perhaps his delay will be to our benefit." At Laurie's uncomprehending look, he explained, "If he were to appear on the scene too quickly, it might be easier for Rossetti to connect him with Arlene. Although Finch assures me we will not know him in his new disguise, the captain has sharp eyes."

Laurie pretended to agree, but she could not help worrying. From what she had been able to discover, Archie did not have much common sense. It would be just like him to forget the time, or even the address.

It was almost five when she heard the rumble that signaled that a number of horses were approaching. Lord Vare looked up from his papers, his eyes keen, and she forced herself to sit still until this time she was sure that whoever was riding by was not going to pass the house. Only then did she run to the window. For a moment she could not believe what she saw, and she gasped. "Come here, John," she called. "Whoever can this be?"

The marquess pulled the drapery back to look out the window, and even in her interest in the scene outside, Laurie was very much aware of him standing so close behind her.

Together they watched amazed as two coaches, attended by a troop of horsemen, drew up before their door. The coaches were mud-spattered, as if they had been traveling hard from a great distance. Laurie could just make out a crest on the door of the lead coach, and as she watched, two grooms in gray livery sprang down from the back and hastened to open the door. They bowed reverently.

The marquess chuckled. "But this is perfect," he said, his voice admiring. "Trust Archie to do the thing up in style."

By this time a number of servants had gotten out of the second coach, and now they sorted themselves out in two lines before the door to the house, looking straight ahead. Laurie was amazed at the size of the group. Counting the

mounted troop, there were some twenty servants in
attendance. Capitano Rossetti's men stood nearby, their
mouths agape in astonishment. Laurie knew just how they
felt. Surely this was an entourage fit for a royal prince.

"I shall never mock Archie again," Lord Vare murmured.
"But you must excuse me, Laurie, while I go and welcome
him in the manner he so richly deserves."

Laurie remained by the window, and so she was the
first to see the man that came down the steps of the coach,
assisted by his bowing footmen. She saw at once that it
was not Archie. This man was much taller and even thinner,
and many years older than Lord Price. He raised an
ornate quizzing glass and proceeded to inspect his surroundings as his servants bowed and curtsied in unison.

The gentleman was dressed all in black, from his hat to
his shining boots. He did not turn or make any acknowl-
edgment of her presence as a lady stepped from the coach
behind him, but he held out his right hand for her in
support. Laurie's eyes widened. The lady wore only
white—a sumptuous silk gown trimmed with snowy er-
mine and mother-of-pearl buttons and beads, and a large
sweeping hat adorned with at least a dozen white roses
and yards of veiling. As a contrast to her escort, she was
magnificent, but Laurie couldn't help but wonder if her
outfit was not very uncomfortable in the heat of an Italian
afternoon. She noticed that the only color about the lady
was her brilliant red hair and sparkling dark eyes.

And then Archie appeared. For a moment she was not
sure it was he as he minced down the steps, clutching an
elaborately embroidered *portefeuille* so tightly, it was obvious he carried important documents. His hair and eyebrows were now dark brown, and he sported a thin
mustache. Although he was tricked out fashionably, from
an elegant cravat and a number of fobs and rings, to a
clouded cane and skintight breeches of a pale primrose
shade, he paled in comparison to the couple who had
preceded him.

Laurie saw John come out of the house, his hand extended in welcome, and then she saw him stop, a fero-
cious frown crossing his face. It was gone in an instant,
although the welcoming smile he had worn at first was

definitely missing as he moved forward to greet his guests.

Outside, Lord Vare had choked back an oath when he saw the company Archie kept. He knew the man in black, of course, for it was none other than the Dandified Duke, a figure all London society knew well. Henry Rothsbottom, the Duke of Delvers, was a man in his late thirties, and so far in his lifetime had found nothing to be of more importance than his own glorious self. He adorned his person with each new whim of fashion, keeping three valets busy all the time. It was said that he often changed his clothes ten or eleven times a day, when the mood was on him. He never wore anything but black or white, but this eccentricity did not keep even the Prince Regent himself from often asking his advice on matters of dress.

John bowed to him, but his eyes went at once to the lady on his right. She smiled at him, a triumphant, glittering smile, as Archie came up and said, his voice excited, "My dear Lord Tench, well met, sir! You do remember Lady Willoughby, do you not?"

Archie put his arm around the lady's waist then, and beamed, and Lord Vare forced himself to bow, although his thoughts were murderous. What was the Lady Pamela Jones-Witherall doing in Milan? And what bad angel had made sure her path and his cousin's would cross?

The lady laughed at him, a silvery trill of complete amusement, and then she said, "I cannot tell you, Lord Tench, how much I have been looking forward to our meeting. I was so sorry to miss your wedding last spring, and I am so anxious to meet your bride! Lord Willoughby has told me *all* about her."

She snuggled closer in Archie's arm. "Indeed, yes! I trust you will forgive us for intruding on your honeymoon, m'lord, but the Duke of Wellington was most insistent that you get the messages we carry." She shrugged, and then she seemed to notice the doge's guard for the first time, especially Capitano Rossetti. The hatred and disappointment in his burning eyes made her pause for a moment, and the Duke of Delvers was able to speak at last.

"Yes, yes, my dear, most true, most true indeed. But

perhaps now we could retire to some more seemly location? It is not at all what I am used to to be kept standing about on the cobbles like a tradesman." Coming from his reed-thin body, his voice was surprisingly deep and booming, and as one, his servants bowed again.

"What? What?" he asked plaintively, and the marquess tore his eyes from Lady Pamela's exultant face and ushered him up the steps, Archie and his fiancée close behind.

"A small establishment you have here, m'lord," the duke complained as he strode past his scraping servants. "But not to worry, sir, not to worry at all. I'll hire the houses on either side for my staff. Higgins? Higgins?"

A small man in gray, clutching a large portfolio, appeared as if by magic from the line of servants, and the duke waved a languid hand. "See to it, at once."

"Certainly, your Grace," Higgins said, stepping backward and bowing even more deeply than before.

Laurie waited in the middle of the salon, her hands clasped before her. She wished she had changed her simple morning gown of peach muslin for the green silk, or even the royal blue that she had been saving for some special occasion, and she wished she had had her new maid redo her hair at some point during the afternoon. Nervously she tucked up a drooping curl, and then she stood quietly again. What difference did it make what she wore? It appeared that Archie had found some friends to help him with his masquerade. After she had met them and they had had tea, they would probably be on their way.

Both doors were flung open then and the newcomers entered, preceded by a thunderous-looking Marquess of Vare. Laurie did not notice him as she inspected the others. She thought Archie seemed strangely excited as he came to her and pressed both her hands. "Laurie, my dear, you must let me make you known to Lady Pam . . . er, I mean, Lady Willoughby," he corrected himself, drawing the lady in white closer. "And darling, this, of course, is Lady Tench."

He looked around, and when he saw the butler had left the room, he whispered, "Not really. This is Lady Laura Lockridge—you remember."

Laurie held out her hand and was surprised to hear the lady's mocking chuckle. Startled, she searched the other woman's face, and she was shocked. Lady Willoughby—whoever she might be—was much older than she had appeared at a distance. Her face was beautiful, but even the heavy makeup she wore could not hide a score of tiny lines around her mouth and eyes. She stared at Laurie, and she seemed vastly amused as her dark eyes slid over the girl's slim figure and short chestnut curls. Laurie felt her face flushing, and her hand dropped to her side.

"So this is Lady Tench. My, my," the mythical Lady Willoughby said, and then she laughed in derision. John came to stand beside Laurie, his face stern. Archie looked from one woman to the other, wondering why Pam was behaving so badly. He could not know that she was jealous of the young girl before her, and afraid that he would compare her to Laurie's fresh innocence, much to her detriment.

"Behave yourself, Pammy," the other stranger boomed, and then he strolled forward and bowed. "Happy to make your acquaintance, Lady Tench, very happy indeed. I see I shall have to tell you that I am the Duke of Delvers, since my host seems to have been struck dumb by some malady I can only hope is not contagious."

"Your Grace," Laurie said, smiling as she sank into a deep curtsy.

"Very nice, very nice indeed, John." The duke beamed. "Can't say I blame you for a minute."

"Now, see here . . ." the marquess began, his face flushed and his eyes indignant.

"No need to come to cuffs with me, sir, no need at all. Assure you, I perfectly understand your chivalry now I have met the lady. By the way, you do have room for us, do you not? Archie told me there would be no problem, but even though I am happy to do all I can for a fellow Englishman—most happy—I will have to go if my comforts are at stake. Even patriotism has its limits, you know."

Laurie stepped forward. "Allow me to take care of it, your Grace. Won't you be seated while I order tea?"

His grace looked gratified at this attention and went to sit down in the most elaborate chair in the salon.

Lady Pamela laughed loudly in disbelief. "Good heavens, girl, we don't want any nursery pap! Order some port and brandy, or at least some wine. Acting is such dry business, is it not, my darling?"

She smiled and stroked Archie's arm. When his letters from abroad had arrived less and less frequently as the weeks passed, Lady Pamela had become alarmed. She was running out of money and credit, and she knew she could not afford to let this wealthy prize slip away. And so she had made arrangements to travel with the Duke of Delvers to Milan, a city Archie had mentioned they would visit, to await him there. She knew the old saying "out of sight, out of mind" to be very true, especially when his cousin, Lord Vare, would be doing everything in his power to bring Archie to his senses. She was sure that when she was with the boy she could rekindle the flame of his passion for her, even to his accepting her traveling with the duke. It was a business arrangement, after all, although she had no intention of mentioning to Lord Price that she had given her favors on the journey, in return for her passage. She had been so convinced of Archie's infatuation, she had felt herself infallible, but now she was not so sure.

Her smile for him was warm and full of barely suppressed ardor. Although Archie returned it, John noticed that he seemed a little taken aback by his fiancée's behavior, and his spirits rose.

Laurie went to give the butler orders to ready some rooms and to bring in not only tea but also decanters and glasses. She tried not to dwell on the rude, flashy woman and her ducal escort as she did so, although she could not help but wonder who they were and why they were here.

When she came back to the salon, she found the lady snuggled close to Lord Price on a sofa, her elaborate bonnet discarded at her feet and her fingers teasing his jawline before they moved to ruffle his hair as she whispered to him. Archie's face was red; he did not look at all comfortable at this intimacy in the presence of others.

Lord Vare was standing before the empty fireplace, his

hands clasped behind his back as he glared at the lady.
The duke was left to conduct a gentle monologue as he
swung one shiny black boot slowly to and fro.

"Happy to assist you, m'lord, and from what Lord Price
has been telling me, you are in dire need of it. Who is this
murderous doge, by the by? But no need to fear him
further, no need at all. We shall remain here until his
suspicions are lulled, and then we will be glad to have you
join our party on the road to Florence. Milan grows dull."

"When did you arrive, your Grace?" the marquess asked,
as Laurie came to sit across from them. She turned her
back on the Lady Pamela, who was now kissing Archie's
ear.

"About a week ago. Brought Pammy out, y'see, at her
insistence. She claimed she could not bear to be separated
from Lord Price for another moment, and begged my
escort. Happy to agree—I was traveling anyway."

He shrugged, his vacant eyes twinkling for a moment
before the drooping lids came down to hide their sudden
shrewd look. "You don't seem to be overjoyed at her
arrival, m'lord. Now, why is that?"

"I shall be glad to tell you, your Grace, when we are in
private," Lord Vare said, his voice colorless, and then the
butler and footmen came in with several trays, and conversation became more general.

When they had all been served, only Lady Pamela
insisting on a large glass of port, Archie told them his
story. In searching for an inn where he might spend the
night, he had seen the duke's carriage and had recognized
the crest at once. Thinking he might enlist his support, he
had entered the restaurant where it waited, to find not
only the Dandified Duke but also Lady Pamela. Laurie
noticed how his eyes shone and his Adam's apple jumped
up and down as he swallowed in his excitement. "Wasn't
that the most fortunate thing, John? For here is the Lady
Willoughby of our cast of characters, and there can be no
question of propriety, not when we are to be married so
shortly."

Laurie set down her cup, her eyes wide with shocked
surprise, and then she lowered them to a plate of cakes as

she passed it to the duke. He smiled at her a little, looking amused.

Lady Pamela laughed and tossed off the rest of her port. "My dearest, Lord Vare is in no position to cry propriety, not now! Why, our being together pales in comparison to his situation with Lady Laura."

"I say, Pam, you don't understand," Archie interrupted, seeing the murderous glare in his cousin's eyes, and Laurie's white face. "There has been nothing anyone could take exception to—why, we have been together all the time."

"All the time?" she asked, chuckling again. "But that is even worse. How crowded you must have been!"

"That will be quite enough, Pammy," the duke ordered, and she subsided, her eyes dancing with malice.

Now Laurie was as furious as Lord Vare, but she knew she had to keep silent unless she was prepared to stoop to this woman's level. But oh, how she longed to tell her exactly what she thought of her! The Lady Pamela was coarse and vicious, and she was much too old for Archie. Why was he engaged to her?

"May I show you to your room, m'lady?" she asked, proud of her even voice. "Perhaps you would care to change? We dine at eight."

Lady Pamela looked as if she wished to refuse, but the duke rose and said, "Run along now, Pammy. You have done enough damage for one afternoon. Besides, you will need the time for your toilette. I want you to wear the white satin gown tonight. Is that quite understood?"

Lady Pamela thrust out her lower lip, looking mutinous, and then Laurie was surprised to see her rise obediently and gather up her belongings. "Very well, Dandy, if you insist," she said, blowing him a kiss. "Archie—until later, my love."

She followed a stiff-backed Laurie from the room, and the duke took his seat again, and drew out a cigar case. "All right to smoke in here, m'lord?" he asked, and at John's nod, offered the case to the others. Archie refused, and settled back in his chair, his eyes troubled.

"I see I have more to do here than I thought, much more indeed," the duke remarked, puffing on his cigar until it began to draw evenly. "Now, what's all this, Archie,

my boy? You—marrying the Lady Pamela Jones-Witherall?
Have you gone quite mad?"

Archie paled, but the duke went on before he could
speak. "I thought it was all a hum when she told me, but I
was perfectly happy to have her come along. She's a
beautiful woman even if she is past her prime. But good
heavens, Archie, you amuse yourself with women like
that, you don't marry 'em! Take it from me, my boy,
there's no need to."

He smiled to himself and then he asked, "Isn't that
right, Lord Vare? Wonder you didn't point that out to this
young idiot yourself. Related, aren't you?"

Archie was stunned. To say he had been shocked to find
his betrothed traveling with the duke was an understatement, but he had tried to be worldly about it. She had
explained it was only a platonic relationship, "because I
had to find you, my love. I have suffered so from loneli-
ness since you went away, I could not bear it," she had
said, her dark eyes filling with tears. He had kissed her
and assured her it did not matter, but if he was not
misreading Dandy's words, the journey had not been platonic at all. And then he had not been able to help
comparing Pamela and Laurie, not only their looks, but
their behavior as well. Pamela had not shown to advantage
in the situation. He reminded himself he was a gentleman,
and he had offered for her after all. He could not retreat
now.

"But . . . but I love her," he said nobly, although he
still looked distraught.

"Obviously you haven't spent much time with her, then,"
the duke remarked. "The tantrums, the screaming—why,
the scenes, and before breakfast, mind you, you would not
believe. I think the lady has a screw loose, she is so
unstable. She is also wild to a fault, undisciplined, decadent,
and wanton. All of which makes her an exciting mistress, if
you can stand the pace, although she would make a terrible wife. Even, my boy, if she were anywhere near your
age, which of course she is not. If you persist, you'll make
a perfect cake of yourself and all London will be laughing
at you. It's such a bad *ton* besides. I shall have to drop
you, indeed I will. Everyone who is anyone will."

The duke paused to puff on his cigar, and then he added, "Much better for you to marry the Lady Laura. Handsome girl, and a good 'un, I can tell."

Lord Vare wondered why such a solution was so repulsive to him as Archie sputtered, "But . . . but . . ."

"Your engagement to Pammy hasn't been announced, has it?" his friend asked. "Well, then, with a few stratagems, you're safe out of it. However, better not mention your changed feelings until we're safely away from here. Wouldn't put it past Pammy to drive straight out to this doge of yours and tell him everything, just out of spite. Nasty woman, very nasty."

The duke rose and stretched. "I must beg to be excused now, if we dine at eight. I shall have only two hours to change, and that's cutting it a bit fine. Now, don't worry, Archie. I'll take care of the Lady P, at least until you have made good your escape. There's sure to be some French or Italian count who'll catch her eye in Rome. And she has done very well for herself—no need to fear I shall leave her destitute. All those gowns and furs and jewels I bought for her have set her up in style for some time to come."

He strolled across the room, leaving a quietly satisfied Lord Vare and a stunned Lord Price staring after him. At the door, he added, those deceptively sleepy eyes gleaming, "You must not think the lady will fall into a sad decline because she loses your love, Archie. If you weren't worth those twenty thousand pounds a year, she'd never have given you so much as a smile, never mind the dubious honor of claiming her often-bestowed hand."

He chuckled and went out, closing the door softly behind him.

Archie groaned and buried his face in his hands. "I . . . I feel such a fool, John!" he mourned. "When I found her with the duke, I was so thrilled to see her again I did not think. She told me she was only traveling with him so she could reach my side, that it was a business arrangement. She even promised me, on her honor, that she had had nothing to do with him. Ha!"

He rose and paced the room, his face bitter. "I see now that it certainly was a business arrangement. I tell you, I have never been so disillusioned or so shocked!"

John wisely bit back a biting retort. "At least you discovered her true colors before you married her, cuz. But I must warn you that the duke is right. On no account are you to let her suspect that your feelings have changed, not at least until we have left Milan."

Archie promised he would not, although Lord Vare knew it would be the hardest acting his cousin had been called on to perform up to now.

# 10

Upstairs, Laurie sighed as she told her maid to lay out the green silk gown. She knew she could not rival the Lady Pamela this evening, no matter what she wore. As she dressed, she wondered why she had to keep meeting beautiful, more experienced women. At least John does not appear to care for this one, she told herself as she sat down to have her hair dressed.

She came downstairs early, for she wanted to be sure that everything was in order. When she saw the duke's servants setting the table in the dining room, and running through the hall, she realized she need not have bothered. Probably the duke's own chef was even now in the kitchen preparing some of his favorite dishes.

When she entered the salon, she found Lord Vare ahead of her. He was leaning against the mantel, looking down at the little fire that had been lit, and as she paused at the door, one hand to her throat in surprise, he straightened up and came to greet her.

"I am glad you are early, Lady Laura," he said, taking her hand and wondering why it trembled in his. "I have been worried about you."

Her hazel eyes searched his blue ones for a moment, and then she looked away. "Worried, m'lord?" she asked as she went to take a seat.

"I thought the Lady Pamela might have upset you," he explained. "You are not to regard her. Although her appearance here can only strengthen our case with the doge, I cannot but regret it. She should not be allowed in the same room with someone as fine as you. I am sorry."

"Is it true that she is going to marry Archie, m'lord?" Laurie asked, ignoring his last words, although her heart had leapt at his praise.

Lord Vare's little frown disappeared in a heartfelt grin of relief. "No, she is not," he said, his voice exultant. "She is not aware of it as yet, but Archie has had second thoughts about the wisdom of such an alliance."

"I am glad," Laurie said simply. "I do not think she is any better than she should be, although she is very beautiful, is she not? But her traveling with the duke makes me wonder about her morals . . ."

Her voice died away and she flushed as she remembered that she herself was traveling with a man—in fact, several of them. The marquess pretended not to notice her confusion.

"The duke, as her present protector, has offered to take her off Archie's hands," he explained, and then he added with another frown, "But I should not be telling you these things. I am sure such knowledge is unsuitable for one of your innocence and tender years."

Angry now, Laurie rose in some agitation. "I wish you would not treat me as a child, m'lord! After meeting the *principessa* I am well aware that there are women like that in the world."

"What has the *principessa* to do with it?" Lord Vare asked, coming to stand before her.

"I saw the way the two of you whispered and laughed together," Laurie could not help retorting. "It is obvious that you were attracted to her." She tried to shrug, as if his behavior did not matter.

The marquess laughed a little. "You may not be a child, Laurie, but you are not very old or very experienced. Women like the *principessa* can make a discussion of the weather seem immoral. I merely went along with her because she expected it. It is the way of the world."

When Laurie would not answer or look at him, he stepped closer to tip her chin up gently. For a moment he was stunned at the unhappiness he saw in her hazel eyes.

"What a touching scene, to be sure," Lady Pamela's voice mocked from the doorway. Laurie whirled as she came in, resplendent in a slim, revealing gown of white satin. "But since you play the husband, m'lord, why not take every advantage of the role? I am sure you have both found it . . . hmm, very exciting!"

Her dark eyes flashed as she took a seat. Laurie was glad when Archie came in just then and went to kiss the lady's hand, and she turned away from them all to go toward the fire, ignoring John's frown.

The duke, dressed impeccably in his customary black, was not far behind, and when the butler announced dinner, he came over to her.

"May I have the honor, Lady Tench?" he asked in his booming voice.

As they crossed the hall to the dining room, they saw a group of servants in the duke's gray livery carrying several trunks and portmanteaus up the stairs. The front door stood open, and Laurie could see a large wagon there, and still more trunks to be brought in.

"All this, for just the two of you, your Grace?" John asked, his voice amused.

The duke seemed surprised at the question. "But of course, m'lord. You did not think I could manage with only those few pieces of baggage you saw this afternoon, did you? I see no reason to lower my standards of dress just because I am on the Continent. After all, I have a reputation to maintain."

Laurie wished she felt more like laughing, but there was still an ache in her heart from Lady Pamela's insinuations. She took her seat at the head of the table with foreboding.

To her surprise, dinner turned out to be very pleasant. The duke was amusing in his rambling, repetitive way, Lord Vare witty and erudite, so Archie's and her silence was not remarked. Even the Lady Pamela behaved herself and had little to contribute to the conversation, although Laurie could see her puzzled glances at Archie's thin, serious face. To draw her attention away from him, Laurie began to ask him about London.

With the servants in the room, they could not talk openly, but the duke seemed determined to treat her with the courtesy that would have been hers if she were truly John's marchioness. The masquerade goes on, she thought, stealing a glance at the opposite end of the table. She saw the marquess watching her, his dark blue eyes intent, as if he were pondering the scene between them before dinner. She lowered her eyes, hoping no one but herself had noticed his steady, serious stare.

When she would have given the signal to withdraw to Lady Pamela, dreading the moment when she would find herself alone with her, she was surprised to see John rising as well, and beckoning to the other men. "Shall we have our port in the drawing room with the ladies this evening, sirs? That way Lady Pamela can enjoy some as well."

The duke agreed, but only on the condition that Lady Laura would allow him to smoke an after-dinner cigar. It was all done smoothly, and with great style, and Laurie was grateful to both of them.

A short time later, she heard a knock on the front door, and remembering last evening, looked to John for reassurance. He smiled, as if he knew what she was thinking, and shook his head. A moment later, the butler knocked and presented a letter that had just arrived. The marquess excused himself while he read it. Laurie watched him anxiously until his expression changed from a frown to a smile.

"But we must celebrate, my friends!" he exclaimed. "I have here a most abject letter of apology from the Doge of Varallo. As arrogant as he is, it must have pained him to have to pen these humble words! He has withdrawn his guard, and he assures me that Capitano Rossetti will be punished for striking Rob and frightening my marchioness. Such wonderful news calls for a celebration—a toast to our freedom."

Laurie smiled, but she wondered if the doge had really given them up. Somehow she did not think he would let them slip out of his net so easily. The duke must have agreed with her, for he said in his booming voice, "Wonderful news, wonderful! But may I suggest, m'lord, that you remain on guard until you have left Italy? You fit the bill too closely for him to allow you to escape, especially since no other suspects have been found."

The marquess nodded, promising he would take care, as

he went to summon the butler. In a short while they were all drinking to their new freedom and making plans to leave Milan in three days' time.

As Laurie prepared to go up to bed, the marquess came to her side. In a low voice he asked her to join him on a tour of the city the following morning. She knew she should not agree, that she should stay as far away from him as she could, but somehow she could not bring herself to deny him. A time was set, and he bowed. As she left the salon, Laurie was very much aware of the others, and of Lady Pamela's mocking laughter.

Although the royal blue was too formal for the morning hours, she could not resist wearing it with its smart plumed bonnet and matching kid slippers. The marquess was waiting for her in the hall when she came down, and he smiled when he saw her. "I am glad you wore that gown, m'lady," he said as he opened the door for her. "It is quite my favorite of all the ones I bought in Biella. I was beginning to think you did not care for it."

"I was saving it for a special occasion, m'lord," she said, and then could have bitten her tongue. Seeing Simmons beside an open landau, waiting to drive them, she smiled and waved, glad she did not have to see the marquess's look of amusement at such childish gaucherie.

But it was such a beautiful morning that her spirits began to rise. None of the doge's guard was there to stare at them and follow, and it was a relief to be free of Lady Pamela for a few hours. She tilted her parasol over her shoulder and prepared to enjoy herself.

As the carriage moved slowly through the streets, Lord Vare pointed out the sights, including a building that he said was the largest theater in the world, the vast Ambrosian.

Laurie found the crowds in the streets more amusing, for they were so different from people in England or even France. Seeing two noblemen wrapped in long black cloaks that covered most of their faces, she asked the marquess why they were dressed that way.

"They look like two conspirators in a dastardly plot, do they not?" he remarked. "However, it is the custom here, as it is for Italian women to wear black. They are never seen in colors after the first year of their marriages."

Laurie was reminded of the *principessa* and Lord Vare's attraction to her, and she was glad when Simmons pulled up before the Palazzo Brera. As she strolled with the marquess through the rooms hung with Raphaels and Titians and Leonardos, she was glad he had engaged a guide called a *laquais de place* to explain the paintings they were seeing. For a moment she wished her father might have been with them. How he would have enjoyed such masterpieces! Lord Vare squeezed her arm gently when he saw the sadness on her face. Laurie was amazed that he could read her thoughts so well.

After the Brera, he took her to the enormous cathedral that was made entirely of white marble, inside and out. It soared above them, its walls adorned with pinnacles and statues and endless decoration. Although the marquess said it had been started in 1387, it was still in the building process. Laurie found it overwhelming, especially one of the chapels that was decorated throughout in glittering silver.

As they were leaving, the marquess suggested luncheon. "Surely we have done our duty as tourists this morning," he said, after telling Simmons to drive them to a café nearby. "And now, completely cultured, we have earned a respite."

Across the small table set among others under a colorful awning, he studied Laurie as she ate, watching the passersby. Although he had suggested the expedition only to separate her from Lady Pamela, he found he had enjoyed himself immensely. Laurie had so many intelligent questions. She was refreshing, for she took such an educated interest in her surroundings. Her early stiffness in his company had soon disappeared, and he himself had forgotten to maintain the wall of formality he had built up between them. As she sipped her coffee and smiled at a little girl and her nursemaid who were walking by, he smiled in turn.

"What would you like to do now, m'lady?" he asked. Laurie turned to him, her hazel eyes glowing with happiness. She had decided to enjoy every moment she was alone with the marquess. She would not think of the future, or her impossible love for him; she would be content to live only in the present, at least until they left Milan.

"But you are my guide, m'lord. I shall allow you to choose," she told him, her lips curling in a smile. The marquess thought she looked beautiful—and happy and relaxed for the first time since she had arrived in Italy. He wished there were some way he could make sure she would never have to be afraid again.

"Then I know exactly what we shall do," he said, rising and holding her chair. He would not tell her where they were going, and so she was surprised a few minutes later when he ordered Simmons to pull up before a row of distinguished shops.

"What is this place, m'lord?" she asked as he helped her down.

"This, Lady Laura, is where people shop for beautiful silk and jewels and trinkets." He felt her stiffen and hold back a little, and he added, "You did leave the choice to me, did you not? I have decided our day would not be complete without some souvenirs of Milan."

Laurie tried to pull away from his strong hand. "But, m'lord! I cannot allow you to buy me anything else, you know I can't. You have spent too much already, and you will not let me repay you."

The marquess ignored her distress. "Have you forgotten the duke's warning? We must behave normally. In Milan we are still the Marquess and Marchioness of Tench. Do you really believe the doge has given up having us watched, even now?"

Laurie looked around. There was a man across the street that she was sure she had seen earlier, and she allowed Lord Vare to escort her into the nearest shop without another word.

She soon forgot to protest after the marquess bought her some amber beads, a cut-glass scent bottle, and a beautiful hand-painted fan. He seemed determined to shower her with gifts. He purchased some delicate lace-trimmed handkerchiefs, a heart-shaped box covered with gold filigree to keep them in, and a large book containing sketches of the city. She managed to dissuade him from buying a gold chain and jeweled locket by saying she could never accept something so expensive, but he was adamant when he saw a length of cream-colored silk that was embroidered all over with a gossamer design in gold thread.

"This will make a beautiful ball gown," he told her. "When we return to England, you must have it made up by the finest *modiste*. And since you insist on repaying me, I shall expect you to save me a waltz and the supper dance as well, at the first ball you attend. Is it a bargain?"

His dark blue eyes teased her, and a little breathlessly she agreed. When they left the shop, Laurie insisted on carrying the silk herself, but she would not let him buy her anything else.

"If you do, m'lord, I shall send Simmons back here later to buy you a remembrance of Milan too," she threatened, and then she laughed. "Even though I am not entirely sure you would care for it."

"What do you mean?" he asked as he handed her into the landau.

"Can it be that you did not see that dear little monkey?" she asked demurely as she settled her skirts. "I know he would make a wonderful pet."

"Don't you dare, Laurie," the marquess growled. "I have no desire to exchange a Capitano Rossetti on my heels for a monkey on my shoulder."

Laurie only laughed again and changed the subject. When they returned home, the marquess had his purchases carried to her room, and after thanking him for her wonderful day, Laurie went upstairs to rest. Although she lay down on her bed and closed her eyes, she did not sleep. Instead, she spent the time remembering how he had looked all day—the sunlight and shadow on his face at the café, the smiles he had given her in the carriage, the feel of his hand and arm as he helped her up the steps of the Brera. And she knew she would never forget the way his blue eyes had laughed at her when she had insisted on feeding the pigeons in the *piazza*, or how they had teased when he asked her to save him the first waltz in her new silk gown. How much she loved him!

She was glad that for the remainder of their stay in Milan, Archie and the duke kept Lady Pamela amused while she and Lord Vare explored this intriguing city by themselves. But, all too soon, the morning of their departure arrived.

There were three coaches now, and Laurie was grateful she did not have to ride with Lady Pamela. Poor Archie, she thought as she took her seat beside the marquess, and smiled at Finch sitting next to her Italian maid opposite. He will be cooped up with her all day. I do not envy him at all, and as for the duke, how can any man want a woman like that? It was something she wished she might ask the marquess about, although she knew that was impossible.

They drove south at a leisurely pace. The duke, predictably, had hired, not one, but two guides called *vetterini* to ride ahead of them and arrange for new teams and accommodations. Since the two men seemed to be competitors, the inns where they stayed were the best to be found.

On the second evening of the journey, as they lingered over their coffee in an inn a few miles north of Piacenza, the duke mentioned that his guards had noticed they were being trailed by four horsemen. Laurie shivered. It seemed the doge had not given them up after all.

"Shall I have them . . . er, discouraged in their pursuit, m'lord?" the duke asked Lord Vare. "Easiest thing in the world to do, y'know."

"No, I think not," John murmured. "That would look too suspicious. I wonder if it would not be better for us to make a dash for the coast, instead of going on with you to Florence. We could take a *feluca* at Genoa for Marseilles, camping out along the shore at night, rather than waiting about for a ship to England. The doge would not expect us to travel that way. Once in France, Laurie will be safe."

Lady Pamela poured herself a glass of wine. "Laurie-Laurie-Laurie! How tedious this has become, this masquerade! But at least since Archie does not go with you, m'lord, he is safe out of it."

"But I must go with them, I must," Archie announced, his high voice cracking a little in his earnestness. "Laurie may need me."

Lady Pamela swallowed a sharp retort about his concern

for such a silly chit, and made herself say reasonably, "But, my darling, you cannot mean to leave me after I have come all this way to be with you! I will not hear of it! Lord Vare has never had any trouble with the female sex before this; he can manage one little girl by himself, I believe. Besides, I am sure he would be wishing you at the devil in short order, would you not, m'lord? Three's a crowd, and not at all what he had in mind."

John glared at her, and Laurie looked down at her lap and counted to ten, and then to twenty.

Lady Pamela laughed at them, as she went to cling to Archie's arm. "Consider the words he used, Archie. They are to make a *dash* for the coast—in the *moonlight*, no doubt, and then they are to sail by native boat *slowly* along the shore, *camping* out at night. Ah, all those soft, romantic Mediterranean nights that they will be lost in each other's arms under the stars! It would be cruel of you to intrude on such an idyll, my love."

The marquess started to rise, his face dark with fury, and the duke reached out and held his arm. "No, m'lord. Do not trouble yourself. Take the Lady Laura outside while Lord Price and I acquaint Pammy with the true state of affairs. I am sure Lady Laura would not care to be present when we do so. Come back in half an hour, for we have many plans to make."

John glared at the redheaded lady who stood staring at him so triumphantly, his hands clenched into two hard fists. For a moment there was silence in the parlor, and then he nodded.

"Come along, Lady Laura," he said, his eyes cold as he went to the door. Laurie followed him, her head held high. The journey, when he had proposed it, had sounded wonderful, until Lady Pamela's sly words had turned it into a sordid interlude. Behind her, she could hear this lady's voice rising in volume as she screamed and cursed, and then there came the sound of shattering glass.

For the first time in an hour, the marquess smiled, albeit grimly. "Hurry, m'lady," he commanded. "Her language should be in no way a part of your education. Poor Archie! I hope he comes out of this with a whole skin."

Outside the inn, they strolled up and down, the mar-

quess strangely silent now. Laurie could have wept. Once
again, she was leading Lord Vare into danger, and he
would not talk to her or discuss it. How he must want to
be rid of her! This dash to the coast that he proposed was
only so he could get her to France as quickly as possible.
Then the burden of caring for her, of being placed in
almost constant peril himself, would be lifted from his
shoulders. She told herself she must remember his
indifference. It was obvious that he did not care for her,
that he thought her a child. She was just a responsibility
to him, a promise he must keep.

For his part, the marquess was wondering if she were
up to the journey he had in mind. If it were to be
successful, they would have to travel hard and fast. Of
course she would have to dress as a boy again. He was
glad now that he had written to Lady Blake a second time
and asked her to come to France and await him in Le
Havre. He only hoped they did not run across any of the
English nobility until he had Laurie safely delivered into
her care.

Finch came to summon them a little while later. His
austere face looked severe in the light of the flambeaux.
"The duke has asked that you rejoin him, m'lord, m'lady.
The Lady Pamela has retired."

"Completely vanquished, one sincerely hopes," Lord
Vare muttered.

"Just so, m'lord, although I regret to say it was necessary for the duke to use force." His disdainful sniff spoke
volumes.

"You have almost made my day, Finch," Lord Vare
remarked. "My cousin is all right?"

"A small cut, m'lord, but nothing serious," Finch assured him as he held the door of the inn for them to enter.

The marquess and Laurie found the duke calmly sipping
wine, while Archie held a napkin to his cheek. He looked
white and horrified as he darted glances at the duke's
servants, who were sweeping up the broken glass that
littered the floor.

"Ah, there you are, my dears," the duke boomed. "Come
in, come in. You had a pleasant walk, I trust?"

Laurie sat down beside Archie, smiling to let him know

how glad she was that he had escaped Lady Pamela at last. His answering smile under the dark brown mustache was weak, for he was still in a state of shock. He had not imagined that Pamela even knew such words as she had used to tell him of her displeasure at being jilted, and only because she had been the duke's mistress for a few weeks.

After the servants had left the room, the duke shook his head. "Bad business, that," he said. "But we will not be disturbed again. Pammy has retired on my orders, and her door is guarded by two stout footmen. Now, m'lord, let us hear more of this plan of yours to make for Genoa. I am still not entirely sure it is the best course. Why not continue south with us until we reach Florence? The doge would never dare to attack such a large, well-armed party."

The marquess frowned. "It might be safer, but it only prolongs the problem. Sooner or later, we must make for some port, alone. And when we do that, Capitano Rossetti will make his move. Besides—and you must forgive me, your Grace—I do not care to have Lady Laura exposed any longer to the language and immorality of Pamela Jones-Witherall. She is young and she has just lost her father. She should not have to bear such vindictive cruelty and coarse behavior."

Laurie clenched her hands together as she cried silently: I am not that young! Why, oh, why do you treat me like a child?

The duke inclined his head, his drooping eyelids hiding the sudden shrewdness of his glance. So, lies the wind in that quarter, does it? he asked himself idly. The Marquess of Vare caught so neatly, and by an innocent babe at that. What an *on-dit* it will make in London!

"No, I thank you for your kindness and concern," the marquess went on, "but I think we will leave you here. If we ride hard, we can be in Genoa in two days' time."

"Are you up to such a strenuous journey, Lady Laura?" the duke asked, smiling at her. "You must forgive me, but you do not look as if you have the strength for it."

Laurie looked from the duke to the marquess and back again. "I shall manage, your Grace, if I am permitted to ride astride."

The marquess's frown did not lighten as he nodded. "Of

course you must masquerade as a boy again, Laurie. That is the only way our escape can succeed. And if we leave here at dawn, we should be well away before the *capitano* misses us."

"Dear sir, you are not thinking," the duke boomed. "Why should he miss you? You were not planning to take your valet with you, were you, or m'lady's maid? They will be in your coach, of course, and it will be the easiest thing in the world to dress up two of my servants to take your place, and the Lady Laura's."

"Of course!" the marquess exclaimed, his sudden smile white in his tanned face. "That way, we shall be long gone before he suspects anything. But I must ask your kindness for my man, your Grace. After our flight is discovered, Finch will need your protection until he is safely aboard a ship for home with our belongings."

The duke waved a careless hand. "Consider it done. Now, how many will be in your party? Pietro, one of my *vetterini*, will go before you to make arrangements for fresh horses at each stop, and for meals as well. It will smooth your way."

"You think of everything, your Grace," Laurie said, her voice admiring.

"I would never have suspected you of being such a good intriguer, sir," the marquess remarked. "With your help, we shall beat the doge and his wicked captain yet!"

The duke looked surprised. "But of course. We are Englishmen, after all. The issue was never in question."

Archie spoke up for the first time. "Is it to be just the three of us, then, cuz?"

"No, we will take Rob and Simmons with us. They're both handy with a pistol. Besides, I doubt very much if I could keep them from coming. They are Lady Laura's servants, and devoted to her, your Grace," he explained.

"Then that is five of you. I shall instruct Higgins to make the arrangements. One more suggestion, if I may. Travel light, carrying only what you will need to reach France. One can always purchase clothes, after all. And do not worry about Lady Pamela, m'lord. I will keep her muzzled until you are safe away."

Laurie looked at the duke in wonder. He had not seemed

a forceful man, but just then, in his quiet words, she had heard a cold sternness and authority that she herself would hesitate to defy. Still, remembering the redheaded virago he traveled with, she prayed he could keep her in check.

The duke rose and wished them all a safe journey as he came to kiss Laurie's hand. "I shall not see you in the morning, m'lady, but know my thoughts will be with you. I look forward to meeting you again in London." He seemed about to add something, and then he shrugged. "Give one of your bonnets and gowns to Higgins before you retire. I have just the maid in mind to impersonate you."

He waved off their thanks as the marquess walked with him to the door to call Finch and the others. In a few minutes the six of them sat around the table of a foreign inn once again, making plans for yet another escape. This time they were all easier in each other's company, and everyone spoke up freely, even Rob.

Finch looked affronted when he learned he was to be left behind, but he could see that it was for the best. He was not a horseman and he would not be able to maintain the pace he knew the marquess meant to set. He could not help worrying that the Lady Laura would not be able to do so either. Upon voicing these fears, he was clapped on the shoulder by Jed Simmons.

"Now, don't you fret about milady, Mr. Finch," he said. "She's been brought up to ride 'ard and long. The earl never mollycoddled 'er, now did 'e, Lady Laura?"

Laurie smiled warmly at the elegant gentleman's gentleman. "I thank you for your concern, Finch, but I will be all right. I may not lead the way, but I shall contrive to keep up. I could never look Rob and Jed in the eye if I did not."

They arranged to leave the inn just before dawn, booted and spurred, and carrying only a few changes of clothing in their saddlebags. Laurie could see that both her servants looked relieved that there was to be some action taken at last. These days had been hard on all of them, but she knew Jed had felt especially helpless to protect her, and as for Rob, he just wanted to get home and never leave England again.

At last Laurie went to her room, and after she gave a bonnet and gown to Higgins, set about packing for the ride. She would need some changes of linen, another pair of breeches, and her boat cloak; the rest could go in the coach with Finch. And of course she would need her pistols and shot. When she had these things assembled, she hesitated, and then she added one more item, wrapped in oilskin and carefully sealed, to the bottom of her bag. The cream-colored silk that the marquess had bought for her in Milan must go with her too. She could not bear to let it out of her sight.

# 11

---

It was late the following morning when they stopped to change horses at Rivergaro on their way to the coast. The marquess made Laurie and Archie wait outside the town while he and the others rode ahead. Laurie was glad to dismount and stretch, and share some of the bread and cheese Finch had given them in the gray, predawn light before they rode away from the inn. She had not been able to resist kissing his cheek for this kindness. Finch had looked a little flustered at the attention, but she did not think he had been displeased.

She had not been sure where the *capitano* and his men were, but she had noticed that the marquess kept the pace to a slow walk until they were some distance away, so the sound of their horses' hooves could not be detected. And then, as the sky slowly lightened, he had ordered them all to a fast gallop. Laurie's gelding was as game as the rest; she was glad she had not been given a gentle mare. After a while, Lord Vare slowed the pace again to give the horses a chance to recover, but he continued to drive them all hard, shortly thereafter.

When the three returned from Rivergaro, on new mounts and trailing two more, Lord Vare studied Laurie carefully. She did not appear to be tiring, although it was difficult to say, for she held herself so erectly in the saddle. In her breeches and with her curls tucked up into a cap and her slender hands hidden in leather gloves, she looked just like a stripling. He hoped she had a boy's stamina as well. As he gave the office to start, he beckoned Simmons to ride beside him.

"I want you to let me know the moment you think Lady Laura is tiring, Jed," he said, so the others could not hear. "I know she is a good rider, and we must make the best time we can, but I would not have her suffer."

The grizzled servant nodded, and a little smile played around his mouth as he said, "I'll watch 'er, milord, never fear, and let you know instanter I feel it's too much for 'er."

He tugged his forelock, laughing to himself. There were muscles and a wiry strength under that soft skin that Lord Vare knew nothing about, but Laurie would show him.

Their way led them along the banks of the Trebbia River, although the marquess was quick to detour if he saw a village or even a farmhouse ahead. The fewer people who saw them, the better. He would have liked to travel at night, but in countryside he did not know, it would be too dangerous. The day was warm, and although there were a few clouds in the sky, it did not threaten rain, for which he was grateful. At times, he looked back to inspect the small troop of horse under his command, to assess their stamina. He knew Rob and Simmons could go on until the horses dropped beneath them, but he noticed Archie's tired, set face as the afternoon wore on. At once his eyes went to Laurie. Her posture was not as erect as it had been earlier, but when she saw him looking at her, she gave him a gallant smile that lighted up her hazel eyes and lifted the corners of her mouth. As he continued to look at her questioningly, she nodded, as if to tell him all was well. The marquess looked away first, thinking again what a brave girl she was.

He had made arrangements with the *vetterino* to change mounts again at Bobbio, and the same procedure as before was followed. This time, when he returned from the village, Laurie and Archie were stretched out full length on the grass. Laurie got to her feet when she saw the weary horses they still rode, and Lord Vare's black frown. Simmons and Rob were also looking grim, she noted.

"What's amiss, m'lord? Were there no horses to be had?" she asked, hoping her voice did not reveal her growing weariness.

"Pietro met us as we approached the village. He says

one of the doge's men is there and he did not dare to
arouse the man's suspicions by ordering five mounts. We
will have to make do with these poor beasts. Come, mount
up! We must be gone."

Laurie was glad to let Archie give her a leg up into the
saddle as the marquess continued, "We will give Bobbio a
wide berth, although it will lengthen the trip, and we will
ride on as long as the horses can carry us. Pietro gave me
some wine and bread, for we will have to camp out tonight
in some deserted spot. Take the lead, Rob, and keep an
eye out for a likely place."

The footman saluted as he wheeled his horse and rode
away.

It was almost seven in the evening before Laurie saw
Rob waiting for them some little distance ahead. They had
not passed a farmhouse for some time, and the land here
was hillier and wilder than any they had seen all day. The
marquess spurred his tired horse.

When the rest came up, she heard her footman say,
"I've looked ahead as well, milord. There's no one near
'ere for miles. I found this forest track that leads up into
the 'ills. There's a brook nearby a clearing where someone
'as been cutting wood. It's the best I could find, sir."

Lord Vare made himself smile at the anxious footman.
"Well done, Rob, lead on!"

The others followed single file, the horses stumbling a
little as the ground rose before them on the narrow track.
Laurie, who was bringing up the rear, found the marquess
waiting for her.

"Are you all right, m'lady?" he asked, his glance intent
on her face.

"I am fine, m'lord," she tried to say casually. "But only
for another fifteen minutes. After that I fall off and lie
senseless on the ground. This roan, in case you haven't
noticed, has a very uncomfortable gait."

Lord Vare smiled at her courage. "When we are home,
I would like to have the mounting of you, Laurie," he
said. "A rider of your caliber deserves the best."

The little glade that Rob had mentioned was reached
after not too many more minutes. It seemed darker in the
woods, lonely and a little frightening after the bright sun-

shine of the cleared land near the river. When Laurie
swung her leg over thankfully, she found the marquess
waiting to catch her in his arms. She put her hands on his
shoulders and tried to come lightly down, but she was so
weary she had to lean against him for a moment. Across
the clearing, Jed watched them, his eyes keen.

"I say, cuz," Archie exclaimed as he looked around as if
to find a waiting groom to attend his horse, "what a
deserted spot! How are we to manage?"

"You'll see, my boy," the marquess said, putting Laurie
away from him and glad of the interruption. Those hazel
eyes and that soft mouth had been much too close for
comfort, and he had had a hard time not to tighten his
arms in support of that slender, tired body.

Laurie began to unsaddle her horse, talking to him
softly all the while and trying to forget how wonderful it
had felt to be held close in John's arms again. The marquess watched her for a moment, and then he cocked his
head and stared at his cousin. Archie flushed, and hurried
to attend to his own mount while the marquess went and
lifted her saddle before Laurie could try to do so.

"It is too heavy for you, m'lady," he explained, his face
impassive. Laurie thanked him, her expressive hazel eyes
carefully indifferent.

"Milord," Rob's voice interrupted, "I'd be glad to set
some snares, if it's all right with you. A couple o' rabbits
would taste good, and I guess it don't matter none. If
we're being accused of murder, wot's a little poachin'
then?"

The marquess laughed and agreed. Rob's welt had faded,
and there was only a red mark left to show the blow he
had taken. With his fair, open face and straw-colored hair,
he looked the complete Englishman. Lord Vare was glad
he had men such as Rob and Simmons with him to protect
the Lady Laurà.

Rob went away to prepare his traps. Jed was already
gathering firewood and twigs, and Laurie began to wipe
down her horse with a handful of grass. Looking stunned,
Archie copied her. It was as if he could not believe that
he, the elegant Lord Price, was engaged in such a plebe-
ian task. As the marquess unsaddled his horse, he said,

"We will take them down to the brook when they have cooled. I'm afraid they'll have to make do with whatever graze they can find, but if Rob is successful, we shall fare much better."

Two hours later, the five sat around a small campfire watching Rob turn three rabbits on the green wood he had cut to use as spits. Laurie couldn't help but be proud of his ingenuity, and of course, of Jed's comforting presence and good sense as well. He and the marquess were discussing the day's ride, and what they might expect on the morrow. Laurie wished she might listen, but Archie turned to her and said, "The skinning and cleaning of rabbits is disgusting! No one with any sensibility at all should be subjected to it!" His voice was peevish with weariness and hunger.

"It is just as well that we don't have to depend on you for our supper then, Archie," Laurie replied from where she was sitting on a fallen tree branch. "I imagine you will change your mind when you taste them. They smell delicious, Rob!"

Archie sniffed. "I hope I can bring myself to eat after the revolting process I observed."

Laurie was very tired, and she lost her patience. "All the more for us if you cannot. These airs and graces you parade are ridiculous in the woods. I wish you would give over, m'lord!"

Archie's face grew red and his mouth dropped open. The marquess interrupted before he could give her a scathing setdown. "I, for one, am glad of Rob's talent in the poaching line. I wonder whose woods these are? Not that it matters. We are safe here tonight, and I suggest we all get as much rest as we can. We must ride hard tomorrow so as to be inside the city by dark."

"We could always camp out again, m'lord," Laurie replied, glancing sideways at Archie.

Lord Vare shook his head, his face grim. "No, that is something that must be avoided at all costs. The countryside around Genoa is riddled with groups of *banditti,* and if travelers are lucky enough to avoid them, they are often set upon by Turkish pirates from the Barbary Coast. They come ashore in bands to plunder and murder."

"What a charming country this is," Laurie remarked. "I am sure we will all be bored when we return to England to peaceful and tranquil lives."

"I, for one, never intend to leave it again," Archie exclaimed.

"Nay, me neither, milord," Rob muttered as he tested one of the rabbits with his knife.

"What is Genoa like, m'lord? And what will we do there?" Laurie asked, leaning forward a little in her eagerness, and ignoring any discussion of England's superiority.

"Genoa is not noted for its ambience, I'm afraid," Lord Vare told her. "The harbor, of course, is magnificent, and you will see some of the finest palaces there, set in orange groves for shade. But you will also see more dirty beggars than anywhere else on the Continent. And you will have a hard time trying to understand the dialect. The city is well known for the terrible Italian that is spoken there. But these are small matters. We do not linger as tourists, and even though the velvets and point lace to be found there are beautiful, we will have no time for shopping." He paused and smiled at her. "You will have to remain a boy until we reach France, Lady Laura. As soon as I can find a suitable *feluca* or small coastal vessel with Pietro's help, we will be off. And then we will be safe, at long last."

"Do not say it yet, m'lord," Laurie pleaded. "It might be bad luck."

"I trust the duke. He will keep Lady Pamela from seeking revenge, and the *capitano* from suspecting our defection as well. Our main danger now comes from pirates and bandits. You have your pistol, Laurie?"

"Both of them," she replied, her eyes wide at his serious tones.

"Keep them close to you at all times," Lord Vare told her.

Although they had no plates or cutlery, and Rob had to use a flat stone as a carving board, everyone, even Archie, ate heartily. In a short time, the rabbits and the bread and wine were gone. Replete, Jed added some more wood to the fire, and said to Lord Vare, "Best we keep the fire going tonight, milord. There may be wild boars."

"I say! Do you really think there are wild boars about?" Archie asked, his blue eyes popping as he edged closer to the fire.

"Wot's a wild boar then, after wot we've been through, milord?" Jed asked, his sympathetic face creased in a rallying smile.

Remembering the doge and Capitano Rossetti, to say nothing of Lady Pamela, Archie silently agreed.

"Just in case, Rob, my boy, let's you and me bring the 'orses closer to the fire," Jed added, rising and stretching. Laurie wondered if everyone was as stiff and tired as she was. She knew she should be thinking of sleep, but she was too weary to move. She rested her elbows on her raised knees and propped up her chin with her hands, while her mind ranged lightly over the past events of this unusual grand tour she was taking. France, Switzerland, and then Italy. Italy, where her life had changed completely in a moment. She had known danger, and sorrow, and loss, but she had also known the beginnings of love. Her eyes were dreamy as she stared into the glowing fire, watching the little tongues of flame lick eagerly at the dry wood.

The marquess, who was seated across from her, studied her, his half-concealed eyes under hooded lids intent as the firelight flickered across her soft, smooth face and tipped each chestnut curl with pure gold.

Suddenly he heard her lazy chuckle, and when she looked at him and saw his inquiring glance, she said, "I was just remembering my aunt, Lady Blake. She did not want my father to bring me on this journey, and had any number of objections. I have already had to deal with the fleas, bedbugs, and wolves she mentioned. I only hope that her other prediction—that I would have to face a wild boar—does not come true."

She chuckled again, and Lord Vare asked, his voice almost satirical, "Were wild animals and hygiene the only things your aunt worried about, Lady Laura?"

Laurie frowned as she remembered her aunt's stiff white face and disapproving airs. "No," she said slowly. "She was sure that my going abroad would toss the entire family into a scandal broth of gossip, and she did her best to dissuade us. She is . . . she is very concerned about the opinion of the *ton*, and social niceties and formal manners." Her frown deepened as she fell silent, sighing a little.

"I think I have met Lady Blake in town," Lord Vare said. "But I do not know her all that well, for our paths seldom cross. Do you like her? Is she a good, kind aunt?"

Laurie appeared to ponder this question, and the marquess noticed that the little frown between her brows did not go away as she said, "I suppose she has always been kind to me. But the Towers near Taunton, where she lives, is a long way from my father's estate, and I did not see her often. My . . . my father shunned London and the Season, while Aunt Margaret lives for it. So does my cousin Rosamunde, who made her come-out this spring, and her brother, Percival, Viscount Blake. To be truthful, we—my father and I—did not have much in common with any of them."

She ducked her head for a moment, and then with a visible effort raised it to stare at him and ask in a stiff voice, "Why do you ask, m'lord?"

"Because it is to Lady Blake that you must go now, Lady Laura. I understand she is your only close relative."

Laurie stared into the fire. "Yes, that is true. I had not thought I would have to live with her. I intended to go home with Jed and Rob, to Lockridge Hall."

"But you can't do that! Don't you know anything? The estate must go to some male relative. You have no place there," Archie interrupted.

Laurie was startled by his voice, for she had forgotten he was sitting beside her, listening. For a few moments there had been only John and herself, in quiet conversation across a campfire in the Italian hills.

"You are only a green, young girl. Naturally you must reside with your aunt," Archie instructed her, his high voice scornful that she did not know even that little bit of society's rules.

Laurie opened her mouth as if to protest, and just as quickly closed it. Of course she must make her home with Aunt Margaret now, but oh, how she dreaded it! There would be nothing but morning calls and manners, shopping trips and stitchery, and the endless Season to be borne. And over it all, a rigid adherence to the conventions and strict rules of the nobility.

Lord Vare saw the misery that washed over her face and then was so quickly hidden, and he felt a pang of regret that Laurie did not care more for her aunt and her family. The woman sounded like a high stickler for society's edicts, edicts he knew Laurie, brought up as she had been, would scorn even though she would be forced to obey them.

He noticed the faint shadows under her hazel eyes, and the way her slender figure drooped on the log, and he went to help her rise. "You must try to sleep now, m'lady," he said, pressing her hand in sympathy a little before he released it. "Jed has put your saddle and blanket over there under that tree."

Laurie nodded, her voice subdued as she said good night.

A short time later, wrapped in her blanket and with her boat cloak spread over her to protect her from the morning dew, she was just dropping off to sleep when she heard Archie say in a soft voice, "Well, here's a mess, cuz! I had not thought of it before, but there will be a scandal broth indeed when the two of us return Lady Laura to her aunt. I hope she does not insist that one of us must marry the chit to observe the proprieties. And if she does, I pray you will not appoint me the victim!"

Even his whisper sounded horrified at such a course, and Laurie strained her ears to hear John's quick reply. "I doubt it will come to that, Archie, but do not worry. You will not be called on to make such a supreme sacrifice!"

Before she could ponder this careless retort, Laurie fell asleep. She was so exhausted that even the hard ground and the absence of any pillow but her saddle did not cause her to stir. She did not know how often Jed or the marquess woke to be sure that all was well, and to add more wood to the fire, and she was not aware of it when very early in the morning the marquess came to kneel beside her to tuck her blanket more closely around her. He stared down into her oval face as he did so. Those expressive eyes were shuttered now by sleep and the long curling lashes that rested on her soft pink cheeks. No one was awake to see the way he shook his head and frowned as he rose and left her side.

When Laurie woke, it was morning. For a moment she lay still and stared up at the leaves fluttering in the slight breeze above her, and listened drowsily to the morning songs of the birds. Then she remembered where she was, and she sat up and stretched.

Jed was already saddling the horses, and he smiled at her as she climbed out of her blanket and tried to stretch her sore muscles. She was stiff, as stiff as she had ever been. The hard earth she had slept on and the forced pace of the previous day had taken their toll. Of Archie and the marquess there was no sign, she noticed as she hobbled over to Jed. He told her they had both gone to the brook to wash.

She saw Rob coming back into the clearing and waved to him. "I take it that there are no rabbits for breakfast, Rob?" she asked. "Oh, how hungry and sore I am!"

Simmons chuckled as he adjusted a cinch. "Lord Vare says we should be in some place 'e called Montaldo di Cosola by midmorning, Lady Laurie. The *vetterino* is to meet us there with fresh mounts and food."

"Thank heaven," Laurie remarked as she prepared to go into the woods herself to wash and tidy up. "I could not bear this roan for many more hours. Pray I get a softer ride from my next mount."

They did not linger in the clearing, for Lord Vare had no desire to be discovered by the woodcutter and forced to explain why they had camped there. The pace he set was just as fast as yesterday's and Laurie gritted her teeth. It was true she was used to riding astride, but this mad race to the coast was harder than anything she had ever done before. She was delighted to see Pietro not only waiting but smiling too, outside the town the marquess had named as their rendezvous. As he led them to an inn, he talked volubly all the while. It was quite safe, none of the doge's men were about, so he had arranged for a private parlor and a hot meal, as well as for new horses. Lord Vare, who was watching Laurie, decreed a rest for an hour. "We are ahead of schedule, and even with this delay, should reach Genoa long before dark," he said as he helped her down in the courtyard of the little inn.

He rubbed his hand over the dark bristles of the beard he had not been able to shave that morning, and added, "We will be able to make ourselves more presentable as well. As it is, I am sure I look worse than any pirate in my present condition. How glad I am that Finch is not here to see me!"

Laurie was glad too to have a chance to wash in hot water and change her linen and comb her curls, and she was happy to sit in a proper chair and eat the hearty meal Pietro had ordered.

When it came time to mount her horse again, she had to steel herself, her muscles were protesting so. She noticed that Archie was also looking grim, and had little to say for himself. Suddenly she remembered his remark last night when he thought she had been asleep, and the misery of her tired body was as nothing to the dismay that stabbed her when she recalled the marquess's careless reply that making the sacrifice of marrying her would not be required. She felt hot tears stinging her eyelids, and defiantly she put up her chin. She did not know why she wanted to cry, for she had known all along that Lord Vare did not care for her. Such weakness must be because she was feeling so worn and pulled. As for Archie, he had nothing to worry about. She would kill herself before she married such a fop.

As they got closer to Genoa that afternoon, they often saw other horsemen, and once a band of men riding toward them from the distance. The marquess ordered them all off the road into a grove of olive trees until the band should pass. He made them dismount and be prepared to silence their horses if they tried to neigh to those riding by, so their concealment would not be noticed. The ruse worked perfectly, and fortunately they did not have to contend with either bandits or pirates. Laurie was relieved, for she did not think she could even lift her pistol, never mind cock and fire it. Her hands in their leather gloves felt as if they had been curled around the reins for days, and her legs and back and neck ached with strain. She stared between the erect ears of her horse, concentrating on remaining in the saddle. She would go on until the marquess told her to stop—she would ask no quarter.

It was early evening when they rode into the city. Laurie was too exhausted to even notice the buildings or the harbor or the crowds of beggars who whined and pleaded as the little group of foreigners passed at a slow walk. Pietro led them to an inn on the waterfront, where eager ostlers came running to take their mounts in charge. Still Laurie sat her horse, too tired even to dismount. And then the marquess was there to lift her down into his arms. She did not protest, but sagged against him, her eyes closed and her hands clutching the lapels of his riding coat. An arrested look came over Lord Vare's face as he stared down at her, and for a moment he did not move, almost as if he had been stunned into silence and immobility by what he was thinking.

"I have never known a braver woman, Lady Laura," he said at last as he carried her into the inn. "But your ordeal is over. From now on you will only have to sit quietly as we sail to France."

Following the beaming innkeeper, he carried her up a flight of stairs, asking, "What would you like to do first? Sleep? Eat? Bathe, perhaps? I shall relay your orders at once."

Laurie sighed, but she did not open her eyes. She could feel the rough cloth of John's riding coat against her cheek, and she could smell his masculine scent again, more marked now after their hard ride. She was content just to lie in his arms, limp and trusting, and let him take care of her.

As he reached the room the innkeeper pointed to, the marquess shook her a little and chuckled softly. "Do not fall asleep just yet, m'lady. Not, at least, until you have told me your desires."

Then I will tell you I desire you, John, for I love you, Laurie thought, and her eyes flew open as if she feared she had spoken out loud. Above her, the marquess's dark head was bent over hers. All she had to do was reach up a little and her lips would be touching his. She felt a stirring deep inside as she stared into those dark blue eyes so close to hers, and all unbidden, her hands crept up to his neck.

Suddenly she found herself lowered to her feet, and she turned away, afraid he would see the deep disappointment in her eyes that he had let her go.

"Well, m'lady?" he asked, and if Laurie had not been so engrossed in her own tumultuous thoughts, she would have heard the husky unevenness of his voice.

"No food—not even a bath, m'lord," she made herself say. "I only wish to sleep—for days!"

The marquess bowed and moved as if to kiss her hand, but she had moved away, so he made himself say as lightly as it was possible to do, "No one shall disturb you until you ring, m'lady. Sleep well."

When she turned around, he was gone, and the door was closing softly behind him.

As he went down the stairs, John pondered his reactions to the lady he had held so willingly in his arms. He had wanted to protect her and comfort her—he had wanted to kiss her and never let her go. His lips curled in a smile. He had been so blind! All this time he had thought of her as an innocent child. A delightful, appealing one, to be sure, but a child nevertheless. These past two days he had come to see her womanly strength, her steadfast courage, and her sweetness. He had always thought her handsome, but he was too old to be swayed merely by a pair of speaking eyes and a slim, pliant body. He wondered how long he had loved her without even guessing that he did, and shook his head at his imperception. It was true that Archie had nothing to worry about, nor did Laurie have to concern herself with her aunt's lectures and strict propriety in the future. No, he would ask her to marry him as soon as she was in her aunt's care. Until that time, he promised himself, he would behave as if he were the distant older uncle he had set himself to be. For a woman like Lady Laura, everything would be done correctly, and in great state. She deserved nothing less when he wooed and won her.

Laurie did not wake until late that night. She was not hungry, but she rose to drink some water and to go and lean on the windowsill that overlooked the harbor. It was still dark and she could see few lights, but she could smell the tar and salt water, and hear the creaking of anchor chains and the little waves that slapped the many hulls. It reminded her of Dover when she had just been starting out, full of excitement and hope. But now, possibly as soon as tomorrow, she would be going home. Home to Lady Blake, and without her beloved father or her beloved Lord Vare. She sighed, and then, as a cool breeze came in the open casement, shivered a little and went back to bed.

In the morning, when she had bathed and dressed, she came down to find Archie alone in the coffee room. After asking how she did, he told her that the marquess and the *vetterino* had gone out to hire a suitable ship for the passage. Laurie was ravenous, and she devoured the rolls, and fruit, and eggs, letting him talk on. Jed was there to serve her, his rough hand pressing her shoulder as he poured her more coffee.

She smiled at him, her eyes serene and rested. "Where is Rob?" she asked.

" 'E's gone out to see the sights, m'lady. 'E won't be long, though, not if wot m'lord told me about the beggars is true. If you want to go out, m'lord said you were to take a chair."

Laurie stretched and yawned. "I don't think I shall, Jed. I find I am still tired, and feeling lazy."

The marquess did not return until late afternoon, and Laurie, who had been reading in the window seat of their parlor, thought his face looked stern and disappointed somehow as he came in. His eyes searched her face first, and he nodded. "I am glad to see you are feeling better, Lady Laura," he said formally as he bowed to her.

"You found a vessel, John?" Archie asked, discarding his game of patience.

"Yes, but it will not be possible to sail until tomorrow morning." He frowned again. "I cannot like the delay. To be sitting here is dangerous. If the duke was not able to control Lady Pamela . . ." His voice died away and then he said more briskly, "However, we have no choice but to wait. Both Pietro and I are agreed that this *feluca* is the best available. It is still unloading cargo and there are some minor repairs to be made. Tomorrow at dawn we shall be rowed out to it, to sail on the morning tide."

Archie shrugged. "I'm in no hurry and will be glad of another night's rest."

Lord Vare took a seat at the table and spread out a map to study their route. "I have no idea how long a sail we shall have, but once we reach Marseilles, we must hire horses again and ride across France to Le Havre. It will be a long journey, but not an arduous one, I promise you."

"At least we will not have to keep looking over our shoulders for pursuers, m'lord," Laurie pointed out, abandoning her book. "How restful that will be!"

"And if we feel the pace you set is too rigorous, cuz, we can always mutiny," Archie threatened.

Laurie smiled, but her face grew still and she jumped to her feet when Lord Vare said, "I expect that Lady Blake will meet us in Le Havre. I wrote some time ago and asked her to await us there."

"How could you do such an infamous thing, m'lord?" Laurie demanded, her voice shaking with anger. "Now he will fuss and scold and carry on. . . . Why couldn't you have waited until we reached England?"

Lord Vare's face and voice were cool. "You are not thinking, m'lady. If you cross the Channel in the company of your aunt, there can be no gossip, no scandal. But to step off a ship into a throng of Englishmen on my arm or Archie's can only give rise to the speculation that your aunt and I are so anxious to avoid."

Laurie swallowed. She knew why John was being so careful. If there were no gossip to contend with, he would not have to offer for her. That was why he had summoned Aunt Margaret. Then too, he would that much sooner be free of the onerous burden of caring for her and seeing to her comfort. She nodded, saying in a colorless voice, "Of course. I understand your concern for my reputation completely, m'lord. Thank you." And then she turned away to take her seat again, her eyes lowered.

Lord Vare stared at her for a moment, and a little muscle moved in his cheek as he said, "Naturally your well-being and reputation are of paramount importance to me, m'lady." He paused as if he would have liked to say more, but she only inclined her head, and he was forced to talk to Archie when she opened her book again.

After dinner that evening, Laurie left the table to take her earlier seat in the window, to sit and stare at the lights of the harbor. Behind her, the marquess and Lord Price were shuffling the cards, preparatory to playing some hands of piquet. Archie had moved the two branches of candles closer, and she sat in the shadows, idly trying to guess which native boat was to be theirs. Suddenly the door to the parlor was thrown open, and a triumphant Capitano Rossetti strode in, pistol in hand. She gasped, and drew farther back out of sight.

"My dear Lord Tench . . . or should I say, more accurately, Lord Vare?" the *capitano* purred. The marquess lowered his cards to the table, and the captain aimed the pistol at his heart. "Do not move even slightly, m'lord, I beg you. It would be such a shame if you had to die so quickly."

He swaggered into the room, slamming the door behind him with his free hand. He was not dressed in his gorgeous livery now, but even in a plain brown suit he looked menacing. Laurie stared at him, horrified, as he continued, "And here we have Lord Price, I believe, alias Arlene the maid, and Lord Willoughby from the English Foreign Office. A fine dance you have led us, m'lords, but your acting days are over now—for good."

"How did you find us?" the marquess asked. Laurie wondered at his even tone, especially since Archie seemed to have lost the power of speech, and was trembling besides.

"The Lady Pamela, m'lord. Although closely watched, she bribed one of the maids at the inn to deliver a letter to me. You should never have underestimated the hatred and ingenuity of a woman scorned. No, she told me of the whole thing; your guilt and your deceit—even where I could find you. I cannot tell you how delighted I am to take you and your cousin prisoner, and of course, the lovely Lady Laura. Where is m'lady, by the way?"

Laurie saw Archie's mouth opening and closing, and was glad when the marquess said, "She is upstairs, resting in her room."

The *capitano* chuckled, his dark eyes gleaming. "How

very fortunate! She will need her strength for the journey and . . . er, what follows."

Seeing his attention was focused completely on the marquess, Laurie moved slowly and carefully to withdraw her pistol from her jacket pocket. She had kept it there ever since they left the duke, and now she was glad she had not put it away in her bag when they reached Genoa. Archie had his back to her, and could not see what she was about, but she thought the marquess must guess, although he could not look at her too obviously.

"May I?" he asked now, indicating his glass of wine. The captain sneered at him, his slight bow ironic.

"But of course, drink while you can, m'lord. My men will be here shortly, and until then, there is nothing to do but wait. I could not restrain myself from riding ahead in my eagerness to capture you."

Slowly Laurie moved sideways until her booted feet were touching the ground, praying her spurs would not betray her. Her breath was coming unevenly now, and she willed herself to be calm. As if he sensed the need to keep the *capitano* occupied, Lord Vare said, "Come join us in a glass of wine, Rossetti. Perhaps there is another way out of this coil that will be to all our benefits. I would be willing to part with a great sum to escape the doge, you know. And when you hear the amount I am about to offer, I am sure it will give you pause." He lifted his wineglass as if to admire the ruby color, and added, "After all, all you have to say is that you could not find us because we had already sailed before you arrived. Even your men will not suspect any trickery."

All the while he had been speaking, Laurie had been getting up slowly and carefully and raising her pistol. Over the *capitano*'s shoulder, Lord Vare could see the glint of the barrel just below her glittering hazel eyes, and suddenly he called, "Now, Laurie!" and threw his wine into the captain's face.

The two guns went off almost simultaneously, and Laurie felt as if her heart had stopped. How could the *capitano* miss at that range, even blinded by the wine?

The *capitano* dropped his pistol and crumpled to the floor, clutching his bleeding shoulder, and then, to Laurie's disbelieving eyes, the marquess rose from behind the table where he had dropped just before the pistols went off. Archie still sat frozen in his chair. Laurie had the irrelevant thought that it was fortunate he had not been in the line of fire, and then, for a moment, was sure she was going to faint, for her head was swimming and she was trembling all over with relief.

Lord Vare kicked the captain's pistol across the room and tossed his own weapon to his cousin. "Cover him, Archie, and shoot to kill if he makes a move," he said crisply, and then he came and grasped Laurie by both arms.

"Steady, Laurie, steady," he said, and she took the first deep breath she had dared for many minutes.

"Are you really all right, my dear?" she whispered. "I was so sure he had killed you!"

"Thanks to your good aim, I am. You fired first, and it made his shot go high and wide. I owe you my life, m'lady!"

His eyes burned into hers, and Laurie tried to smile. "You said once you could wish no better man beside you in a fight, m'lord. I had that reputation to uphold," she said, trying to jest.

The marquess squeezed her arms, and then, with one arm tight around her waist, he led her to a chair and went to pour her a glass of wine. Archie never looked away from the captain, his thin face set and determined in his task of guarding him.

And then there was a bustle and stir outside the door, and both Jed and Rob burst in, along with Pietro and the innkeeper and what seemed to be every servant in the place, all talking and exclaiming.

The marquess took charge, demanding silence. "This man is a thief and a murderer," he told the innkeeper when he could make himself heard. "I want him arrested and taken away at once!"

"He lies! I am the Doge of Varallo's captain of the guard," Rossetti screamed in pain and anger.

"A likely story," the marquess said, his voice rich with scorn. "These scum will say anything to escape the prison hulks in the harbor, isn't that so, *padrone?*"

Thus directly appealed to, the innkeeper nodded, his fat face shining with perspiration and excitement. "Your worship's pardon! That such a thing should happen in my inn," he mourned.

"It can all be sifted after he is taken to the police," Lord Vare went on. "Do not concern yourself. And now I am tired of this whole distasteful affair. Do me the favor of taking him away."

There were many willing hands to drag the captain from the room. He screamed curses and threats of reprisals, for the servants were none too gentle. As soon as everyone had gone but Jed and Rob and the *vetterino*, the marquess dropped his scornful air and spoke quickly. "Make haste! Rossetti will be free before long, for his men are right behind him. We must away! Pietro, go and arrange for rowing boats to take us out to *feluca*. We will spend the night on board."

He saw Laurie hurrying from the room, and called, "Never mind your things, m'lady. We haven't time!"

But Laurie was already running up the stairs. She didn't care about her other belongings, but there was no way after carrying it this far that she was going to leave the cream-colored silk behind.

# 12

Early one October afternoon some three weeks later, two English noblemen and a youth, attended by two servants, rode into the Channel port of Le Havre. They had little baggage, but the landlord at the hotel they chose to honor with their custom was sure that a coach, or even two, must be following with their belongings. The elder gentleman did not enlighten him.

"Perhaps you have an Englishwoman staying here, my good man?" he inquired. "A Lady Blake?"

The landlord regretted that he could not instantly produce this lady for the tall, stern-featured man who had such a look of authority and wealth, in spite of his small entourage.

"No matter. There are other hotels," the marquess murmured, and then confirmed the landlord's opinion of his consequence by ordering separate rooms for the three of them, and one for their servants, and a private parlor as well. Behind him, Laurie leaned against the doorjamb, trying not to feel so miserable that they were at journey's end at last.

Archie had not been amused at the length of time that it had taken, and had often protested the nursery pace. It was obvious that he was anxious to return home, where he planned to cut a great figure with his friends, stunning them with tales of his numerous adventures, from which all mention of the Lady Laura would be deleted, at his cousin's orders.

Laurie, on the other hand, felt the days had sped by, and to her their arrival in Le Havre only meant her final

parting from the marquess and her return to Aunt Margaret.
She wished the trip might have taken twice as long.

They had escaped from Genoa just as the dawn was
breaking. Laurie had stared back at the harbor for a long
time, almost as if she could not believe even now that the
*capitano* would not manage to stop them and force them
to return. At first, the three-masted *feluca* had ghosted
along, but as soon as the morning wind came up, the
lateen sails bellied out to starboard, and, heeled over, the
vessel gathered speed until she felt they were flying.

By noontime she was glad to seek the shade under the
awning that covered the middle of the deck, and join the
others for lunch. Archie was feeling cock-of-the-walk after
their near-escape, and joked with Rob and Simmons as if
they were his old friends. Laurie was quiet, as was the
marquess, and once in a while she would look up to find
his somber gaze studying the horizon, and she would look
away. The sun glinting off the water was hot, and although
the wind rose through the afternoon, she soon removed
her riding coat and loosened her stock, as the others had
done earlier. She was sure the sailors, dressed as they
were only in ragged trousers, and barefoot, were much
more comfortable.

There were no cabins on the *feluca*, for such vessels
were fairly primitive, but the marquess had arranged for
her to have some privacy from the men by having a small
tent placed just before the center mast. As the days went
by, she spent most of her time there alone, her brooding
glance fixed on the blue-green water they sailed through.
She found herself listening for John's deep voice among
the others, and wondered why he never bothered to come
and speak to her.

She did not know that the marquess did not trust himself alone in her company. He had never doubted that she
had the courage to fire the shot at Rossetti that saved him,
but when it was over and he went to her to make sure she
was all right, he found himself trembling. What a marvelous woman she was! How hard it was not to tell her at
once of his feelings, his plans for the future they would
share, to make love to her with his eyes, his words, his
gestures. Since he knew he must not do this, and since it

was easier when he was not with her, he stayed away. He was glad that Jed was often by her side to sit with her through the long, hot afternoons at sea, talking quietly to her as if he were her second father indeed, and not a servant at all.

They spoke of many things: the earl and the heart condition he had been hiding from Laurie but which Jed knew about very well, their adventures abroad, and Lockridge Hall and all its memories.

It was with her head on Jed's shoulder that she cried for her father, and it was his hand that patted her back and comforted her, and his rallying words that made her wipe her eyes and try to smile at last.

But they did not speak of the Marquess of Vare. Jed mentioned him many times, for he suspected that Lady Laurie was in love with him, and he knew he was the fine man the earl would have approved for his daughter's husband, as he did himself. But Laurie, so open in other ways, was strangely reticent now, and would not confide in her old friend.

Jed had more than a suspicion that Lord Vare loved her too, and he wondered why he did not tell her, until he heard his plans to take her to her aunt, Lady Blake. Then he smiled to himself, glad he was such an honorable man.

Both Laurie and Archie, with their fair skins, tended to sunburn under the strong Mediterranean sun, but the marquess tanned so deeply that Archie said he looked like a blackamoor. Privately, Laurie thought his bronzed skin was magnificent. With his blue eyes and slashing white grin, he looked like a handsome pirate.

The *feluca* stopped briefly at Noli and Imperia, but none of their party went ashore.

"This is still Italy, my friends, and so we cannot camp out onshore," Lord Vare pointed out one evening as they sat at anchor under the stars. "And even if, all thanks to Lady Laura, Capitano Rossetti is not capable of trailing us himself, I would not bet a *scuda* that the doge has not sent his men to do so in his place. No, best we stay aboard until we reach France."

When they dropped anchor in Nice at last, where some cargo had to be unloaded, he took Laurie and Archie to see the sights. Both of them laughed when they found themselves staggering after their days at sea. The ground seemed to rise and fall just like the deck of the ship. As soon as they regained their land legs, they went shopping to replenish their wardrobes, and after a stroll along the beachfront, repaired to a café to enjoy a cool drink and the sound of French being spoken once again.

"I say, what a delightful spot this is," Archie said, squinting against the sun as two very pretty girls strolled by their table. They tilted their parasols and giggled when they saw they had caught his attention. "Very delightful!" he enthused, and Laurie saw the marquess's smile.

But all too soon, in spite of these pleasant interludes, the *feluca* deposited them in Marseilles, and they repaired to an inn ashore to make plans for the trip across France.

Lord Vare asked Laurie if she preferred to ride or travel by coach, and when she hesitated, he said, "Of course, riding will be much faster, if you feel up to it, m'lady."

Laurie put up her chin. "By all means let us ride," she said. "I know how anxious you are to find my aunt, m'lord."

"Indeed I am. You cannot imagine how much I long for that day," the marquess said, his face unsmiling. If Laurie had not turned away so quickly, determined he would not know how his words hurt her, she might have seen the fervent gleam in his blue eyes before it was so quickly masked.

True to his promise to himself, Lord Vare had behaved in an exemplary fashion. Not even by the smallest sign did he show his true feelings for her. His hand did not linger on hers, nor did his gaze too often seek her face, and his words to her, when he had to speak to her directly, were cool and controlled. Sometimes he had trouble sleeping, and then he would smile wryly to himself. Although the others might be done with playacting, he and Laurie were still engaged in it—she pretending to be a boy, and he struggling to maintain the role of uncle and mentor, when all he longed to do was catch her up in his arms and kiss her, and never let her go.

But as anxious as he was to bring Laurie under Lady Blake's wing, and so end this pretext of indifference, the marquess tried to make the journey across France a pleasure rather than an ordeal. They did not start too early in the morning, and they lingered over their luncheons. Very often they stopped for the day by midafternoon. The marquess was quick to point out anything of interest he thought Laurie would enjoy. When he saw how fascinated she was with the antiquities and the Roman aqueduct at Arles, he delayed their departure for two days in order to show her the town. It seemed to be the only time she was happy, and sometimes he would frown when he caught sight of her sad face when she thought no one was looking. He wondered at her lack of vivacity, until he remembered how arduous a time she had had of it. Then too, he told himself, surely she had never shot a man before. It was no wonder she brooded and was so reserved, for she was, after all, in spite of all her daring and spirit, a tenderly reared gentlewoman. He remembered too how she had said that she would not mourn her father until after they had escaped the doge. Perhaps she was mourning him now.

Of necessity, they avoided the more traveled routes. There were many Englishmen here in the south of France, and the marquess was careful to avoid them. As they traveled farther and farther northwest, such precautions were not necessary, but he knew a deep sense of relief when at last they rode into Le Havre without a single slip along the way.

That evening, over a festive meal that had the landlord rubbing his hands together in glee, Lord Vare poured a glass of wine for Jed and Rob, and beckoned them to come and sit down at the table one more time.

"A toast, my friends, to our success," he said, and Laurie thought that with his eyes blazing with satisfaction, and his smile lighting his tanned face, he had never looked more handsome.

"Hear, hear!" Archie echoed.

"And I drink to the company as well," the marquess continued. "Without each and every one of you, and the absent Finch too, we would never have won through. No wonder England is such a formidable enemy, so often victorious in battle. Why, even her women are superlative!"

He bowed to Laurie and raised his glass to her alone.

For the first time, he let his mask slip and his eyes caressed her face and tumbled chestnut curls. Soon, my love, he thought, soon. Laurie, her head lowered, did not notice.

For the next hour they all reminisced about their journey. Even Rob, after two glasses of wine, was brave enough to join in, and Jed Simmons stood and proposed a toast to the marquess in turn.

It was late when the party broke up. As she was leaving, Lord Vare came up to Laurie and took her hand. "We shall set about finding your aunt tomorrow, m'lady," he said.

Laurie noted his complacent voice, and then she asked, "And what will we do if she has not come, m'lord?"

She watched the light fade from his face. "Since I am sure she had my letter long ago, there will be nothing for it but to take you to England myself. But for your sake, m'lady, I pray she has come."

Laurie withdrew her hand. "And for yours too, Lord Vare. I am well aware that caring for me has been irksome and that you are anxious to return to your own pursuits."

The marquess put out his hand, somewhat stunned at her bitter words, but she had whirled and run from the room. Absently he poured another glass of wine and went to lean against the mantel, to brood down at the fire. It appeared from her words that his make-believe had succeeded only too well. He rubbed his jaw and tried to grin. Perhaps he would have a harder time than he had thought, wooing the Lady Laura. But even though she misunderstood his motives, he meant to begin his search for her aunt early the next morning. Time enough to explain why he had behaved as he had, when he was free to take her in his arms for the telling.

But no search was necessary. Laurie, wakeful through most of the night, rose early and dressed in her boy's clothes—the travel-worn breeches and scratched boots, with her riding coat over a white cambric shirt. She pushed up her curls under her cap and left the inn. She would walk for a while, she thought, and try to decide what she would say to Aunt Margaret when John found her, as she was sure he would. The October morning was gray with

clouds scudding overhead, and there was a chill wind
blowing from the Channel, damp and salty and cold. Even
the cries of the gulls, wheeling and diving over the harbor,
seemed muted and forlorn, as if they knew that soon it
would be winter.

Laurie came back to the inn at midmorning, no wiser
than she had been before, to see the marquess waiting for
her. And then a coach that had been passing was suddenly
pulled to a halt, and the moment Laurie had been dreading was upon her.

Her aunt's scandalized face appeared in one of the
windows, and in a horrified voice she exclaimed, "Laura
Lockridge! Can it really be you? In *breeches?*"

Her blond head in its modish bonnet disappeared as
she screamed, and in a moment Percival Blake opened the
door of the coach and stepped down into the street, too
distraught to even wait for his footmen to let down the
steps.

"So it is you, you shameless girl!" he exclaimed in a
loud voice. "See what you have done! My mother has
fainted, and if this shock is not the death of her, I, for one,
will be surprised. Why are you dressed like that? It is a
scandal, a scandal, I tell you!"

Still Laurie stood frozen to the spot, until she heard
Lord Vare's stern, harsh voice behind her. "It will certainly become one immediately, sir, if you continue to
shout it far and wide."

Lord Blake looked away from his brazen cousin to stare,
somewhat astounded, into the scowling face of the Marquess of Vare.

"M'lord, can it be that you . . . *you* have been a party to
this . . . this . . ." He waved one elegantly gloved hand in
Laurie's direction, and then he covered his eyes, as if he
could no longer bear to look at her.

"Go inside, Lady Laura," the marquess ordered quietly.
"I will bring your aunt to you presently."

He turned back to Lord Blake and said, "I suggest you
would be better occupied reviving your mother, m'lord,
so we can repair to my rooms. I find I take exception to
your advertising Lady Laura's sex, especially since I have
just brought her all the way across France without a single

soul guessing she was not a boy. Come, I must insist on your silence until we are private."

Lord Blake retreated before the carefully controlled fury of the marquess. Muttering to himself and shaking his head, he climbed back into the coach. A few minutes later he helped his mother and his sister to alight.

Wisely, the marquess did not try to observe the amenities, for by this time the landlord and several of the inn servants had arrived on the scene, two ladies who had been passing by on the other side of the street had stopped to point and whisper, and the inevitable beggars were assembling in force.

Bowing slightly, he took Lady Blake's arm, and motioning for the others to follow him, led her into the inn. "You will soon feel more the thing after you have had a restorative, m'lady," he said with a conviction he was not feeling. "Landlord! Some of your best Madeira at once!"

The landlord scurried away, and the servants dispersed, whispering to each other. Lady Blake moaned as he took her up the stairs, and, impatient with this sign of weakness, he put his arm around her waist and half-carried her up the flight.

In his private parlor, they found Laurie standing in the middle of the floor, a bewildered Archie and a protective Jed behind her. The marquess led Lady Blake to a chair as the others came in. Bowing, he said, "Thank you for coming in response to my letter, m'lady. I believe we have met in London—I'm Vare, you know."

Lady Blake extended a trembling hand and he kissed it punctiliously. Then he turned and asked the red and furious viscount, "And you, sir, are Lord Blake?"

He smiled a little at the beautiful little blond beside him, until Percival, recalled to his manners, mumbled, "My sister, Lady Rosamunde."

Lady Rosamunde blushed and curtsied, her lashes hiding a pair of shocked, astonished eyes. Lord Vare begged her to be seated.

In the sudden silence that fell after all the formalities had been observed, the landlord knocked, and until the wine had been served and he had bowed himself out most reluctantly, there was silence in the room.

John went to stand before the hearth. "Now, m'lady, I realize that you have had a shock, but I think when you have heard me out and consider the circumstances, you will come to see that there was no other way for Lady Laura to dress. If I may?"

At her icy nod, he proceeded to give Laurie's relatives a much-abbreviated and highly expurgated account of their adventures. He began with Lord Lockridge's death, claiming he himself had shot the prince. The doge was the same revengeful villain of the piece, but Lady Pamela Jones-Witherall did not enter the story at all, nor did the Duke of Delvers or the wounded *capitano*. Laurie noted that he also forgot to mention that he had posed as her husband and the father of her child, and there was no account given of their night spent camping out in the woods, or their journey by *feluca*.

"I am sure you must all be proud of your niece and cousin when you consider what she has had to bear, and how brave she has been," he concluded. Looking from Lady Blake's white face to her son's flushed one, and the little round O of astonishment that was Lady Rosamunde's mouth, he could see they were not proud at all, and braced himself.

"Breeches!" Lady Blake moaned, pressing her handkerchief to her brow and ignoring every other aspect of Lord Vare's explanation. "It was not enough for you to cut your beautiful hair, Laura, you have been wearing breeches as well. I shall never recover from the shock!"

The marquess felt his temper rising. Hadn't the woman heard a word he had said? "Lady Blake, think!" he demanded. "You cannot seriously have imagined that she could travel across two countries in the company of a group of men, dressed as a young girl?"

"I never expected her to travel with a group of men at all," Lady Blake retorted, her thin nose in the air. "Was there no gentlewoman you could have found to act as chaperon?"

"I must remind you, m'lady, we were fleeing for our lives, and it was a very near thing. If we had lingered to observe the proprieties, I am sure none of us would have escaped alive."

Lady Blake looked as if she thought death preferable to dishonor, and she sniffed.

"And she is in mourning, too," Lord Blake pointed out, his voice contemptuous. "We shall never live this down."

Lady Blake's eyes went to her silent niece again, and she shuddered. Then she looked around at all the other people in the room, and seemed to notice Archie for the first time. "And who might this be?" she asked, raising a haughty pince-nez.

"Allow me to present my cousin, Lord Price," the marquess said. Archie hastened forward and gave the lady his best bow, and then he turned to Rosamunde and breathed reverently, "M'lady!"

If Laurie had not been so upset, she might have laughed at him. His blue eyes were popping and his smile was eager as he bowed again to the most beautiful little lady he had ever seen. Lord Vare's expression was ironic. I fear I shall return Archie to his mama deep in love again, he thought, but at least she cannot take exception to a young lady from what most certainly appears to be England's most proper family.

Lady Blake became aware that the strange young lord was ogling her daughter, for she drew herself up sharply and said, "You and Laura may retire, Rosamunde, until I send for you. I assume my niece has a private room, sir?"

Lord Vare looked suddenly dangerous, and as he leaned forward and his dark blue eyes blazed, she cringed back in her chair.

Laurie, who had been silent all this time, found her voice at last. Her tone was indignant as she said, "You insult me, Aunt Margaret, and you insult the marquess as well. If it had not been for his kindness and concern, I would not be with you today. No one could have been more the gentleman since my father gave me into his care." Her eyes flashed with contempt as she added, "You say you are ashamed of me. Well, after today, I am ashamed of my family!"

Lady Blake looked a little self-conscious that she had been caught in such a *faux pas*, and waved a dismissive hand.

"How dare you speak to my mother that way, you

shameless chit?" Percival asked. "This whole thing is disgraceful! On previous occasions I have called you and your father eccentric, Laura, but after this . . . this escapade, I cannot find words bad enough to describe you!"

"And that is just as well, m'lord, if you value your continued good health," the marquess remarked, his voice dangerous. "Leave us now, Lady Laura. I think when you come back you will find the situation vastly improved. Simmons? Archie? If you would be so good . . . ?"

He moved to open the door, and everyone filed past him. Laurie was the last, and as she drew abreast, she raised her eyes to his face. Eyes, he noted bitterly, that were swimming with tears, although she held her chin up and her back was ramrod straight. He smiled, trying to show her his concern, but Laurie, who could barely see, did not notice.

Lord Vare closed the door behind them, wishing there was some way he could have dispensed with the viscount's presence too, as he came and took a seat next to Lady Blake. "I wish you had not gone about things in quite the manner you did, ma'am," he began. "Lady Laura is very young. There has been no question in her mind about the proprieties, and I can assure you I have taken every care, not only of her, but of her reputation as well."

The viscount snorted, and the marquess's dark blue eyes fell on his flushed face and haughty mien. "I should be glad to excuse you, m'lord, as well," he said, and although his voice was soft, the viscount flushed an even deeper red. "Just so. Sit down, man, and listen, and try to forget your precious decorum for a moment!

"No one knows that Laurie has been dressed as a boy these past few weeks, and there is no reason anyone should ever know. You will certainly never mention it, and you have my word that neither my cousin nor I shall do so either. Therefore we need not worry about the *ton*'s gossip."

A shrewd look came over Lady Blake's face, and her pale blue eyes narrowed as the marquess went on, "Now that you are here, it will be a simple matter to transfer Laurie from my care to yours. After she is properly attired again, you can take her home. Who could see anything wrong in that? To the *beau monde* you simply say that Laurie has been staying abroad with some friends of her father's until you were able to reach her side. All aboveboard, and the soul of conventionality."

"But still I wonder you did not feel the need to ask the girl to marry you." The viscount sneered. "It is what any gentleman would do."

"I am sure you would have insisted on it at once, m'lord," the marquess replied. "Thereby forcing her into an even more sensitive position, and alive to all the evils of her situation. You forget, I think, that Laurie had just lost a much-beloved father and was in shock. No, my functioning as a kindly uncle was much the better course."

Lord Blake still looked indignant, but his mother said slowly, "I suppose it can be carried out as you say, m'lord, if you are quite sure that no one knows what she has been up to—what you *all* have been up to these past weeks. If this should ever come out, we will be ruined!" She sighed and added, "I told my brother the same before the start of this imprudent journey he was so set on, but of course he would not listen. And now we see the results! Bandits, and murderers, and wicked doges! I do not know how Laura survived. I am sure Rosamunde or any other gently bred girl would have succumbed to hysteria long since."

The marquess's bow was ironic. "There were also wolves, fleas, and bedbugs, but fortunately, no wild boars."

Lady Blake looked at him as if she suspected he had suddenly gone mad. And then John's blinding smile lit up the harsh features of his face. "But the Lady Laura managed to cope with all of them. I am glad that you recognize she cannot be compared to other girls. In fact, I would go further and call her unique."

Lady Blake's eyes widened and she seemed lost in thought at his words, but the viscount did not appear to agree with this compliment to his cousin.

"And now we are to be saddled with her!" he exclaimed, his voice shrill. "I warn you, Mother, our peace will be all cut up from this day forward! And what of her influence on my impressionable sister, who has always been such a good, biddable girl? Is her company not likely to contaminate Rosamunde as well? It is too bad! Not only have we missed the better part of the Little Season in coming to her rescue, we also find ourselves in the unenviable position of having to house this bold girl under our roof. And, I might point out, probably forever. You will never find a husband for her now, madam."

John made an effort to relax the two hard fists he had made during this impassioned speech as he said coldly, "I should be very distressed if Lady Blake did so, m'lord. You see, I have every intention of marrying Laurie myself."

"But . . . but . . . *you* . . . *now*?" the viscount asked, completely bewildered.

"The nuances that made me wait to court her until she was under her aunt's care are perhaps too subtle for you to understand. Yes, I am sure that is it. But know that there will be no need for you to house her, husband-hunt for her, or be horrified that her outrageous behavior will reflect on your honorable name. I suggest you make all speed back to London and your Little Season. Laurie's future will be safe in *my* hands now!"

His jaw was hard set, and his eyes blazed with his anger, and the viscount retreated.

"Well, if you are serious, there is no more to be said. I must say I honor you—"

"You would be most unwise to do so, sir," the marquess snapped, "unless you want to find yourself stretched out on the floor unconscious!"

"Percival, dear son, I think it would be best if you left Lord Vare and me alone now," Lady Blake declared, rising to lead her speechless son to the door. "Do go and see what Rosamunde is doing. I cannot like to leave her alone all this time in a public inn abroad. And then there is Lord Price . . ."

The viscount bowed. He could see that if he did not leave of his own accord, the marquess would be delighted to assist him in doing so, at a great loss to his dignity. He left the room, snapping the door shut behind him to let the man know his displeasure.

It was quite half an hour later before Laurie was summoned to rejoin her aunt. She looked from the marquess to Lady Blake, wondering why Aunt Margaret looked so smug and why there was no expression at all on John's taut, harsh-featured face.

"My dear, come in and let us begin again," Lady Blake said, smiling a little as she held out her arms. "I was so grieved to hear about my dear brother's death, and I have been so worried about you. Forgive me for the way I treated you at first, please."

Laurie ran into her arms, the tears she had been keeping firmly in check falling down her cheeks. Whatever John had said, it had made a vast improvement in her aunt's behavior, she thought, as Lady Blake patted her back and murmured to her.

Laurie had spent the intervening time in her room with Rosamunde, trying to ignore her cousin's disapproving manner and breathless questions. It was only after she had the good sense to ask her about the Season and her beaux that the conversation was easier. She had been feeling heartsick at the things her family had said and implied, and now, in relief, she mopped her eyes with the handkerchief Lady Blake gave her. Her aunt bade her collect her things and run down to the carriage at once.

"We shall be very busy today, my dear," she said as she gathered up her own belongings. "Somehow, we must find you something in Le Havre to wear, if both Percival and I are not to go into fits of apoplexy."

Laurie hesitated, her eyes going to John's face where he had retreated to the hearth again. She went up to him and held out her hand. "M'lord, I would thank you for all your kindness . . ." she began, but Lady Blake was beside her, a firm hand on her arm.

"Come along at once, Laura! You shall see Lord Vare again before we sail, and give him your thanks then. Indeed, we shall all thank him."

Laurie stared at the marquess, trying to memorize his face and hoping that her own did not betray the sadness she felt at leaving him. For a moment his blue eyes held her prisoner, and then he bowed over her hand.

"Go with your aunt, Lady Laurie," he said, his deep voice curiously gentle. "I shall call on you, my promise on it."

Laurie had to be satisfied with this as she allowed herself to be led away.

The rest of the day passed slowly. She was driven to the Blakes' hotel, and, wrapped in Lord Blake's cloak, bundled up the stairs to her cousin Rosamunde's room. And then she was left to stare out the window or pace the floor for what seemed like hours until her aunt and her cousins returned from an extensive shopping trip. Lady Blake shook her head over the two black dresses she had found, bemoaning the fit, for they had been made for a much larger lady, but she seemed happier when Laurie was attired in one of them.

Laurie and Rosamunde were set the task of remaking the evening gown of black silk so it would become her better. By teatime Laurie was heartily sick of the gown, her relatives, and her situation. She was missing the marquess and she had been lectured by her aunt, quizzed by Rosamunde, and when not ignored by Percival, treated to his most disdainful looks. It was a very subdued young lady who went away to dress for dinner.

After the meal, she discovered that her aunt expected her to begin altering the daytime dress, since she claimed she could not take her to England in anything so loose and unbecoming. Laurie sighed, and threaded her needle. In her mind's eye she could see the lovely cream-colored silk that John had given her. She wondered when she would ever have a chance to wear it, for from Aunt Margaret's disclosures, it appeared she was to be kept in full mourning black for several months.

Percival had left the ladies shortly after dinner, for which Laurie could only be grateful, and soon Lady Blake took Rosamunde to her room as well. Alone, Laurie was engaged in making some darts at the waistline of the gown when a knock came on the door, and it opened to disclose the Marquess of Vare. Her scissors fell to the floor unheeded as he came in and bowed. His dark face was serious, but when he saw her in one black gown, and busy sewing another one, one eyebrow rose and he smiled at her.

Laurie sat and watched him wide-eyed as he came and picked up the shears and put them on a table nearby, before he took her sewing from her unresisting hands and drew her to her feet.

"So you have already been set to domestic tasks suitable to a young lady, Laurie," he remarked. "Are you fond of sewing?"

"I hate it," Laurie whispered, her throat dry.

"Good! It is not an occupation I would care to see you engage in very often. I see your aunt has lost no time decking you out in black."

His dark blue eyes smiled down at her and she imagined she could see a tiny light somewhere deep inside them. Feeling breathless, she said, "I must look like a crow! I am sure my father would not have wanted me to dress like this, but Aunt Margaret says—"

"Would it distress you very much to learn that you will not have to heed what Aunt Margaret says much longer, Laurie?"

He reached down and took her hands in his, and she shivered at the warmth of his touch. "Although I will expect you to heed what I say when we are married, of course," he added.

"When we are . . . Oh, no!" Laurie cried as she pulled her hands away.

The marquess made no move to recapture them. "No?" he asked softly, and the little light in his eyes burned stronger. "Are you quite sure of that, m'lady?"

"I will not marry you, John, not this way," Laurie said, wishing she could look away from those compelling eyes.

John leaned back against the center table, crossing his arms over his chest. "What way is 'this'?" he asked, his voice casual.

"I know very well that Aunt Margaret and Percival made you ask me, for the sake of propriety," she said hotly. "And since you are a gentleman, you feel you have to!"

John stood up and came toward her, and Laurie backed up until she felt the wall behind her. He stood very close, but he did not touch her, and Laurie concentrated on not trembling.

"It is no compliment to me, Laurie, to say your cousin Percival could make me do anything. The man's an idiot!"

He looked disdainful, and then he said, his voice serious now, "No, dear love, I do not *have* to. I *want* to."

Laurie drew a shaky breath. "It is very nice of you to pretend, John, but I do not believe you. If you love me, why didn't you tell me before? No, you have treated me as if I were no more than two-and-ten, and either spoken to me coldly or ignored me ever since we left Genoa. How can I believe you now?"

Suddenly John pulled her roughly into his arms, one hand tipping up her chin and his dark head bending until his lips touched hers. Touched them lightly, and then came down in a passionate, all-absorbing kiss. Laurie, who had never thought to know that kiss again, trembled, and his arms tightened around her. She felt as if she would break into a million little pieces if he let her go, and when at last he relaxed his embrace, she threw her arms around his neck and begged him with her soft lips not to stop. At once he lifted her off her feet to hold her tight against him, while he kissed her even more fervently.

When he stopped at last, she was breathless, and she took little gasps of air as he put his hard cheek against hers and murmured in her ear, "Do you believe me now, love?"

Laurie sank against him, her eyes closed. All her senses seemed heightened. She could smell not only the masculine scent of his skin and the lotion he used but also the starch of his cravat. And she could feel the warmth and strength of him from her head to her toes, his strong, supportive arms and caressing hands, the broad chest and powerful thighs and the hard contours of his face that was pressed against her own. In her mouth she could still taste his kiss.

And then he shook her a little, and she opened her eyes. John caught his breath at the delight in those wide-spaced hazel eyes that shown like two stars.

"Well, m'lady?" he asked, his deep voice husky.

"Mmm . . . well, what?" she murmured.

The marquess laughed and lowered her to her feet, and she leaned back against the circle of his arms, looking puzzled.

"A very short time ago, I asked you if you believed I loved you now. Do you, my dearest?"

"I must believe you, John," she said, and then, after considering for a moment, she added, "But not as much as I love you."

He put back his head and laughed. "We shall see," he said when he was able to speak again, and then he picked her up in his arms and carried her to a big armchair to sit down with her on his knee. Laurie snuggled against him and sighed.

"But why didn't you tell me before, John?" she asked. "I have been so unhappy, for I have loved you for such a long time—ever since you kissed me at the Villa d'Emillio."

"Your cousin, Lord Blake, is not the only nobleman with scruples, m'lady," John admonished her. "How could I tell you of my love, situated as we were? I had your reputation to consider."

Laurie waved her hand. "Pooh! I am not so missish that I care about that," she said airily.

The marquess sat her up and took her face in both of his hands so she was forced to look at him. She wondered at the seriousness of his expression.

"But I cared," he said. "I cared because I loved you so much that I knew that nothing but the deepest homage would do for my lady."

This called for another kiss, and more whispered endearments, and then Laurie asked, "But why didn't you tell me this morning, John?"

She looked puzzled until he said meekly, "I was not allowed to, my dear. Your aunt would not hear of my proposing until you were properly clad. What, the Lady Laura Lockridge to be asked for her hand while clothed in breeches? My dear!"

Laurie ignored the laughter in his voice. "Do you mean to tell me that you let me suffer this entire horrid day just because of Aunt Margaret's silly notions of gentility? Oh, I could kill you!"

John leaned back in pretended horror. "I beg you will not, love! I know your prowess with a gun. Punish me some other way."

Laurie appeared to consider this rash offer seriously, and then she laughed a little and put her hands back around his neck. "I am sure I will be able to think of something," she said demurely, her eyes dancing, and John buried his face in her chestnut curls.

When Laurie pulled away again, his eyebrow rose. "But, John, Aunt Margaret says I must wear mourning for at least a year, and after that, black gloves, and—"

The marquess put a big hand over her mouth. "Aunt Margaret says, Aunt Margaret says! In this matter, I am sure I can convince her a year is much too long. Besides, I shall have Lord Blake on my side once I point out that he would have to house you all that time. Heaven knows what trouble you might get into. No, we shall be married at once!"

Laurie admired his air of stern authority and his determined blue eyes, even as she shook her head.

"We shall be married as soon as I can have the cream-colored silk you bought me made into a wedding gown, m'lord," she said, just as sternly.

"But that is with Finch, and I have no idea when he will be back in London. You cannot be so cruel, love—"

Now it was Laurie's turn to put her hand over his mouth. As he kissed it softly, and then moved to brush the soft skin of her wrist and inner arm, she felt a tingle where his warm lips touched her. A little breathless now, she said, "I have it safe. I brought it with me in my saddlebags, John, for I could not bear to part with it."

As the marquess raised his head to smile at her, she added, "And when you plan our real honeymoon, m'lord, I pray you will take me to—"

"*Not* Italy!" he interrupted.

"Anywhere *but* Italy!" she agreed.

## About the Author

Although Barbara Hazard is a New England Yankee by birth, upbringing, and education, she is of English descent on both sides of her family and has many relatives in that country. The Regency period has always been a special favorite of hers, and when she began to write seven years ago, she gravitated to it naturally, feeling perfectly at home there.

Barbara Hazard now lives in New York State. She has been a musician and an artist, and although writing is her first love, she also enjoys listening to classical music, reading, quilting, cross-country skiing and paddle tennis.